broken

by Joseph Kiel

Copyright and Legal Notice

'Broken Melody'

Copyright © 2018 Richard Joseph Dutton

Second edition copyright © 2020 Richard Joseph Dutton

ISBN: 9781977043603

www.josephkiel.com

Chapter 1

I'd had some hangovers in my time, but this one was the worst. My head pounded as though last night's debauchery had bruised my brain, the yucky taste of stale vodka staining my tongue. I knew this would take a whole day to wear off, but what was worrying me the most was that I couldn't remember anything of what the hell I was doing.

I mean, I remembered the start of it, of course, the stage before we'd gone out and got trashed, despite having plenty of pre-drinks. It was Veronica's birthday, and we'd hit the city to celebrate. I don't really like Veronica, I have to admit. I find her a bit stuck up and the sarcastic tone she always talks in rather grates on me. But we have a mutual friend, Rachel, and it was Rachel who twisted my arm and made me come along. On a Thursday night, too, when I had a lecture and a seminar to attend the next day. But, hey, we're students. It doesn't matter what night the party is. Every night is party night.

But this one I was regretting saying yes to as I dared to dangle my feet outside the bed in search of my slippers. I held my head in my hands, admittedly a little frightened that my brain would slop out of my ear holes. My heavy eyes glanced at my bedside clock. Oh crap. It was a quarter to ten. Only fifteen minutes till my lecture. I had to move. I'd missed way too many lectures in my first semester. In the new year I'd made a resolution I wouldn't miss any at all for the rest of the year. I didn't want them to fail me for poor attendance. It was only my first year at Meridian University.

The adrenaline kicked in and helped ease the pain of my headache slightly. I stood up and quickly rummaged through my wardrobe for something to wear, anything. I couldn't be a picky diva this morning. As I reached for the first thing, I noticed some ink on my hand, like someone had stamped me. So possibly we'd been to some nightclub last night? And we'd popped outside for a cigarette or something and they'd marked us with this so they'd let us back in again? I didn't recognise the symbol though. It was

3

a black circle with a cross in the middle. It was still vivid on my skin, not having faded with sweat or soap, but then for all I knew, we were probably in this club only a few hours ago. I didn't have time to think about it.

I put on a thick jumper, and some jeans, then took a quick look in the mirror. Thankfully, my subtle makeup was still holding up. No surprise that I'd been too paralytic to wipe it off when I'd returned home. I should be thankful I'd even made it back to my own bed.

There. Just a couple of minutes and I was ready to go. I'd really smashed a stereotype this morning. I reckoned I even had a spare moment to write Rachel a quick text before I left my dorm room.

Girl, what in God's name did you do to me last night??? X

I hoped she'd be able to fill me in, a reassuring natter where she'd tell me she'd been with me all night and we'd done nothing stupid at all. Waking up alone, it was apparent I hadn't brought back some pervy married pensioner and he'd had the biggest thrill in decades; my body certainly wasn't telling me I'd been up to any shenanigans last night. And I didn't *sense* that anyone else had recently been in my room and in my bed. But the thought lingered that someone had potentially taken advantage before I'd arrived back home. I needed Rachel to help me piece together the events.

I knew I wouldn't get a reply before my lecture. She would be snoring soundly in her room for the next few hours at least. The lucky cow; she didn't have any lectures or anything on a Friday. The weekend had already started for her.

I grabbed my key off the holder – I'd somehow had the wherewithal to hang it up there in my drunkenness – picked up my bag positioned by the door, filled with the relevant folders and stationary. Like I said, I've done this partying thing before and learnt that if you're going out, it's worth spending a few minutes before it all gets going to get everything in place ready for whatever's on the timetable the next day.

I spotted a solitary red apple sitting in the fruit

bowl. Great. There was breakfast. It must have been there since Tuesday when I'd last gone shopping, so it should still be juicy. The perfect thing to eat on the go.

I grabbed my coat, a scarf, and a woolly hat with cute eyes and ears on it, then trotted out of the halls of residence towards the lecture theatre, the apple in hand. As soon as I stepped outside, the daylight prickled my eyeballs, not that it was a bright morning at all; the skies were actually as clouded as my head. It wasn't a lengthy walk, but as I dashed through the underpass, the icy February air hit me and my brain seemed as if it was swimming in acid.

Honestly, I'd never known a hangover like this one. I felt... different. Had we taken something? Boy, I'm not really the adventurous sort like that. Sure, I'd smoked a bit of weed now and again, but that was about my limits. I remembered one evening, another drunken occasion, Rachel had mentioned we should try a legal high one day, that her boyfriend took this certain one all the time and he'd recounted to her in great detail how amazing it was. Triple Rainbow, it was apparently called, and he tripped out that he was a mermaid swimming in a giant fish tank. However, even then I had no appetite for getting into that bullshit. But maybe last night she'd presented me with a pill and twisted my arm again?

I supposed it would make sense. To be fair, I'd rather Rachel had made me take some chemical crap than some stranger slipping some shit into my drink. Oh God. I couldn't even entertain that thought. I dwelled on that for any amount of time and I really would spew up then and there in the lecture hall.

Or perhaps that apple would have me retching. On taking a bite of it, it occurred to me I really should start storing the things in the fridge, as it had now reached that yucky mealy stage where it tasted of soggy cardboard. With one bite mark exposing its sallow flesh, I tossed that thing in the dustbin outside the campus lecture hall, and scooted on inside, as much as I would have loved to collapse to the ground and sleep like Snow White.

I took my seat on the end row, so glad it was dimly lit back there. The darkness was soothing on my fragile state, and no one could look at me and see how terrible I appeared. With any luck, if I held my notepad on my lap and kept my hat on, no one would be able to tell if I fell asleep. Hey, my New Year's resolution was to attend all my lectures. I made no vows to myself about being conscious within them and actually absorbing any information. There was little hope of that happening today.

I was already drowsy by the time the lecturer stepped up to the podium, feeling snug underneath my silly panda hat. A moment later though, the adrenaline suddenly surged again as the lecturer was interrupted by the sound of my mobile phone announcing a text message.

Awesome. The entire audience turned round to stare at me and I wished my seat was actually the tongue of some giant furniture monster that would mercifully swallow me up.

'Sorry,' I muttered sheepishly, before the lecturer carried on lecturing and reclaimed everyone's focus.

With all eyes off me, I pulled my phone out of my pocket, quickly switched it to silent, then opened the message. Great! She was awake. It was from Rachel.

FML. Send me a paramedic coz I am literally dying. We totally need to do this again tonight x

Fucking drama queen. Do *what* again tonight!? Can't you just answer the question and let me know what happened?

Even though the lecturer was in full swing by now and throwing around all his big academic words that I should have been scribbling down, I quickly typed out another text for Rachel, again asking her the question. I then rested the phone on my notepad, waiting patiently for the answer to appear. It was inevitable, right? Rachel was now awake. She'd already texted me mere seconds before. Yet even though I desperately wanted to know the answer to this very simple question, there were no more texts imminently appearing on my screen.

Thanks, Rachel! Just go back to sleep, why don't you? Honestly, the modern-day equivalent of waiting for a watched kettle to boil is waiting for your phone to buzz with the message you want. I pinged her another.

Wake up you lazy cow! X

I knew it was a waste of time though. I had a lecture to put my mind to somehow. Or, most likely, I would do the same as Rachel had done and fall back to sleep as well. I again regarded that ink stamp on my hand and tried rubbing it off. What was that symbol supposed to mean, anyway? Was it a crosshair? A Jesus thing? What kind of place were we in? Damn thing wasn't coming off either. Seemed like I needed to get some serious detergent on it. I sensed this mysterious symbol was the riddle, and for some unknown reason my subconscious was screaming to me to solve it. And soon.

Chapter 2

I had only an hour to listen to the lecturer talking about the social development of children. My mind drifted in and out as he mentioned such things as self-harming and social media bullying and I even coordinated my hand to scrawl down a few words on my notepad, but aside from that I was counting the seconds until I could get out of there. It was purgatory, like the big guy had sat me down and told me to think about what I'd done to myself last night. Except I still didn't know the answer to that one! Oh well. My best hope was that I would download the lecturer's notes later on and when I read through them, it would bring it all back to me. I'd *heard* his every word, even though my consciousness had been fading out. It was all in there *somewhere*, right?

With the lecture over I wanted nothing more but to bang on Rachel's door till she woke up, but immediately afterwards I had a seminar to go to. Another hour of academia, and I definitely wouldn't be able to sleep through that one and, worse still, would even have to *contribute* stuff back to my tutor's questions. Give thoughts on the lecture that I'd slept through and had virtually no notes on. Awesome.

It was days like this that made me question what I was doing with my life. What a state to be in when I was supposed to be applying myself to my further education. It seemed more and more about just getting by for me. I'd bullshit my way through the seminar, peer out the corner of my eye at my fellow students' notes, somehow make it *appear* as though I'd read the song sheet. In two years' time I was confident I'd leave the University of Meridian with a piece of paper and a photograph of me wearing a silly square hat.

See, there were plenty of other students who were even worse than me. I observed how some hardly attended any lectures, left their assignments till the last days before the deadline, and still they scraped through. So my reckoning was I only needed to do a little better than them and I would be fine too. Simple. If this subject I was studying was my primary passion in life then sure, I'd be approaching this all completely differently, but it's not. I have another dream. I have something else I want out of life rather than being a social worker or an occupational therapist. But when your Plan A is a long shot, it makes sense to have a Plan B up your sleeve. Hence why I'm a student.

As I sat down in the circle in the seminar room, I felt a vibration against my leg. My phone buzzing with what I hoped was Rachel's next text. At least, I hoped that's what it was. Sometimes I imagined I'd received a notification, but when I'd gone to check, there was nothing on the screen. Phantom vibration syndrome, I think that's called. Somewhere in the world there's someone doing a study on it, I'm sure. Unfortunately for me I couldn't check because as soon as we'd all sat down, the tutor started talking, and it would have been a tad rude to get my phone out at this precise moment.

So I waited. A whole hour of intolerable discussion and engaging my brain that wasn't just out of gear, wasn't just stalled, but had been towed to the scrap yard and crushed in a compactor. I didn't have a dark corner of a lecture theatre to hide away in. I had to participate. It was torture.

And then when it had finally finished, and I was able to check my phone to read Rachel's text, I discovered it wasn't even from her at all. It was some crappy spam message from my local gym back home. Great! I already knew I was a reckless boozer, now the universe was telling me I was an exercise-deficient slob. I didn't think I could get any more deflated today.

That was it. Time to go knock her door down. I started calling up her number too. Hopefully she didn't have her phone switched to silent, and she'd be woken up by her annoying ring tone; she'd set it to *Happy* by Pharrell Williams a few months back, you see. She used to love that song. However, whenever you set your ringtone to your favourite song, it always gets worn out and you start hating it. Rachel wasn't good with technology and she couldn't figure out how to switch it back. Anyway, Pharrell or not,

9

she really wasn't going to be so cosmic hot air balloon-happy when she saw me.

Her room was in the same dormitory as mine, a few numbers down the hall. I stormed up to her door, my fists already clenched, ready to thump them on it. But when I got there, I was surprised to find the door was open. I peered inside. No sign of her. Had she really called for an ambulance or something? Was she even more ill than I was? As I stepped into her bedroom, I saw her duvet laying in a sad and crumpled heap on her bed, the usual clothes and dirty coffee mugs strewn about the place. But no Rachel.

Perhaps we had taken something last night? Sure would explain a lot. I noticed her phone sitting on the bedside cabinet. There were three missed calls on it and eight unread text messages. Definitely not all from me. How do I get hold of her now? It occurred to me Veronica might know. I reached for my phone, caught in an internal debate of whether I really had it within me right now to deal with that sarcy sod, before I heard someone behind me.

I turned round and there was Rachel, a towel in hand, her long hair damp and ruffled. We didn't have any luxurious ensuite facilities in this hall. It was all communal showers and toilets and always someone in there when you wanted to use them.

'Oh. Hey pumpkin,' she said with a cheerful tone that contrasted with my mood.

'So you are alive then. Too busy pampering yourself to answer my text?'

'Huh?' She seemed genuinely confused for a moment before glancing at her phone to see all the messages she needed to catch up on. 'Oh yeah, I thought I had a memory of you texting me this morning. I couldn't tell if it was a dream or not.'

'Too hungover to check your phone again before you got out of bed?'

'Darling, you weren't here,' she advised me. 'I really needed that shower. You honestly didn't...'

'Yeah, I don't want to hear the details,' I cut in to shut her up.

She was already reading through her texts. Funny how responding to digitally mediated messages always seemed more compelling than engaging with people who were right in front of you.

'Can you just tell me what happened last night, Rach? I've never felt so off colour in my entire life. Did we take anything?'

'We just went into town, darling.'

'I feel like I had a bit more than several WKD Blues. Assuming that's what I even drank. I can't remember anything.'

'What, like, really? Or are you over-dramatising this?'

'No!' I cried, now employing some actual drama. 'I don't remember what the hell we did. I know we were in here drinking your nasty wine, I have a vague memory of walking into the city, but after that? Absolutely nothing.'

'Well, calm down, deary. There isn't that much to tell.'

'Okay, so...?'

She paused for a second, staring away from her phone screen, seemingly trying to drag the memories out of her sluggish brain.

'So we went into the city...'

'Already established that myself.'

'And first off we called in at that craphole place, you know, the one we don't like but Veronica does coz she likes the guy that works there.'

'*The Fog*?'

'That's the one. Had to go there coz she wanted to gorge on the eye candy.'

'And did she?'

'I guess. Starting to get hazy for me too, actually.'

'Okay, where did we go after that?' I pressed her.

'Pretty sure it was *Silver Moon* next, then shots at *Walkabout*. Any of this coming back yet?'

'Not at all.'

'Jesus, girl, you really took a hammering.'

'So after *Walkabout*?' I prompted her.

'After that...' Her eyes glazed over. 'Damn. I'm not

sure even I remember.'

'Great.'

She stood there, her tongue running along her top teeth, ready to go again once she'd retrieved the memories and could put them into words. But nothing came. Christ, maybe we were both drugged. Come on, Rachel! Piece this together for me!

I held up the back of my hand. 'What about this? Was this a nightclub we ended up in?'

'Oh!' she said, her eyes alight as though that had unlocked it all. 'Snap!' She raised her hand and sure enough, she had that strange marking on it too.

'So where do they stamp you like that?'

Her eyes deadened again. 'I don't know.' Boy, she was useless. 'In fact, I don't know anywhere that does that.'

'Veronica get one of these too?' I asked, but she didn't answer me.

'Okay, I have an idea,' she resumed at long last. 'Let's go back to *The Silver Moon* and see if it triggers anything. You know? Retrace our footsteps. I'm sure it'll soon come back to me.'

Any excuse to go drinking. As crazy as it sounded, and as terrible as I felt right now, perhaps it wasn't such a bad idea. One or two hairs of the dog might actually help my head. Perhaps the best thing to do was to switch my mind off from this for a few hours and we'd hopefully solve the mystery in the process.

'Maybe,' I replied. 'But some of us haven't been able to have a lie in, so first I need some beauty sleep before I turn into Princess Fiona, and then I'll think about it.'

I pulled my scarf away from my neck, unconsciously preparing to get back into bed.

'Turn into Princess Fiona? I think it looks like you're going to turn into Count fucking Dracula. Where did you get those marks on your neck?'

'What?' I stepped over to her fancy make-up mirror that was all lit up with lightbulbs around the edge. Sure enough, there were two marks on my flesh. 'Huh. Look at that.'

She joined me at the mirror, and we stood there in

silence for a moment.

'Do you think this place has a flea infestation?' she mused.

'Totally wouldn't be a surprise. Yeah, that's what it must be.'

'Hmmm,' she replied closed-mouth.

'Anyway, Rach, I absolutely need to get some sleep,' I said as I moved towards the door.

'Oh, that was it. It suddenly all came back to me. We ended up in *The Titty Twister* last night.'

I threw her a blank look but then then I got it. *The Titty Twister*. That place in Mexico where George Clooney and Quentin Tarantino go and unexpectedly end up fighting a bunch of vampires.

'*From Dusk Till Dawn*. Yeah, nice one, Rach. I'm off to bed,' I replied sarcastically as I headed out of her room.

'Want me to get you a coffin?' I heard her shout to me as I walked on down the hall.

Chapter 3

I managed about two hours of catnapping. You'd expect it would be difficult to sleep during the day, but this was a university dorm and Friday daytime was actually a pretty quiet time round here, most students nursing hangovers, or if they weren't doing that, they were square-bears and so were busy reading. However, I just couldn't switch off. I had no idea why. I hadn't been drinking any caffeine. It was like my brain was buzzing, electrical charges firing off like some Fourth of July fireworks display, unable to settle.

My phone alarm went off at 7pm and I crawled out of my shallow sleep. I needed a quick coffee to perk myself up. I assumed that nothing had changed and Rachel was still willing to go back into the city tonight to retrace our footsteps, so I got myself ready.

I grabbed my towel and some clean clothes and scooted down the hall to the shower which, by some miracle, was vacant. First time for everything. I slipped off my clothes and got under the jet of water. The water pressure may have been feeble but at least with this place being so old they hadn't fitted any stupid thermostatic valves and you could set these showers real hot. By the time I'd finished, my skin was red raw, the steam rising off me. Although I felt refreshed, I still hadn't managed to remove that mark on my hand. What the hell kind of ink did they use? I'd assumed it was a simple surface stamp but I couldn't dismiss the possibility we'd got ourselves tattooed last night. Admittedly, it was a very strange choice of design, but the more I examined that symbol, the more it seemed a permanent branding.

After my shower I put on my blue dress and a cardie, then made my way back to my room to sort out my hair and apply some makeup. My mirror wasn't as fancy as Rachel's. She was a Drama student, you see. That thing of hers folded up and she could take it with her whenever the Media students roped her into any film shoot. I envied that about her, her headstrong pursuit of her dream to become an actress. She wasn't distracted by a Plan B that fed into doubts and undermined her Plan A. She wanted to be a star and so that was what she would be.

By 8.30pm I was ready to go again, however Rachel messaged me to say she needed another half hour, so I lay down on my bed and read a bit more of my current novel. Although I got through two more chapters, the narrative really wasn't registering in my brain and I couldn't have told you anything about it.

My thoughts centred on the mystery of our forgotten night out, and another friend popped into my head. I wondered whether I should buzz him to see if he had been around and knew anything of our activities. However, I always felt awkward texting Olly, ever since we'd split up right before Christmas. I didn't want to give him the impression he was on my mind. I mean, of course he'd inevitably been on my mind at points, but it wasn't because I missed him, and so I didn't want him to get the impression I might be trying to rekindle anything.

He was a great guy and on paper we seemed a perfect match as we had so much in common. I'd soon come to the conclusion that we were better off as friends though. I guess he was my first proper relationship since being at university, and if I was to be completely honest, I didn't I want to be exclusive to anyone at this early stage of my higher education life.

It had all happened too quickly between us anyway, like *really* quick. We were at some rowdy party thrown by some second-year students and Olly had turned up with his girlfriend while they were in the middle of an argument. Rachel and I witnessed the death of their relationship right there in the kitchen with a slap and a door slam, and then somehow, no longer than an hour later, I disappeared upstairs with Olly and had sex with him.

Because of that sordid fact, it had become increasingly weird between us as our relationship developed over the following month or so, the unmoveable thought in my brain that I was just the rebound girl, and literally the first thing he'd seen after his girlfriend had stormed out of his life. Not that I could make any complaint myself about moving on quickly or being promiscuous. Olly may very well have slept with two different people on that same day, perhaps having some morning sex with that ex and capping it off with a drunken shag with a fresher, whereas I knew for certain he wasn't the only guy I'd slept with that day.

It wasn't that I endeavoured to get my bedposts full of notches since I'd come to Meridian, that I was a raging nymphomaniac that needed to fornicate with a different person each day of the week. It just so happened that two opportunities had come along at the same time on that particular day. Waiting for a bus syndrome. Hey, sometimes that rule applies to partners too.

I shook off my worries as I started typing out a text to him. We still did stuff with each other, not *sexual* stuff, I don't mean. We had a common interest in something, you see, something completely innocent, and he could do the *just friends* thing with me as we pursued it. In fact, I wondered why I was even worried about contacting him in the first place. It was stupid, come to think of it. The speed at which Olly could move on, it really wouldn't be any surprise if he was now onto the eighth girl since me. Surely I was flattering myself if I wondered whether he might still hanker after me.

I didn't get to press send on the message though, for there was a knock at the door.

'Mel? I'm ready!' It was Rachel.

I deleted my words and jumped off the bed, but Rachel opened the door before I got to it. She had a luscious shade of lipstick on, and she looked radiant, just like a film star.

'*Silver Moon* first then? Or do you want to start at the very beginning?' she asked.

'*The Fog* seems an appropriate starting point today,' I replied.

So that's where we headed. Only for one drink. Neither of us really liked the place and normally without Veronica with us we wouldn't have gone anywhere near it, but this time it was necessary, because tonight we were living the chick version of *The Hangover*.

As we trailed across the city, I reflected on our freshers' week when you were forever being helped by students who were older and much wiser, assisting you with getting settled in and used to living away from home for the first time. Along with all the vouchers and leaflets and sexual health advice they dished out, one piece of advice that had seemed overcooked was about being careful about going out on your own in the city. It took me a couple of weeks to find out exactly what they were getting at with that one.

Apparently Meridian used to have a serial killer who preyed on young, beautiful women, and apparently he would only strike during the lead-up to Christmas. But that had all stopped a few years back before I'd come here, and so it wasn't something that I gave a great deal of thought to. There was also the factor that being from a sleepy rural town, I didn't really have the brain for anticipating being the victim of a serious crime. It was hopelessly naïve of me to be that way, I know, but the worst crime that happened where I came from was someone parking in a cycle lane. Even then the police didn't give a shit.

But if I was honest with myself, it played on my mind at this precise moment for some reason. Not that I thought that Rachel and I had been murdered last night and we were in fact now ghosts wandering the earth. That was *obviously* ridiculous because this serial killer only struck in December, and right now we were in the safe zone of February. Not to mention that this killer, the Christmas Reaper they called him, had apparently retired, so his spectre of fear had dispersed. Unless he were to come out of retirement and reinvent himself as the Valentine Reaper?

It occurred to me I should have perhaps texted Olly earlier, that maybe Rachel and I would have been better off with a male companion on our quest. Heading back into the metropolis that had created this enigmatic void in our memories probably should have been tackled with a bit more of a plan. Something was off. Perhaps we needed the assistance of someone older and wiser than some sheltered fresher and her ditz of a friend. However, no bloodthirsty maniacs made an appearance before we arrived at the first pub in our memory-jogging crawl.

'One glass of true blood for the vamp,' Rachel said, breaking my thoughts, as she turned away from the bar with a glass of what looked like thick blood.

'What the fuck is that?'

'Relax, sweetie. It's a bloody Mary. Tomato juice. Trust me, it's great for hangovers.' She grabbed another glass of the stuff off the counter and took a sip. Reluctantly, I copied her. Well, it was a crap bar. May as well have a crap drink to go with it.

Being on the edge of the city centre, *The Fog* was nearer the rough end of town so the clientele there could be pretty grufty. Plus, there were plenty of underage drinkers there, and together with all the dirty old men, they all probably had boners at the site of us two wandering into their territory. Thankfully we weren't staying long. We stood there idly surveying the room, our cardies folded over our arms. It smelt sweaty and stale in there.

'Oh no, look! Don't tell Veronica but her bit of stuff is on tonight,' Rachel said as she spotted a guy with a black beard collecting glasses from the table nearby. It wasn't one of those hipster type beards, more like one of those *I just can't be bothered to shave* beards.

'So it is. Not going to call her to let her know?'

'Heck no. She came out worse than all of us. Said she's had her head down the toilet all day.'

'Poor thing,' I said... or rather I *acted*. Boy, I should have signed up for Drama Studies as well. I could be pretty good at it sometimes.

'But when the cat is away...' Rachel handed me her cardigan and her eyes twinkled.

'No, Rach...'

'Hey, he might be able to fill us in on what we were doing here yesterday,' she replied with a wink.

Already she was walking over to Mr Glass Collector, leaving me all alone like a vulnerable lonesome deer in a jungle filled with jackals and hyenas. Thanks, Rachel. I hate standing on my own in pubs. I instantly felt awkward and self-conscious as though everyone was now peering at me and thinking, *'Oh my God, get a load of that loser all on her own. Aww the poor thing has got no friends'*. I did the usual thing of checking my phone, as though doing that somehow justifies my existence. It's not like you can stand there on your own gawping at other people or just staring into space. Seriously, where are you supposed to look when you're on your own in a pub?

I had no new texts, so I tried connecting to the pub's Wi-Fi before I realised it had no Wi-Fi, so I resorted to reading through *old* texts. I've been there plenty of times before, either doing that or perusing old photos, attempting to project a look on my face that suggested I was doing something really important and I didn't want to be bothered.

Eventually I glanced over to Rachel to see how she was getting on stealing Veronica's fancy man. To be brutally honest, I don't think Veronica stood anything of a chance with him. He was cute, actually way too classy for this place. His eyes seemed to be forever swirling around in his eye sockets, analysing everything, the tranquil surface of deep waters.

Suddenly they were on me. Rachel continued to talk to him, but I couldn't read anything in her face because she had her back to me. But even though I could see her gesticulating and her head moving from her busy mouth, he fixed his gaze on me. It was like he looked right through me, like he was daydreaming and staring into space and I just happened to be what was in line of his eyes.

I returned my attention to my phone. Something about that whole moment felt eerie. I turned my back to him too, although my shoes had practically stuck to this horrible beer-stained floor. I'd had enough of this place already, so I started drinking my yucky drink in bigger gulps. It was like watered down supermarket brand ketchup. It struck me how tasteless it was. I thought they put all sorts of spices and things in bloody Marys. Great night this was turning out to be. First my friend gives me this piss to glug, and then she ditches me. And so far it was doing nothing to jog my memory. I'd almost forgotten what we'd come here for.

When I first came to Meridian, this pub was

19

actually one of the first places I checked out. Being new in town I needed somewhere to play, and I soon discovered that every Sunday evening they had an open mic night so I turned up with my guitar and played some of my songs.

You see, that's my plan A. Well, not playing guitar in a craphole pub. No, I mean trying to be the next Lily Allen or Gabrielle Aplin, except really I'm not trying to *be* like anyone. I'm just trying to be the first Melody Freeman. Can you believe that? I want to be a musical star, and my name is Melody? Sometimes people are born with the name that fits their destiny, like William Wordsworth or Thomas Crapper. Or maybe it's some power of suggestion thing. My parents named me Melody and my subconscious thought I'd better make some. It helped that my parents were kind of musical and passed on their talents to me. Well, my mother did. She played flute in the local concert band. My father, on the other hand? He was a prison warden. Can you believe that too? In charge of keeping prisoners locked up, and he has *that* surname?

I used to think we were some sort of weird quirk, until one day I read about something fancy called 'nominative determinism' in some crap blog and found out it's an actual thing. It's so typical. You go about thinking you're unique and special and then you discover that you're not; we're subconsciously just narcissistic egoists. I bet anyone with the name Richard but was called Rich by their parents ended up loaded like Richard Branson. Poor sods, those Richards who were called Dicks.

So, anyway, I came here and played a total of four songs and while I performed the last one, a cover of *Set Fire to the Rain*, I had the feeling the crowd weren't watching me because they were enthralled with my rendition of Adele's song but instead were mentally undressing me. And then some poser came on after me and played a Maroon 5 cover and the place suddenly came to life, and that was the exact moment I realised this venue and its patrons weren't for me.

There was no wonder I didn't have any memory of last night. The way I felt about this pub, it was obvious my mind had tried to blank it out.

'Well, that was odd,' Rachel said.

Her voice startled me but I was relieved to have her standing with me again. 'What's that?'

'Maybe I should text Veronica and see how she is.'

'Why?' I asked in a very deliberate manner, prolonging the syllable.

She didn't seem to register it though, too busy tapping away on her screen. 'What? Oh, I asked Glass Collector guy if he remembers us three in here, and he said yes, he recalled talking to Veronica. I think they must know each other better than I realised.'

'What? Like, he knows her in the Biblical sense?'

'Huh? No, he's not religious...'

I rolled my eyes. 'Doesn't matter. So, he spoke to Veronica...'

'Apparently. He said my friend was really ill, like there's something really wrong with her...'

Her phone buzzed. 'Oh, that's her.' But she didn't read the message back.

Although she was busy composing a reply, I interrupted anyway: 'So did he shed any light on my little problem?'

'What?' she asked, bringing her attention back to me. 'Oh, no, I didn't get anything else at all that I didn't know already.'

'So we came here for nothing.'

'Pretty much. Should we make like a Hill Valley nerd and get out of here?'

I took one last sip of that nastiness, then ditched my glass on top of a nearby fruit machine. Rachel, however, was keen to consume every last drop of alcohol so continued to sip at hers. And it was at that exact moment something suddenly dawned on me.

'Oh my God!' I chirped, as if my excitement alone would enlighten Rachel into the brainwave.

'What?'

I felt so stupid. I'd just had my phone in my hand going through the old stuff on there and I hadn't thought to check what visual evidence we may have gathered.

'Have a flick through your phone. We may have

taken some photos!'

'Oh yeah,' Rachel replied, then duh'd herself. We both quickly swiped through to our stored images and immediately I could see that I had some with today's date, taken throughout the early hours.

'I've got some,' I told her.

'Me too! Where the hell was *this* place?'

She tilted her screen towards me and I squinted as I analysed the image. We were obviously in some club and evidently appeared to be enjoying ourselves. I was standing there smiling and winking at the camera while Rachel pouted sexily, or rather what she thought was a sexy pose but really made her look like a drunken student. The place we were in was weird. It had one of those trendy vintage vibes going on, the bar area full of what I assumed were spirits but seemed more like potions.

She swiped to another photo: Rachel had a bottle halfway down her throat like a porn star as we sat at a table. I held a bottle in my hand and was laughing at her antics. I really hoped no one had put any rogue substances in them.

She swiped again to another picture that was blatantly out of focus and automatically swiped on before I stopped her.

'Let me see that one again.'

'I don't think this one is going to win a photography award, honey. It's a wonder they're not all like that.'

'Look in the background though,' I told her as I continued to scrutinise it. We were the blurry figures in the foreground, but right behind us was some guy facing the camera too. It was difficult to make out much else. He might be handsome, he might look like the Elephant Man. There was no telling with how the picture had turned out. He seemed to have shocking hair though, spread out like a lion's mane, and I was pretty sure that wasn't solely down to the lens blur. He had the same kind of style as an eighties rock star.

'Who is he?' I asked.

'God knows. Let me see if there are any more.' She continued to swipe through the rest of them. There were a few more of that strange club, some taken out in the street, then some of a bar that I did recognise.

'*The Mercury Lounge!*' I announced. There was no mistaking that funky place with its trippy paintings all over the walls and music videos looping on large plasma screens. She searched on, and we recognised the *Silver Moon Inn*, which is where our trail had run cold. Great! We were getting somewhere after all.

'All right,' Rachel said. 'Good call, Mel. We are starting to put the pieces...' She suddenly stopped as she swiped on to a photograph that was clearly taken on a completely different occasion as it involved Rachel and her boyfriend who were both in a state of undress. 'Oh wait, you do not want to see these.'

I smirked, but she didn't seem that embarrassed. She slipped her phone away, drank the last of her drink and turned to me.

'Ready?' she asked.

I nodded, and we headed on out of there, the desperate-looking clientele gazing on at us sorrowfully as we left them. We trailed towards the city centre and our next bar, the *Silver Moon Inn*, that overlooked a market square. This bar, an old stone building, had been a traditional English pub until it had gone under but recently it had been taken over by young owners who had given it a makeover and brought it into the twenty-first century. It was clean and homely inside, and they never played the music so loud in there that you couldn't hold a conversation.

We had some proper drinks there, vodka and lemonade, and as I drained my glass, I could feel the alcohol erasing my hangover, although I was only really postponing it until tomorrow, like getting into debt but getting another credit card and doing a balance transfer. Oh well. Live for the moment. I'm sure in forty years' time I'll only be reminiscing about how I could live like this. By my second drink I was starting to relax a little more. That nagging thought in my head telling me to find out what we'd got up to last night had quietened, but then I glanced at my watch and that weird stamp on my hand stared me in the face again and brought back the worry.

'I'm hungry. Are you hungry?' I asked Rachel, suddenly feeling pangs in my stomach, and realising I had eaten nothing all day, not unless you counted one mouthful of that apple. It didn't seem too bright an idea to keep drinking without putting some food in my belly.

'Nah, I had a sandwich earlier,' she replied, her face back in her phone.

'Want to come with me somewhere? I need to eat.'

'Yeah, sure, pumpkin.' Her phone pinged. 'Ooh, looks like Ziggy might join us for a bit.'

That was her boyfriend. Ziggy. He wasn't a student, he didn't have a job. He was just some dosser who acted like a pimp. I don't think their relationship was entirely that serious, but they would probably be the first to admit it.

'Righto,' I replied neutrally. I couldn't see how that would help us with our quest. But then again... 'Maybe he was around last night?'

Rachel stared into space again for a moment as she tried to place him in the missing narrative. She shrugged.

I finished my drink. 'Anyway, I'm going to go to that café near here.' All of a sudden I was ravenous.

'What, *Joe's Parlour*? You know it has a really shit hygiene rating.'

She may have been right about that, but I had a soft spot for the place, and right now my hunger was too much to ignore.

'Whatever. I really need to sink my teeth into something or I might start eating you.'

'Kinky bitch,' she replied as we made for the door.

Chapter 4

The greasy spoon dump owned by Joe (whoever the hell he was) was a quiet little escape from the frenetic energy of a night out, a place for people to have a peaceful bite of soggy kebabs and chips before returning home, or a refuge for the casualties of the night to get a coffee and sober up from their inebriated states as they rested their heads on the table. The café was always open. Surely that's why it was so grimy and the wallpaper was fifty years out of date; they never had the opportunity to get in there and freshen up the nightmare. It was probably too far gone even for Gordon Ramsey now.

Rachel didn't come in there with me. She hovered around out the front, talking to Ziggy on her phone. I wouldn't have been surprised to go back out and her tell me she was going to abandon the evening and go round to his place, but I hoped it wasn't a booty call I was leaving her to.

Inside, I grabbed a ketchup-stained menu. The all day brunch caught my interest for some reason. I guessed because it was full of calories and meat, but I particularly had a craving for the black pudding that it came with. I placed my order with the same languid young man who was always behind the counter and always glumly waiting around for his never ending shift to end. I then took a seat at the back next to some antique jukebox. Easy going music played here, but it didn't originate from the jukebox. That thing was just decoration.

As I waited, I rested my chin on my palm and people-watched. The only other diners was a group of three chavvy lads who looked a little underage, but I sensed they'd been drinking alcohol tonight one way or another. They sat around a large pizza and were probably concocting plans to source more booze before the night was through.

A bell jingled as the front door opened, and in stepped a man wrapped up in a vivid green coat. He walked over to the counter and ordered a banana milkshake. While the cheerless garçon trudged off to make it, I suddenly shuddered with cold, a draught invading the room. The green coat guy hadn't closed the door properly. I was just starting an internal debate of whether suffering the cold or being lazy and not getting up to close it was most important to me when the green coat dude shut it himself, as though picking up on my thoughts. As he turned back, I twigged who he was. It was Mr Glass Collector from the first bar we'd gone to tonight. It had already gone eleven, so presumably *The Fog* was closed and he'd finished work for the night. Rachel was still busy yapping on the phone so probably hadn't noticed him enter. Certainly she would have made her way in here and been all over him if she'd seen him.

Once he'd got his milkshake, the man sat down at a table and did the same as I had done, and studied the rest of the patrons. I watched him take a sip of his drink, a tickling in my brain from that sense of synchronicity that I should bump into him again tonight, like the universe was nudging us together for some mysterious reason.

It wasn't something I consciously made the decision to do every time I came into the city for a night out, but if I was honest, it was always something that was there in my mind. Is this the night I meet the man of my dreams? Mr Right? Even when I felt as rough as I had done today, and every part of my body told me I really needed to stay in and have a rest as I watched crap on television, I never wanted to spurn that chance of going out. If I did that it may deny myself of that fateful opportunity. I was young and single and carefree, and had to remain open-minded and ready for anything.

I enjoyed dolling up and putting myself out there just as much as the next girl. I enjoyed the attention of wandering eyes, and yes, a couple of times already in my fledgling university career, I had met a guy and gone back to his place and never seen him again. Well, possibly more than twice. And possibly one time we didn't even make it back to his place at all. And then there was Olly, too. These were all stepping stones to finding the right one, of course. I was still open to something meaningful. Every girl is, no matter how much they might say they're not, how often you hear people singing in songs about finding love when they weren't looking for it. When you're eighteen stone, wearing a tent and share a house with eight cats, *then* you can make that claim.

Besides, I needed to do this, to live like this, because it was experience for my music career. To be a successful singer-songwriter, you had to do this kind of stuff. Adele surely didn't write all those number one songs without going through some genuine heartbreak. So all this was really my duty.

The glass collector guy in the green coat made eye contact with me. Immediately he averted his gaze, staring into his milkshake. However, I could sense that his attention remained on me. It just felt like he was still scrutinising me, that sensation of being watched, of being churned around in someone's brain, even though I could see that neither he nor anyone else currently had me in their sight.

I continued to study him, noting the concentration in his face, his head slightly cocked as though he was listening out to something beyond the tinny music that chirped on the speakers. His facial expression seemed to morph into one of burden, suggesting he was chewing on an important thought.

For some reason, I had a really random memory about living back at home and how, now and again, I would go into another room because I would be looking for something, but when I walked into that room I would see that one of the cats had puked on the carpet, and I was the lucky household member who'd made that delightful discovery. I could have carried on without searching for that lost guitar pick. I could have picked up my instrument and used my finger nails instead and been blissfully unaware that there was a pile of cat vomit lying somewhere in the house, yet fate had decided to bring me to this discovery. And at such an important juncture in my life as that, I had the choice of ignoring this cat vomit and going back to my guitar and waiting for someone else to discover it, leaving the lovely task of cleaning it up to them, and I could have employed my latent acting skills as I sympathised, *'Oh no, the cat hasn't been sick again, has it?'* or I could just do the right thing and go and fill a bowl with hot water and disinfectant.

That was the look on his face. So had he entered this café and discovered something he'd much rather he hadn't? And was I therefore that pile of cat vomit in the corner of the room? I would have liked to have passed this off as some cute romantic encounter, where he'd seen me and I was the woman of his dreams, I was the beautiful angel on the subway that James Blunt had met for a fleeting moment but would never be his, or I was the maid working at Number 10 that the prime minister was falling in love with and had to redistribute because their working together was highly inappropriate. But that's not how it sensed to me. I didn't feel like the girl. I felt like cat sick.

He raised his head again, looked directly at me, and for a moment I saw a flicker of a cringe, like he really was staring at a pile of semi-digested Whiskas. Right then I started to feel weirded out, vulnerable, as though by looking at me, this man had opened my drawer in my bedroom and discovered my journal and was quietly reading through it, learning all my secrets. Perhaps that's effectively what he was doing. Perhaps he had some sort of ability and was peering into my mind and observing all my private thoughts for his own secret, voyeuristic purposes.

Okay, stranger from The Fog, *if you really are reading my mind right now, take another sip of your drink.*

He didn't. But he did shake his head and sigh. Was he telepathic? Or was I just drunk? Why were these strange notions finding a place in my head like this? I contemplated going over and having a little chat with him at least. He knew my friends. I had a reason to talk to him. Sort of.

He certainly wasn't going to approach me anytime soon, to do his duty of 'clearing up the cat sick'. He didn't seem the type to talk to anyone. I could certainly think of far worse individuals to make conversation with randomly, and, like I said, he wasn't completely random, anyway. Besides, there wasn't much else to do while I waited for my food to arrive.

I got up and walked over to his table. Seeing me

approach, he seemed uncomfortable, like this sort of thing had never happened before, the cafe rat about to be cornered.

'You work at *The Fog*, don't you?' I asked him.

He nodded.

'I saw you talking to my friend earlier,' I went on, nodding towards Rachel who continued to yap on her phone as she perched herself on the windowsill outside. 'Mind if I take a seat?'

'Go ahead.'

'Got a name?'

'I'm Xander.'

'Hi Xander. So I'm not sure if Rachel said to you, but we're trying to piece together what we did last night. I woke up this morning and hardly remembered a thing. I know. We're students...'

'Yeah, she was asking if I saw you in the bar.'

'Cool.' He really didn't look like he wanted to talk at all. He seemed about as relaxed as someone having a candlelit dinner with a vomit monster. 'So how well do you know Veronica, our other friend?'

'She comes to *The Fog* now and again.'

'Did you talk to her today? She tell you she was ill?'

'No,' he replied. Which question was he answering? Both, perhaps?

'Oh,' I said, emphasising my confusion with a ponderous frown on my face. I hoped it would prompt him to speak more, but it didn't seem to be doing the trick. Boy, this guy was hard work.

Behind me I heard the listless café worker enter from the kitchen area. I turned around to see he had a plate of food in his hand. He hovered at my table by the jukebox before realising I'd relocated.

I pointed to him to put it down where he was and he did so. 'Well, dinner's ready,' I said as I started to get up.

'Wait,' Xander said. He placed his hand on mine so naturally I paused in anticipation. 'This may sound strange...'

'What?'

'I don't often intervene like this. Can lead to all

sorts of problems, so I've found. But since you came over to me...' He trailed off again, but I sat there patiently, already wondering what he meant by *intervening*. Why would he feel a need to do that with some girl he barely knew anything about? Intervene regarding *what*?

'You're in trouble,' he resumed. 'Really bad trouble. And you don't have much time.'

What the hell? How did he know that? He took a couple of glances at me this evening and he knew just by looking that I was knee deep? I realised I'd been feeling rough today, but still... I didn't look so rough that I was dying, did I?

I gazed into his eyes, searching for more insight. It was like I was sitting at the table with the fortune teller and the milkshake in front of him was his crystal ball.

'What kind of trouble?' I asked him.

He slid his fingers over my hand and I could almost believe it was a tender caress, but then he tapped his finger on my flesh and I realised he was referring to the strange symbol on it.

'I can't uncover all the information you search for. There's an emptiness in your head, a void.'

'You're reading my mind?' I had to ask, even though I could already tell that was what was going on.

'You need to find the people who put this sign on your hand. Or there might be a chance they'll reach you in time. But it's important you keep searching. Don't go home. Don't give up. You need to get to them before the night is over. Before the sun starts to rise. Do you understand what I'm saying, Melody?'

'Yeah. I got it. Who are they?'

He closed his eyes and concentrated hard, stroking the back of my hand as he did so.

'Do you have a pen?'

I quickly rummaged through my handbag for my fancy Harry Potter pen that I'd picked up at Kings Cross one time. He took it from me and began scrawling on a napkin, as though he was the conduit for receiving this message from some unknown plain. He wrote four letters, then drew a pair of what looked like wings.

'What does that say?' I asked him.

'They're called the Vihn Angels.'

'Who are they?'

'I don't know. But they might be able to save you.'

'Save me?'

'You're very ill and you don't have very long left.'

Ill? Okay, so I accepted I had a hangover but hangovers don't *kill* you, do they?

'Where do I find them?'

The bell jingled again, and in walked Rachel. 'All righty, ready to roll yet, pumpkin? Oh, hey there!' She'd seen that I was talking to the hot glass collector guy and as she sat next to me, it seemed she wanted in on that as well. Rachel's crap timing immediately killed our intense conversation and Xander reverted to his typical uncomfortable disposition.

'Hi,' he muttered. 'I was just leaving.'

'Wait,' I stopped him. 'Can you help me? Help me find these people?'

'I'm sorry. I have to go. Good luck.'

'Please...'

But already he was on his way, abandoning his half-empty glass of milkshake. The bell on the door jingled again, and we heard it close.

'Well,' Rachel huffed, rolling her eyes. 'Was it something I said?'

I stood up and returned to my original table, although did I still have my appetite after that random little bombshell? Rachel followed me over there like a puppy.

'Are you going to tell me what the hell that was all about? Who do we need to find?' she asked.

I stabbed a fork in the black pudding and took a big mouthful. 'That guy is weird,' I mumbled. 'Xander he's called. Did you know that?' I continued to prod at my food. Maybe I was still hungry after all.

'Oh. Yeah. Yeah, I knew that. He is a bit strange. Mysterious. That's not such a bad thing, is it? Did you get his number?'

'Did it look like it?' I wasn't sure whether to tell Rachel exactly what had happened. It seemed a private

31

moment. Intimate. Having someone peer inside my mind like that. And would she really believe it? She wasn't *there*. She wouldn't understand. I decided I would water it down a bit.

'He knew something about this,' I informed her as I held up my hand with the strange stamp.

'Oh cool. Did he tell you where we got them?'

'The Vihn Angels. Does that mean anything to you?'

'The what?'

'Didn't think so. Perhaps Veronica does?'

'I don't know whether I should bother her.'

'She might not be as ill as we thought.'

'Really?' She shrugged and already started texting her.

'When you're done writing that, try Google as well.'

I left her to all that as I continued to chow down, processing that strange conversation. As if I didn't need any more confirmation I'd just been through some supernatural psychic experience, I suddenly realised Xander had called me Melody. I certainly hadn't given him my name. It was possible Rachel mentioned it earlier, but, even so, he did well to remember it at such a seemingly significant moment.

Before I knew it, I'd cleared my plate, but I was still hungry. I was blessed with one of those constitutions that I could eat whatever I wanted and never put on weight. I think it comes with using so much mental power on worrying and fretting that I burn up all my calories that way, and perhaps with what Xander had told me and the way my brain was going round in circles, I'd already burnt up the junk I'd just eaten.

'Well, I can't find shit,' Rachel announced as she put down her phone.

'I need to find them,' I said. I really did. He'd practically warned me that my life depended on it. The nagging in my brain I'd endured all day told me the same thing.

'All right, well, let's head on in to the city if you've finished scoffing. Ziggy's expecting us.'

'Really? Do we have to, Rach?'

'Come on, relax, sweetie. We're supposed to be having fun.'

'We're supposed to be finding out what trouble we got into last night.'

'Jees, why do you always think the worst?'

Because you weren't just talking to a mind reader who said I was really ill!

'All right. We'll make a quick diversion and go see your shagpiece.'

She frowned at me, but then it shamelessly turned into a look of *well, actually, you might have a point.* I doubted visiting Ziggy would help me in my quest in any way. He hadn't been around last night, and even if he was, he probably would have been so fucked on drugs that he didn't remember it either.

Rachel leaned over the table, conspiratorially. 'So. How about riding the Triple Rainbow tonight?'

'Rachel? Seriously? Is that why we're going there?' It made sense. Ziggy tempting her over with promises of carnal activity and some legal high thrown in for good measure. She told me he got that shit over the internet. Hell, I thought. Apparently I was dying. I should just go with the flow and ride the tornado all the way to Oz with my friend and dance a jig with the Lollipop Guild. More chemicals might help soften the blow.

Besides, Xander had said I had until sunrise tomorrow. There were still plenty of hours until then. Or was I getting even worse at trying to justify my actions?

'What time does the sun rise tomorrow morning?' I asked her.

'Do I look like Paul fucking Hudson?'

'Well Google it, you divvy bitch!'

'You fucking Google it.'

So I did. Fortunately, *Joe's Parlour* had Wi-Fi, so I got connected and discovered that on Saturday morning the sun would be up at 7.43. Which meant I had a little over eight hours to work this one out. And what would happen at 7.43 tomorrow morning? Christ, perhaps Rachel was right. Maybe I was about to turn into a vampire or a werewolf or the Incredible frickin' Hulk. I wished that Xander hadn't disappeared. I had so many more questions, and he was the only one who seemed to have the answers. If only I'd gotten his number. I could always try to catch him at his pub again, but that wouldn't be until tomorrow night at least, and that fateful occurrence of tomorrow's sunrise would have already taken place. Was I overthinking this? Could I send a thought out there, call him up psychically, and he might show up again?

Or maybe he was just a weirdo who got off on saying creepy shit like this to people to spook them out. There was probably nothing wrong with me at all. Maybe I should go along with Rachel and let my hair down some more and forget all about this nonsense.

'All right. Are we going to go then?' I asked.

'All the way across the sky, baby! Come on, let's blow this slop shop.'

Chapter 5

It never ceased to amaze me how a band like Happy Mondays could make such cool music when they had such a wanker as Shaun Ryder as their frontman. Songs like *Step On* and *Kinky Afro* were real classics that never got old. Ziggy was always playing Happy Mondays CDs whenever we were at his place, so I was pretty familiar with them. I'd even tried strumming a few of their tunes on my guitar and considered them for my set list.

Not that this band was my era. Not that they were quite Ziggy's era either, despite him being a fair bit older than us. I think he was in his thirties somewhere. He may have been really young when they were about. Regardless, their music suited him, encapsulating his existence like it was the soundtrack to his life, mainly because Ziggy was a total wanker as well.

We sat in his lounge, cigarette smoke hanging in the air. The purple carpet was threadbare and hadn't been vacuumed in months. Ash-filled ashtrays lay on the coffee cup-stained coffee table, but I was staring up at the damp yellow ceiling that used to be white. I don't know why Rachel was complaining about *Joe's Parlour*. You took a load off on Ziggy's settee and you might catch a disease.

I sat next to Rachel, Ziggy on the other side of her with an arm draped over her shoulders. Two of his friends slopped around on the carpet as they vaped, looking like fire breathers. They gave the vibe that they weren't allowed to sit on the sofa, as though they were both Ziggy's pets, not that anyone would want a pair of slothful guttersnipes like these two lurking about their house. No one except for Ziggy, that was.

Other than Happy Mondays, his other obsession was cars. He was actually pretty smart when it came to fixing them, and could easily get a job and earn a decent wage working as a mechanic, but that meant *working*, and Ziggy wasn't a worker. He was a dosser. Instead, he and his mates did up vehicles outside their carports just for fun. I was sure they occasionally earnt money doing this from satisfied friends looking for a cheap fix for their vehicles. But when they weren't doing that, they were busy dossing. They didn't want the commitment of a job because that might get in the way of their dossing. That was the only thing they were committed to.

'So, Milady Melody, have I introduced you to The Bluetones yet?' Ziggy asked me. This was one of his things. Well, two of them: firstly calling me Milady Melody where my name was pronounced *Mel-owe-dee* to match the rhythm of *Milady*, and secondly he liked to play the musical aficionado who educated the wannabe musician. Both quirks annoyed the crap out of me, more so the second thing because although he was a know-it-all, what he told me was actually useful education.

I guessed that really he was quite jealous of my accomplishments. You see, beyond the real world I was doing well with my music, in the infinity of the World Wide Web, I mean. I had a decently subscribed YouTube channel where I posted regular guitar or piano covers. Those would always get decent hits. More so than the videos of my own compositions.

I also had a Facebook page with plenty of likes and a Twitter account with a distinct imbalance between followers and following. Melody Freeman of the internet had a presence. That's how so many artists start these days, so I was on the right lines, waiting for that request to use one of my songs in a television advert or a Hollywood film, but recently there had been too many distractions from making more progress. Namely studying for a degree I didn't want and partying too hard.

'I don't think I've heard of them,' I replied.

'Arguably the most underrated band of the nineties. Go back to the Britpop era and all people think about now is Oasis and Blur, and occasionally Pulp, but The Bluetones were better than all of them put together. Hidden away in 1996, the eye of the golden era, you'll find *Expecting To Fly*, an album of effortless and understated genius. It was so sublime that they never quite hit that same level again, although their follow-up album came close, and let's not forget the spill-over EP *Marblehead Johnson*. Painfully underrated. With no Gallagher arrogance or Albarn's je ne sais quoi, it was so easy to brush them aside. The Small Faces of the nineties.'

'You'll have to lend me their CD.'

'You can lend me your ears, Milady. Time for us to take flight. Track nine is my particular favourite.'

He got up and skimmed through his stacks of CDs on the bookshelf. His house was a total train wreck, yet his music collection was all arranged in alphabetical order, and so he quickly came to the album in question. He put it in his player and hit go, and for a moment I thought we'd suddenly transported to Heathrow Airport. The song eventually kicked in, but Ziggy skipped on a few songs to what was presumably track nine. He grooved along to the easygoing jangling of guitars as he crouched down at the coffee table and opened a small wooden container.

'Never mind the blue pill, Neo, never mind the red pill. This one gives you all that those two can and so much more.' Inside the box was a quantity of multi-coloured pills. Undoubtedly Triple Rainbow. 'Who's off to see the Wizard with me?'

'Going to ask him for a brain?' I muttered, but no one heard me. 'Oh shit!' I said as some totally random thought somehow found its way into my head.

'What?' Rachel asked.

I rummaged through my bag, but I knew it was futile. 'My Harry Potter pen. I lent it to Xander back at *Joe's* and I forgot to pick it up again. Fuck!'

She patted my knee. 'Never mind, darling. We'll get you a new pen.'

I zipped up my bag again just as Ziggy placed one of the rainbow pills on the end of his tongue that protruded from his mouth like the head of a snake. Rachel giggled then crawled over to him, leaning over the coffee table as they engaged in a hungry smooch, gobbling the pill from him. She broke off from him and swallowed. Ziggy took another of the pills, which he washed down with some whiskey from the bottle. He offered the box to the fire breathers and they both grabbed one.

'One left, Milady.'

I wasn't in the mood for this. I'd never taken anything like this before and I had no idea what was in those things. But the more I thought about that weird encounter with Xander back in the café, the more it depressed me. I was crestfallen with myself, really. Why do I go down these paths so easily? How do I get myself in these situations? I needed to sort my life out, but with it being such a mess, maybe this would be a welcome escape. Until coming to Meridian, I'd been a right goody two shoes, working hard at school, having goals, and making my parents proud. But I'd grown tired of trying all the time. I needed to relax more.

I held my hand out. Ziggy grinned and placed the remaining Triple Rainbow pill in my palm. I knocked it to the back of my throat and swallowed. To hell with it.

So then we all just sat there, everyone smiling curiously at each other as they tried to look for signs of the drug taking effect, madness appearing in the eyes as though looking within them they might detect the outlandish journey their mind was experiencing, turning the dials of their radio as they could now perceive other stations of existence as they flew with the fairies or roamed with dark spirits and ghouls that usually lay beyond the real world, the turning inside out of the optical illusion, the other side of the thing that was impossible to perceive because it was impossible to exist, manifesting the imaginations that remain suppressed in the world of rain and concrete and traffic and supermarket queues and swiping through the endless banality of social media feeds.

I suspected it would take longer to kick in with me because I'd just eaten. I closed my eyes and rubbed my head, then suddenly opened them again, fearing that time had slipped away from me in that momentary disconnection and now it was morning and my time had run out, but everyone was still there as they had been seconds before.

Rachel stood up, her drooping head lost in her hair. She swayed around for a moment, then stepped over me as she walked out of the room. Ziggy followed her and I naturally assumed they were about to embark on a session of psychedelic sex. It left me alone with the two fire breathers. Awesome. They looked like regulars, their bodies battered by a relentless stream of substances, their complexions pallid and their teeth rotten. The skin on their faces was so sunken you could practically make out the skull beneath it. They probably took drugs like I sprinkled sugar on my cornflakes.

With the pill yet to take effect, I wondered about getting out of there, whether I was better off in the city on my own or whether Spud and Sick Boy represented a more appealing situation. Unfortunately, the latter seemed the best option, even though I risked waking up the next morning with another bout of amnesia and a fantasy land-inspired new life conceived inside me and forever debating which smackhead was the father of the flying monkey.

Crap. Already what Xander had told me was slipping from my mind. What was the name of the people he said I had to find? The something Angels? The Angels of Nimh? No, wait... Vihn. The Vihn Angels. I quickly got my phone out and typed it in a text to Rachel in case I'd forget it by the time the high had worn off.

'Say, fellas, have you heard of the Vihn Angels?' It was worth a shot asking them.

One of them made a phlegm-filtered cough. 'Oh yeah. Weird bunch they are,' he replied, the one on the left, whatever he was called. 'Mate of mine went there once. Up near Chapman Hall.'

'Up near where now?'

'They run that club. What's the name of the place?' he asked as he turned to his buddy.

'*The Hooded Claw*?'

'Nooooo,' he chuckled. 'That was... whatsit? *Wacky Races*?'

'*Stop the Pigeon*?'

'I can't remember. *Pigeon Street*, Long Distance Clara, Mr fucking Jupiter and his massive telescope. The Hooded Claw could be one of the people you might meet.'

They giggled to each other, but I was completely lost. I feared they were well on their trip by now.

'So...' I began, attempting to salvage this abortion of

a conversation.

'It's *The Hooded Claw*. They changed the name,' insisted the one on the right.

'Isn't that from a song?' I asked.

'Nah, it's a club. Vihn Angels are there.'

'And how do I find it?'

'Want me to give you a ride?' the one on the left said, before grinning at his mate. Neither of them had made eye contact with me once since I'd been there. I don't think they were used to talking to young women, or perhaps they were just afraid that I was Medusa.

'Yeah. He goes pretty fast, but you'll enjoy every second,' the other said, their inane banter getting into full swing.

'Please, I really need to find this place...'

'What's it worth?' he sneered. It was at that very moment I knew I had to get out of here.

I stood up, and they both laughed as I struggled to find my balance. The light in this room was so dim, it was almost like I had to feel my way out of there, but thankfully I eventually found the door and closed it shut, leaving those grinning idiots behind me.

Chapter 6

I saw the front door ahead of me. This was my chance to escape before anything crazy happened. It made sense to go back to the sanctuary of *Joe's Parlour* with all the other drunken dropouts and wait for the effects to wear off. A strong coffee might help matters.

I didn't want to leave without at least talking to Rachel first, so I carefully navigated my way past all the boxes and clothes and junk on the stairs. At the top I called her name in a quiet but not quiet manner, but I got no reply. I stood there silently, listening out for signs of passion, but I heard nothing. Which room was Ziggy's? I'd never been up here before. It sure smelt worse than it did downstairs.

'Rachel? Where are you?' I called out again.

I decided I would try all the doors until I found her and if I should walk in and find her butt naked, then it was nothing I hadn't seen before. The first door revealed an empty bathroom. On the second door I knocked, the chances increased that it must be a bedroom. On receiving no response, I opened it and was taken by surprise as the light immediately stung my eyes.

I had not expected to find this up here. The room was completely different to the rest of Ziggy's house. There was a grand piano on the opposite side by the window, and a four-poster bed lushly furnished with expensive linen. It was like the setting of a photoshoot for a glossy magazine, ready and waiting for a beautiful model and a photographer to come along and make use of it. Rich daylight streamed through stainless windows, and somewhere in my brain a thought tried to emerge: the sun had risen and yet I was okay.

I stepped inside, instinctively gravitating towards the piano. There was a tremendous view from this room, and I knew for certain I was no longer in Meridian here. We were high in the mountains, candyfloss clouds drifting past the window, a crystal blue lake glinting invitingly at the foot of the valley. It was a fairy tale vista before me, a herd of wild horses munching on the grass of the hills where I could almost imagine Julie Andrews and a flock of children running along with her gaily.

A man joined me at the window, and I had to squint to take him in. As my eyes adjusted, I could see he was very handsome, neatly groomed, his hair slicked back, and he smelt divine. I was sure I gasped as I came to the realisation this man was Ziggy.

'Where am I?' I asked him.

'You tell me,' he replied, stepping closer to me. He smiled warmly. He seemed such a gentleman all of a sudden.

'What are you doing in here?'

'I was waiting for you, Melody. Waiting for you to help you find your dream, to find your destiny.'

'Right,' I replied, folding my arms.

'You have exceptional talent, Melody. The world wants you. It yearns for more of you than you're giving it. But I'm here to help you on that.' He ran the backs of his fingertips down my face as he gazed down at me tenderly. 'Your music is as beautiful as you are, Melody.'

I didn't know he could be such a charmer. Really helped when he wasn't giving me that annoying *Milady* rubbish. I looked him up and down. Gone were his trashy clothes, and he now wore gleaming black shoes, black trousers and a rich blue shirt. I couldn't believe he could seem so classy. It was like he'd swiftly undergone a dramatic transformation on some daytime TV show.

'Will you play for me?' he asked.

I sat down at the piano, and my fingers hovered over the black and white keys. This wasn't my first instrument of choice; I knew my chords, knew how to bring out the melody, but I never did anything flashy in my videos. Here, however, was a much different story. Here I was like Chopin, my hands gliding up and down the keys, wrapping around all sorts of fat chords and intricate sequences.

'Wonderful,' Ziggy gushed as I finished with a delicate glissando. 'Now let's capture this for the world to see. An intimate performance with Melody Freeman.' Right then he held up some little video camera. He stepped behind me.

'What do you want me to play?' I asked.

'Whatever comes to you. Let the music express yourself. Let's really get to know what's underneath.' I felt his free hand rest on my shoulder and he caressed it as I melted into his touch. I could tell he was reaching for the zip on the back of my dress. The air brushed my naked flesh as he undid it. 'Take it off, Melody. Take it all off.'

His charm had hypnotised me, and the idea of following his orders and getting naked in front of him really turned me on. I'd never thought about making a video like this before. I stood, and my dress fell to my feet. I reached behind my back and unclasped my bra, freeing my breasts as Ziggy gazed upon them.

'Everything?' I asked. He nodded, and so I slid my panties down my legs too. I saw him point the camera at me as the red light turned on. It felt so erotic, knowing I was sharing my nakedness with him and my entire audience, whoever should see this. With that I sat back down and proceeded with my performance, Ziggy circling me with the camera as he eagerly captured it all, my nervous fingers dancing over the keys. I hit all the right notes though. In fact, I'd never made such sweet music before in my whole life. I could imagine my viewing figures going wild with this show. Why had I never thought of it before?

Ziggy moved behind me so I couldn't see what he was doing as I continued to play. I assumed he was still recording me, getting every angle as I sat there naked, my long hair splayed out down my back. Suddenly though, his hand slid up my side and reached for my left breast. It proved too much of a distraction and I had to stop playing as he tweaked my nipple between his finger and thumb. I closed my eyes and sighed. I felt him kissing my neck, then lightly biting me as he continued to fondle me.

His other hand reached forward and placed the camera on top of the piano, angled towards us. I turned round and then noticed he'd removed his clothes too, removed everything. I was so turned on. I needed him right now, needed him to ease the tension inside. It seemed the faintest touch from him would send me right away into ecstasy. I stood, hungrily kissing him while I grabbed his manhood and made sure it was perfectly rigid for me.

He led me towards the bed, grabbing the camera so the conclusion of this scandalous performance would be captured too. He placed me down on top of the thick duvet which sat on the sheets like heavenly clouds, then pushed my legs apart as he slid himself inside me. As he pointed the lens down at me, he expertly built up his rhythm, and then I was aware of something beside me. Was there someone else there with us, lost in the marshmallow duvet? Eventually a sleepy face appeared.

'Hey, Melody,' Rachel said.

Had she seen what I was doing? Having sex with her sort-of-boyfriend? It suddenly struck me that that's what she must have been doing with him moments before I'd come into the room. She propped herself up, her head resting on her hand, and casually watched Ziggy as he continued to thrust at me. Okay, so that obviously wasn't a concern for her, that I was messing around with her man. No wonder they'd never seemed that serious an item.

'Playing with my toy, Melody, hmm?' she asked. 'I suppose it's only friendly to share with you.'

I couldn't form a reply for her right now, my breath getting away with itself as Ziggy continued to send me towards a climax. He'd soon got me so close. Rachel smiled at me then leant in, connecting her lips with mine. We'd never done anything like that before, but it felt so good, Ziggy's manhood ferociously penetrating me as Rachel kissed me. That did it. I was sent over the edge in such an all-encompassing orgasm that shuddered through every part of my body, wrapping my legs around Ziggy and pulling him into me as he also came.

I gasped for air as Rachel released herself from our embrace as she now kissed Ziggy. This was the most twisted passion I'd ever shared with anyone, and already I wondered how I would face her again, knowing what we were doing. Although, the more I considered it, the more I realised I didn't care. I figured I could live with it.

Ziggy detached himself from me and disappeared. I

slid myself towards the end of the bed so I could sit myself up. My head was really spinning after all that. Rachel nuzzled in next to me. Were we going to be lovers now? Moved out of a friendzone that neither of us were actually trying to get out of? I didn't even know she went this way. I didn't know *I* did. We'd spoken nothing of this sort before. I cared for her though. She was my friend. Sure, she was a bit of a ditz, but she was adorable. Maybe we would experience each other like this again.

'Fucking awesome pill, huh?'

And then it hit me. Shit. Where the hell was my head after that Triple Rainbow mindtwister we'd just taken? Was this really happening?

To add a discordant note to this unexpected episode of passion, my stomach gurgled, and I wondered how wise it was to have been lying down like this and having my body jolted around so much after having had such a big meal. Sharp pains suddenly stabbed throughout my guts.

'Rachel, where's the bathroom?' I got no answer as she seemed to doze off again. 'No matter. I already know.'

I sprang out of bed but nearly fell right over my arse as my vision wobbled. I felt terrible, this moment of fantasy quickly turning into one of horror as that familiar sensation of panic rose from my centre. Time was running out, an explosion about to erupt, an awareness that being inside my body was the absolute worst place to be right now as I wished I was far outside it.

With no time to put any clothes on, I darted out of the room.

Chapter 7

I flung myself into the bathroom, slamming the palm of my hand onto the switch as the harsh strands of tungsten light stung my eyes and further prickled the gagging in the back of my throat.

Along with the overwhelming nausea that had suddenly swelled, also came the incredible self-loathing for the cocktail of crap I'd put inside me tonight. Why did I do this to myself? I so wished I'd stayed at home instead. What I would have given to be there right now, to at least cushion myself with some degree of comfort while I was about to be ill, rather than being in this filthy cesspit of grime. I crouched down at the toilet. The lid was already open, naturally, and I hunched my neck over the bowl, as though putting my head into the mouth of some squalor monster, its stool-stained maw yawning at me and about to swallow my sorry self away with all the other yucky detritus.

I retched and a forceful stream of vomit spewed from my throat, plunging into the germ-ridden water of the toilet, splashing back up into my face, chunks of partially digested food clinging to my hair. I continued to hurl, the puke splattering from my mouth like a kaleidoscopic waterfall and for a moment I feared it would go on forever and my brain would starve of oxygen. As it receded, there came bliss, and I finally drew some air back into my lungs, that even in this rotten stinking hole of a bathroom, felt like the sweetest air I had ever breathed.

With no care I rested my head against the rim of the toilet, the thought of whatever matter had been splashed onto it and multiplied on this petri dish from hell a much more attractive experience to what I had just gone through. I panted, partly in relief, and partly through shock from having gone from such sensual tenderness to this wretched mess. And then, from behind me, came the sound of the door opening.

'Please go away,' I said to the unlucky intruder, but then I heard that phlegmy voice speaking.

'Feeling a little off colour, angel?' I turned to see

one of the fire breathers lurking in the doorway, like some ugly troll that had climbed the castle walls and invaded my realm.

'Clear off!' I pleaded, but I knew it was futile. I hunched my body even more to protect my nakedness, so he wouldn't be able to store any images of me in his brain for his own gratification later.

He stepped inside and closed the door, crouching down behind me. I could smell his foul stench of fag breath even above the stench of my vomit.

'Want me to make you feel better, darling?' He reached a hand towards me and grabbed my breast, his breaths on my skin deepening. If I'd had any more vomit in me, I surely would have been unloading it into the toilet. All I could do was hide my head in my arm as I clutched it tightly around the rim, like it was some lifebuoy ring, the only thing I had to cling on to to save me from the sea of horror I was now about to drown in.

He licked his yellow tongue up the side of my face, even though it was splattered in puke. This loser had probably never felt up a girl before in his whole life, and growing up in such a cesspit he'd obviously developed no sense of hygiene. A chance was a chance for this freak. I sobbed, before mustering some force within my body as I started screaming, but the perv kept going.

The door slammed open again and there stood Ziggy in a t-shirt and boxers. 'Hey, what the fuck, dude?'

The fire breather clutched me even tighter, like I was a toy he'd found and wouldn't give up.

'Get the fuck off her,' Ziggy growled, before picking him off me and swiftly ejecting him. 'Are you okay?' he asked me, grimacing at the sorry state I was in.

'No,' I muttered.

Rachel burst in there too. 'What's going on, chick?' Her eyes opened wide at the explosion of vomit and immediately ushered Ziggy out of the room, leaving us alone.

'Lock the door,' I ordered her, and she did so.

'Where are your clothes, honey?'

'In the next room, I hope.'

47

I wondered why she'd asked me that. Didn't she know? Wasn't she aware of what had been going on right before I'd rushed to the bathroom? Perhaps all of that had never happened. Or perhaps that was just Rachel being a ditz again.

'I need to clean myself up.' I hobbled to my feet and pressed the flush on the toilet. However, it was absolutely no surprise that it wasn't working. Oh well. A little souvenir for them. I turned to the bathtub and saw a shower head over it. Hopefully that would work. I twisted the taps, and water sprayed out. As soon as it got to a tepid temperature, I stood in the tub and rinsed all that horridness away, the vomit, the germs, the touch of that filthy goblin. There wasn't any soap in there, but the water was good enough.

'Here,' Rachel said as she handed me a small bottle of something she'd grabbed out of her cardigan pocket. 'It's hand sanitiser. Best we're going to find in here.'

'Thanks,' I replied. It was a first for me, showering in alcohol gel, but it was like a gift sent from heaven.

I didn't care that I was doing all this right in front of her. It didn't seem a biggie after what we'd been doing in the other room, or at least what I thought we'd been doing. Taking a shower in the presence of my best friend was way further down on the kink levels compared to kissing her while her boyfriend penetrated me. But had that actually happened? I was sure as hell there was no four-poster bed or a grand piano in the room next door. What else of it was real? Had Ziggy filmed us? Was there now some sex tape of a drugged-up Melody Freeman sitting on a memory card waiting for the time when I was famous and he could make a killing by releasing it to some porn site?

'Any better now?' Rachel asked me.

I was as clean as I was going to get and yes, I did feel a damn lot better than I was a few minutes earlier. I nodded to her, but my relief was short-lived as I searched for something to dry myself off. All I could find was some rag of a hand towel that looked like it hadn't been washed in years. There was no way I would press that thing to my body.

'I need a towel,' I said as I turned off the tap.

'Let me go look for one. I'll get your clothes as well.' She left the room, and I locked the door behind her. I then stood there shivering and dripping onto the scum-ridden floor. The shivering almost triggered my retching again, but I managed to swallow it back. Eventually there was a knock.

'It's me,' Rachel said. I let her in. She'd found a clean towel thankfully, so I patted myself dry. She then held out my underwear and dress for me and I quickly slipped into them. I tied my damp hair up and wrapped the towel around it.

'I don't know about you, Rach, but I seriously want to get the hell out of here.'

'Yeah, I think it's time we ought to get going,' she replied with faux casualness.

Before we left though, I had to know exactly what had happened earlier. I needed to know if my best friend had turned into one with lesbian benefits, or whether that was all a product of some repressed subconscious I would have to unravel at some more suitable time.

'So... back there in the bedroom...' I began.

'Oh, we were totally mashed, darling,' she replied, smiling as though I was triggering a happy memory.

'And what did we do exactly?'

She shrugged. 'Nothing I regret.'

'Look, Rach, did Ziggy have a video camera? Was he filming us?'

She pursed her lips together, looking pretty clueless. 'To be fair... I wouldn't put it past him.'

'Okay, I need to get that camera. I know I make lots of videos myself, but I'm not sure I want to branch out into that area just yet.'

'All right. I'll see if I can get it off him. Wait here.'

She left, and I listened in anticipation for any audible sign that she might be successful in her operation. I thought I could detect her going back into the bedroom, but then came footsteps outside the bathroom again. They were heavy. I hoped they belonged to Ziggy rather than either of the fire breathers. They seemed to stop right on the other side of the door and as I looked down, I saw the handle turn. Shit. I was just about to slam the lock shut when I heard Rachel's voice.

'Oh, hey. There you are.'

'How's Milady?'

'Think it was a bad trip, Zig.'

'Sorry about that, Rach. Some people do react the wrong way to those pills.'

'I'm sure she'll live. I was just helping her clean up.'

'Okay. I'm making a brew. Come down when you're ready, won't you?'

'Oh totally.' I desperately hoped Rachel was acting when she said that. I didn't want to spend any longer in this place.

'I think you should both stay here tonight, especially as Milady is so off colour. Have a brew then sleep it off, yeah?'

'Great idea, Zig.'

I heard Ziggy walking off back downstairs. The door handle turned again, and Rachel entered. She breathed a sigh of relief.

'I'm not staying for a cup of bloody tea,' I immediately told her.

'Fuck that. Those two dipshit friends of his are still down there. What fucking creepazoids. They'll probably drug us and rape us.' Why the hell did she ever hang around with Ziggy? Then again, I couldn't really talk, having only just had sex with him. Or so I thought. That sure wasn't the real Ziggy I'd experienced back in that room.

I started mentally planning our escape. The front door was right at the foot of the stairs, but I really didn't want to risk going down there. Plus, there was something else we needed to see to first.

'Wait, did you find that camera?'

'Yeah.'

'Great. You got it?'

'Nah.'

'Rachel!'

'But I got this.' She held up a memory card.

'You lifesaver!' I felt like I could kiss her. Again. I grabbed it off her and slid it into my bra. Maybe I'd watch it later. Maybe I'd smash it under the heel of my shoe...

Speaking of which, I suddenly noticed I was still barefoot.

'Oh, and I got these for you,' Rachel said on cue as she held up my shoes and also my bag. I didn't have my cardigan, but I really didn't care about seeing that cheap Primarni garment again.

'Thanks, Rach.' I slid my flats on and ripped the towel off my head and threw it into the bath. 'Ready to make a run for it?'

She squinted, peering beyond me. What the hell was she looking at?

'How about climbing out the window?'

I turned round to assess her idea. It was certainly big enough to climb through. I put down the lid of the toilet, realising I should have perhaps done that already, then stood on it and leant through the frame. Was I really going to do this?

I remembered back to the fire talks we'd had in school, how they hammered into us about being safe and having contingencies if the unthinkable should happen. I could still picture the fire officer talking about assessing your home to form a plan, looking out your bedroom window and seeing what you could use to clamber down, perhaps using the drainpipes or jumping on something to break your fall. It was dark as I peered outside, but my eyes adjusted to make out the mosaic of tiny gardens lining the back of the terrace, a jungle of rundown housing beyond them. I had no idea how we would get out of the garden once we dropped into it. Fortunately, I spotted an old shed right beneath us.

'I think we can do this,' I said. I started to climb into the window, knocking over empty deodorant cans and a toothbrush holder as I did so. 'There's a shed we'll jump onto.' I turned round and eased myself through, holding onto the sill as I lowered myself out.

'Be careful, hon,' Rachel said.

I didn't need care. All I needed was determination, and I had plenty of that. I shoved myself away from the wall and landed with a thud onto the shed roof. I moved over and beckoned to Rachel. She was looking markedly less brave than me, however.

'Come on, Rach. You can do it.'

Reluctantly she followed my same motions, dangling herself out of the window where she hovered, hesitating, too scared to make the jump.

'Do it! It's not far at all. I'll catch you!'

She pushed herself away and screamed as she landed next to me. I clutched onto her arm before she slid off the roof. I just knew someone would have heard her scream so there was no time for hanging around. I could see the light on in the kitchen where Ziggy would be making his drinks.

'Come on, Rach, we need to run.'

I led her across the roof of the shed and jumped from it into the neighbour's garden. Rachel did the same.

'Where now?' she asked.

I feared this was an endless terrace of housing and we'd have to climb fence after fence until we reached the end, but then I noticed an alleyway. I grabbed Rachel's hand as I led us across the garden. Through the archway I saw the welcome sight of the road. Freedom. We'd escaped.

'Come on,' I said, the sense of triumph rising. But wasn't this the moment when we would run into the road and just when we thought we'd made our escape, Ziggy and the troglodyte fire breathers would be standing there and immediately capture us again?

Regardless, we sprinted into the street. I glanced towards Ziggy's house and saw his door was still shut. With that I tugged on Rachel's arm again and we both ran along the pavement and kept running until we were far enough away that the adrenaline started to abate with the thought that we'd reached a safe enough distance and so we sat down on a welcome bench and caught our breath.

Chapter 8

I gazed towards the heavens, my slowing breath rising from me like my spirit was escaping me. We were in some little council park, yet despite still being in the middle of the city, I could see a brilliant array of stars glinting above me. It seemed my irises were adjusting to the dark as, one by one, each star was emerging from the blackness. I'd never seen so many before. Perhaps it was a residual effect of the drug we'd taken, relaxing the muscles in my eyes or something.

'Right, I'm going to call us a taxi,' Rachel announced. 'Time to get you home, Miss Freeman.' She got out her phone.

'No, wait. I can't go back yet.'

'What? You've just taken a legal high, violently thrown your guts up, been molested by some grotty lowlife, and now you want to carry on partying?'

'I still need to work out...'

'Yeah, yeah, what we did last night. Well, if tonight is anything to go by, maybe it's something we're better off not knowing.'

'That's just it, Rachel. I *need* to know. I know this sounds weird, but I have this overwhelming urge to find out. It's like I can sense there's some important discovery to be made.'

'But, darling... it's so late.'

I suddenly felt a wave of panic. Just what time was it? It hadn't seemed like we'd spent a long time at Ziggy's. Taking the Triple Rainbow, going up to his room, puking in the bathroom and then making our escape... all of that was only, what? Half an hour? Forty-five minutes at most?

As I checked my watch, it was like someone was messing with my mind. It was almost a quarter past two. What the hell? We were at Ziggy's for nearly three hours! How was that possible?

'Shit,' I sighed. 'I'm running out of time, Rach.'

'Huh?' she replied sleepily. 'Let's just go back home.'

'I'm not going. I'll carry on without you if I have to.'

'Carry on where? Look, we pretty much worked out where we went last night.'

'I've only got about five and a half hours!'

'Till fucking what?'

'Till the sun comes out. Hell, maybe I did get bitten by a vampire and by sunrise I'll be dead.'

Rachel laughed. 'Oh, my days. Are you still tripping, pumpkin? Come on.' She stood up, as if this was some sort of parental style technique to encourage me to comply with her. I remained where I was and she folded her arms and sighed when I threw her a defiantly unimpressed look. 'Where the hell do you think you want to go next?'

'There's a club I need to visit.'

'What club?'

Crap. I'd forgotten. I cast my mind back, put myself back in that room with the two fire breathers. What was the name of that place? I remembered they were rambling on about cartoons and stuff.

'Come on, Mel, we're just wasting valuable sleep time now.'

'*The Hooded Claw*!' It had suddenly come to me out of nowhere.

'And where the hell is that?'

I didn't have the answer to that one either, could discern the emptiness in my brain where it should be, yet somehow I found my mouth uttering the words, 'Chapman Hall. It's near there.' I hoped to hell Rachel understood what I meant by 'Chapman Hall' because I had no idea whatever it was exactly.

'That's a business centre. I remember Veronica saying she did some temping there over Christmas for some consultancy firm, I think.'

'It's near that building apparently,' I told her. 'Do you know how to get there?'

'Yeah, because I've got an inbuilt sat nav system in my brain. I'm sure your average Meridian taxi driver can get us there.'

I smiled. 'Coming with me then?'

Fifteen minutes later we were sitting in the back of

a taxi on our way towards *The Hooded Claw*. The driver had never heard of it, but he did know where the Chapman Hall Business Centre was and that was good enough for me. I didn't know what we were going to find there, or whether this mysterious club was still open at this ungodly hour, but I was determined to go there. It had become an obsession for me.

Rachel sat in silence, thumbing her phone screen. The poor lass looked so tired and I felt a little guilty for dragging her along on my crazy escapade. I peered out of the corner of my eye at her phone. Perhaps Ziggy had texted her, and she was replying. I hoped she wasn't about to tell him what we were up to, where we were going to. However, it seemed she was looking at the photos she'd taken last night... our blackout night, now two nights ago technically, of course. She held the screen up and squinted.

'What?' I asked. It was that blurry photo with that strange person with the eighties glam rock hair lurking behind us.

'Nothing.'

'Let me see.' I could tell something about it bothered her. I knew her well enough by now. Knew her better than most people after tonight. 'Do you remember him?'

'Not one bit,' she replied. 'It's just...'

'It's just...?'

'*My, what big teeth you have, Grandma.*'

Instantly, I saw what she meant. Within the bleary smear of pixels I could definitely see this mysterious Bon Jovi stranger was smiling for the camera, and his mouth really did seem to be endowed with rather long fangs.

'Must be motion blur,' she said, although it seemed like she was saying it to reassure herself. 'You know, stretched his teeth out?'

'Hmm,' I sounded, unconvinced. Not that I wanted to contemplate the theory that we had run into a vampire last night. I didn't believe in the things. They didn't exist. I mean, I certainly understood a lot about them, reading books and following countless television shows revolving around them. Nearly all of these vampire-dwelling universes took the idea that these beings could compel you, make you do things. Make you forget.

My fingertips stroked the marks on my neck, the puncture wounds. Were they really caused by a blood-drinking creature of the undead sinking its fangs into my artery? If we were about to go back to this club we'd apparently stumbled upon last night, were we going to run into this vampire again? Risk another encounter with him where he'd compel us to forget everything we'd done tonight, and I'd wake up again later and do this all again like some gothic version of *Groundhog Day*?

'Chapman Hall,' the taxi driver announced. 'Eight eighty, please.'

I handed over my debit card, and he slapped it on his card reader. 'Thanks.'

'Enjoy the rest of your evening, ladies.'

'Adios,' Rachel said as we got out. The taxi drove off into the night and we stood there taking in our surroundings.

'That's the business centre,' Rachel told me, pointing up to some spooky block of offices. It looked a tired place, somewhere that offered cheap rent for struggling businesses. Outside it there was a paved area where revellers lingered, eating kebabs and fried chicken wings. We headed towards them. I glanced up and down the road as we crossed it, looking out for some swaying sign, a neon light above a doorway flashing off and on in bright red as it enticed passers-by into the enigmatic establishment known as *The Hooded Claw*. However, I could find none of the sort.

'Let's ask someone,' I suggested.

'May as well,' Rachel replied as we approached some random people.

Suddenly I paused though, and seeing I had done so, Rachel stopped and looked at me enquiringly. Perhaps somewhere deep down in my brain a trapped bubble of a memory had been roused and coursed to the surface. Perhaps a faint cloud of familiarity had drifted into my mind, because from out of nowhere I felt a compulsion to head across the concourse. I heard Rachel's slow footsteps behind me.

I entered a gloomy street, off the beaten track of revellers crawling from bar to bar. The sort of street where you could imagine unsavoury characters lurking in the shadows. There were a few shops boarded up for the night in metal shutters next to boring-looking establishments that, in the day, would house solicitors or accountants.

'This hardly seems like party central, hon,' Rachel said. 'Let me go ask...'

'Wait. Do you recognise any of this?'

'Nah-uh. It's not down here.'

But I continued my wandering, and she had no choice but to follow. Eventually, I stopped. I knew I had arrived there, but there was no enticing sign anywhere, no colourful lights, no names of drinks emblazoned on any window nearby. I stepped farther towards a door made of big wooden panels like it was the gate of a stable.

'That's it. It's in there,' I announced. I knew there were people beyond that door, as though I could smell them.

'I don't think there's anything going on in there, babe. Come on, there isn't even a handle.'

She was right. But then I peered closer at a wooden plaque above the door. Letters had been etched into it in small writing, big enough so that people would read it only if they were particularly looking for it, if they *knew* to look for it. This place was indeed called *The Hooded Claw*. Perhaps it was closed for the night but, despite that, I decided to knock.

'Nothing,' Rachel said after only a few seconds. 'There's no one here. Let's go.'

I was just about to give up when we heard a bolt slide. The adrenaline surged within me. What had I done? Who was on the other side of that door? I could have led us right up to the home of the vampire and he would stand there in a cloak, his fangs extending as he smiled, and in a lightning move he'd grab us and take us into his lair and drain us of all our blood.

The door creaked open, a dull crimson light illuminating a figure who stepped forward. It was a woman, taller than either of us. She was exquisite, wearing red lipstick, her hair intricately tied up as it sat on her head like swirls of sand, a silver cross dangling from a necklace. She wore a corset-style dress and striped stockings, and there was absolutely no hint of a smile on her face as she cast her eyes over us.

'Yes?' she asked. She certainly hadn't just got out of bed to answer the door, but it seemed like we'd interrupted her. Perhaps some lucky guy was about to peel all her clothes off.

'Sorry to bother you,' I began nervously. Boy, we really must have looked like a pair of silly lost girls to her. 'Is this the right place to find...? You see, I'm looking for... Someone told me that...'

'What do you want?' she asked me sternly.

'Does the Vihn Angels mean anything to you?' I decided to just come straight out with it.

'Who are you?'

'I think we came here last night. Is this your stamp?'

Her eyes widened as I showed her the marking on my hand.

'Oh. You need to come inside right now.'

Chapter 9

Once we'd entered, I could see there were indeed more signs of life. A corridor extended before us, what seemed like a long tunnel, candles burning in lanterns that lined the length of it. At the end, there appeared to be a lounge area.

'This way,' the lady said as she led us inside. It seemed to be an old building, like some sort of haunted mansion, portraits of important-looking luminaries on the walls, their eyes probably following us as we walked past. I wondered if we'd stepped into a spooky attraction, and soon the floors would be spinning or ghostly characters would jump out at us.

As I'd sensed, the lounge area had an abundant population of people, most of whom turned their heads to look us over as we walked among them. Was this a private club? There was a mixture of ages here, young, middle-aged, one or two elderly folk. They sat around in comfy chairs, while some played pool, a couple even playing chess, a vigorous fire blazing in the centre of the room. Meat Loaf rang out from speakers, only loud enough so you could hear, not so overpowering that it smothered conversation.

'Get yourself a drink,' our host told us. 'Kerrish will speak to you shortly.'

Before I had a chance to ask who Kerrish was, the elegant lady with the coiled hair walked away, leaving us on our own at the bar. Some people returned to sipping their drinks, others still cast a scrutinising eye our way. I perched myself on a stool.

'This place is giving me the creeps,' Rachel whispered in my ear.

'Is it triggering any memories for you?'

'Not a thing, hon. Think it's a bit too sophisticated for us.'

'What can I get you?' a man behind the bar asked us. I didn't really feel like drinking, certainly nothing alcoholic.

'What the hell is a snake wine?' Rachel asked as she picked up a drinks list.

'Why don't you try one? If you dare,' the bartender replied hammily.

'Okay, sod it, give me a snake wine.'

He turned to me.

'Just a regular, unadventurous lemonade,' I said.

He nodded, then stepped aside to prepare our drinks. We glanced around to continue taking in our strange surroundings. I was trying, but it really wasn't triggering anything within me either. Going on my instinct, which is all I had to go on, and which had served me pretty well so far, I sensed that I'd never been here before.

'How did you hear about this place, anyway?' Rachel asked.

'One of Ziggy's friends told me this is where the Vihn Angels are.'

'One of those two maggots? You're really following the word of someone who molested you?'

'We made it here though, didn't we?'

'I suppose. We definitely didn't come here last night. I mean, what would we have been doing in this part of town to begin with? And none of this delightful décor matches up with any of the photos on our phones.'

I had to agree, with all of it. The bartender interrupted again as he presented us with our drinks. I opened my purse to get some money.

'It's okay. It's on the house,' he said.

'Oh. Okay. Thanks,' I replied. I looked at the disgusting green drink he'd placed in front of Rachel. 'Good luck with that one. Looks like poison.'

'Bottoms up,' she said as she raised the cocktail glass and took a big gulp. Didn't take her long to get back into the party spirit.

'So is this your first time at *The Hooded Claw*?' came a voice the other side of us. We turned to see an older guy standing there wearing a black suit and a mac. He held a whisky glass and had a Sean Connery smile that was clearly attempting to charm.

'Uh yes,' I replied. 'Are you Kerrish?'

'No,' he said. Great. Now I'm about to get chatted up by a dirty old man, I thought. 'My name's David. I work across the street from here. Well, used to work there, I should say. I'm semi-retired now.'

'So, come here often?' I asked, the sarcasm surely coming through.

'Let's just say I have a certain area of expertise that goes hand in hand with the folk here, certain skills.'

'Are you a pimp?' Rachel brazenly put to him. He took it in good humour though and laughed.

'No, no. I'm sure Kerrish will fill you in on what they do. Although, I can let you in on one little secret.'

'Mm-hmm? What's that?' Rachel asked.

'This is my first time here too. I often used to sit in my office over the way and wonder what was on the other side of the door here. *The Hooded Claw*, I saw it was called. How mysterious! I'm usually pretty good at finding things out about people, but not with this clandestine place.'

'What did you work as?' I asked him.

'I was a private investigator. What do you two do?'

'We're students,' we both said in unison.

'Oh really? My daughter is at Meridian University. Never thought she would get there, but she continues to surprise us.'

I was softening to him. Perhaps he was a genuine guy, after all. It didn't seem like he was about to ask us back to his place when it seemed we'd just established we were the same age as his daughter.

'What does she study?' Rachel asked.

'Drama,' he said, feigning a bit of embarrassment with his answer.

'That's what I do! What's her name?'

'Sam. Sam Sherborne.'

'Oh yeah! I know her!'

'Well, that is remarkable. Two million people in this city, and yet sometimes it seems a small world, full of intriguing interweaving.'

'She's a nice girl is Sam. You should be proud,' Rachel went on.

'We are. Although I hope you two don't teach her any of these bad habits, staying out till these unholy hours.'

'How come all you lot are here though at this time

of day?' I asked. Although it was fascinating to realise this synchronistical meeting, I still urgently needed answers, and the mention of the time again reminded me that the grains of sand were rapidly running out for me.

David seemed coy, uneasy. 'I'm sure Kerrish will explain.'

'But what is it you do here?' I persisted.

He stood there silently for a moment, wondering how to answer. He had just opened his mouth when a younger man dressed in a leather jacket approached.

'David, please introduce me to your two friends,' he said.

'Oh. I didn't actually get your names,' he replied.

'I'm Melody. She's Rachel. And I have a feeling you're Kerrish.'

'Indeed, I am,' Kerrish replied. 'David, excuse us, I must take our new friends aside for a moment.'

Friends? Well, I suppose he seemed friendly. More so than the lady who'd answered the door. I got off my stool. I didn't have time to be mistrustful of this stranger, and, besides, I had Rachel with me.

'You can leave your drinks here.'

'Sure,' I replied as we put them back down on the bar.

He led us through the lounge area, all the clientele casting suspicious looks our way, as though we were riffraff that the bouncers were throwing out. At the back of the room we reached another darkened corridor lined with old bricks like we were in a cellar. As we walked down it in single file I had the sensation the passageway sloped downwards.

'Through here,' Kerrish said as we came to a door. I guessed he was taking us to a private area of the club. I certainly wasn't expecting it would be another bedroom. I didn't think lightning would strike twice like that tonight.

As he opened the door, I immediately locked eyes with the mardy woman with the coiled hair who was waiting for us inside. Her mood had now changed though, a warm smile lighting her face like she was an air stewardess and was welcoming us aboard the flight.

'Please step this way,' she said, as though leading us to our seats. We stepped towards an arched alcove, what looked like it may have been a wine cellar at some point. Pinned to the back of the wall I could make out a pair of candid photographs, and I instantly knew they were what we were here to see.

'That's us,' Rachel exclaimed as we rushed up to them, magnetised. What better way to get someone's attention than by something as personal as their own photograph? But why the hell would they have these? They were taken while we were out in a bar, and judging by the clothes we were wearing they must have been taken last night.

'Who took these?' I asked, turning round to Kerrish and the woman. Punctuating my question was the sound of a gate being closed as Kerrish then slid a large bolt to lock us into the alcove, our cell. We both immediately rushed up to the bars and instinctively grabbed them.

'What the hell are you doing?' Rachel cried.

'I'm sorry,' he replied. 'You have been marked.'

'Let us out of here! I'll bloody scream till someone hears us!' she shouted as she rattled the bars.

'They won't come for you, so don't bother.'

'Why are you doing this?' I asked, trying to be as calm as I could, cutting through Rachel's hysteria.

Kerrish approached me and looked down into my eyes as though he was seeing much more than some harmless young woman before him.

'To protect this town. To stem the spread of this scourge.'

'*What?*' Rachel asked.

He stepped away from the bars, checking a message on his phone, chewing over some other thought, nodding to the woman with the coiled hair that now looked like a bundle of snakes. He seemed a man with a million things to do, and locking up two student girls was just a routine occurrence on a Friday night for him.

'Last night our undercover spies observed you as they were out in the city. They marked you with that symbol on your hands so we would be able to identify you.'

'Are you the Vihn Angels then?' I asked. 'This is hardly angelic behaviour, is it?'

Rachel rubbed at the stamp on her hand. 'What is this stuff, anyway? How does it come off?' she asked, as though that was the most important thing right now. *Shut up, Rach!*

'It usually fades in a few days... That's if you make it that long.'

'What are you going to do to us, you bastards?' I spat at him. I was really starting to despise him. We would have been better off just staying at Ziggy's. At least we could deal with him and his fire breathers.

'Don't play the victim with me, young lady. I'm not doing this because I'm a sadist. I do this because it's necessary.'

'Locking up people against their will?'

'Hmm. Well, to prove I'm not the bad guy that you think I am, I will offer you the chance to gain your freedom again.'

'Oh really? How nice of you,' I shot at him. 'Let's do it then.'

His mind seemed distracted, other issues to attend to, things more important than dealing with kidnapped students.

'Patience, Melody. That chance will come. For now, I need to leave you be, so you can reflect on how your waywardness has cost you so dearly.'

Patronising bastard. I watched him leave the room, that smarmy snake-haired woman throwing us a sneer as though we were a couple of scumbags, before she too left us in our dingy dungeon.

Chapter 10

Time passed, and I feared the swelling anxiety would send me mad. I was still locked up in this cell and there was nothing I could do about it, the air growing thick with the pressure that must have been emanating from my brain, as though this room was the cooker and I was a kitten in a microwave about to explode in a mush of flesh. I sat down on the cold floor rocking impatiently from side to side, Rachel lying opposite me, probably asleep.

Right after being left alone in the cell, we'd naturally tried to call someone on our phones, but neither of us had any reception. I kept checking for bars every ten seconds in case my signal should decide to come back (it was my device's typical behaviour) but none appeared. So it didn't appear we would get hold of the police.

I wondered if that man we'd met in the lounge, David, was still there. I wondered if he would help us if he was aware of what Kerrish had done to us. We'd only just shared some friendly small talk with him and five seconds later we'd become kidnapped right under his nose. If only I had some psychic ability like that mysterious guy in the café, Xander, and I could somehow mentally project my cry for help to him. Surely with a daughter of his own the same age as us, one of our peers in fact, he would be the first to respond by immediately storming in with a machine gun and taking everyone down with his particular set of skills like he was Liam Neeson. This was the fantasy going through my mind. If only our phones were working and Rachel could text David's daughter and get her to relay the score to him. Technology always seemed to let you down when you needed it most!

Was I a magnet for attracting dickheads or something? I really did seem to be making a glorious run of that tonight. I looked at my watch. It was ten past three. Just over four and a half hours now. I still didn't understand what was supposed to happen on the moment of sunrise but, with my luck, I knew it would not be good. The dreadful feeling persisted that it may even be the last sunrise I would live through. I certainly wouldn't see it if I remained in this place!

'I know this is a pretty bad situation right now,' Rachel muttered, 'but is it wrong of me to say that Kerrish guy is kind of hot?'

Oh my God. Only she could come out with that. 'We haven't been locked up more than half an hour and already you have Stockholm Syndrome?'

'Well, obviously I'm not happy that he's done this, and I'm really not rating any long-term prospects with him, but it doesn't hide the fact that he's a total dish. I mean, come on, if you were in different circumstances with him, would you be disappointed if you woke up next to him?'

'Jees, Rach, I really can't put my mind into that mode right now.'

'Look, I'm just saying this situation could be a lot worse. Imagine if he looked like Harvey Weinstein.'

'I wasn't getting the vibe from Kerrish that he was about to drop his bathrobe and masturbate in front of us.'

'Oh no, he's too much of a prep. He doesn't have anything predatory about him. That's why we need to use our charms. Come on, you're following the glitterball of showbiz like me. You need to get used to thinking like this to get ahead.'

'Rach... no. Just no. That's fucked up.'

She shut up, sensing I wasn't in the mood for entertaining her thoughts. The girl just wasn't bothered about using her body that way, practically prostituting herself so she could get where she needed to be, whether it would be a role in a movie, or the other side of the bars as was the case for us right now. I wasn't sure if that resulted from her already being conditioned by the patriarchal worlds out there, or whether she was so highly sexed that she just didn't care and was making practical use of it.

Either way, I had no doubt she would do well in life. I already knew she was going to be a star. It was like she already saw herself as someone, and the universe automatically moved around her to fulfil her ambition, rather than how it was with me, that I was trying too much to make the universe recognise my dream. Maybe that's what attracted me to her the most. I subconsciously recognised her as a success story and perhaps her natural abilities to succeed would rub off on me.

There was only one little detail about Rachel that undermined her destiny, one tiny crack in the glamour of her status, one thing that she would have to sort out before she wanted the showbiz world to take her seriously. It was her surname. I admitted I didn't have the best of surnames. It was pretty humdrum. But hers? It was a disaster. Rachel Dickfloss was her full name.

Dickfloss. How could anyone have even invented a surname like that in the first place? It was impossible for her to tell people her name without provoking some seriously twisted mental imagery in them, to the extent that sometimes people thought she was taking the piss, so she'd told me.

Knowing Rachel as I knew her, perhaps there was some nominative determinism going on with her too. The way she talked, I could well imagine she'd undergone a flossing motion with numerous dicks in her already short lifetime. But if she would indeed fulfil a serious career as an actress, she was unlikely to get any Shakespearean roles with the surname Dickfloss. More likely she would end up in porn. Granted, she had the constitution for that, certainly if tonight's earlier activities were anything to go by, but thankfully even Rachel realised she was capable of much more.

Until then, she needed to change her surname and as yet she hadn't found a satisfactory substitute to adopt. Occasionally we would throw ideas out there, try on names like she was trying on clothes, but nothing seemed to sit on her right.

Just as I was enjoying the silence, Rachel turned to me and asked, 'So do you think he's ripped?'

I buried my head in my arms. On some level, though, I was glad that she was here. As inappropriate as her thoughts were, at least they dispelled *some* of the direness of our predicament. But her next stream of consciousness that came spewing out of her mouth really didn't help.

'Are we in some sort of *Hostel* scenario?' she asked, nonchalantly. I began to wonder if there had been something else in that snake drink she'd had. 'We're enticed inside and locked up, and there's these regular business men type who come here, and maybe they're all normal family people on the surface, go home to their wives and eat cottage pie and watch *Monday Night Football*, but underneath they have this sick urge to butcher up young women. It all kind of fits, doesn't it?'

I looked up at her, incredulousness in my face, but I think it was lost in the gloom. I peered through the bars at the rest of the room. I couldn't see any power tools or torture devices, no dark stains of blood decorating the walls and floor. Still, I couldn't dismiss the idea, what with how crazy this night had already been.

'I don't think they would offer us our chance of freedom again if they wanted to use us as torture victims,' I said.

'Good point. I wish he'd get the fuck on with that.'

As though he'd just heard her, the door opened, and in walked Kerrish. He approached our cell flanked by two people: Snake Head, of course, and some nerdy guy dressed in vaguely steampunk attire with wire-rimmed glasses and a moustache that looked like it was being cultivated into a handlebar style.

'Sorry for the delay, ladies,' Kerrish said. He gestured to the nerd. 'Allow me to introduce my colleague Manny Mantella.' *Pffft* was the sound that went through my head. Manny Mantella? He was about as manly as Conchita Wurst. 'And I can't remember if I introduced you to Donna.'

'En-fucking-chante,' I said.

'Delightful. Now, Mantella is going to be your best friend here so you should be really nice to him. He's the one who can determine whether I can set either of you free, once you have taken his little test.'

'Why have you even got us here?' I demanded. I raised my hand at him. 'Please tell me what is going on, and what is with these damned symbols?'

Kerrish got comfy, sitting down at a table as he put his feet on it. Donna and Mantella disappeared into the corner of the room beyond our field of vision.

'Okay,' he began. 'It seemed you two had a bit of a wild time of it last night, didn't you?'

'I don't know. We can't remember.'

'That's absolutely no surprise. You see, our agents saw you mixing with a very wrong sort, and let's just say we fear you're now infected with a... fatal disease.'

'What kind of *disease*?' I asked.

'We're both very careful people,' Rachel added, her mind seemingly in a very different place still.

'There are some rather insalubrious characters that are... polluting our city here, and it's threatening to become an epidemic.'

'You better not be talking about refugees or Eastern Europeans or whatever,' Rachel said, 'because that is *so* not cool. We both voted Remain, FYI!'

'No, no, no, Rachel. Vampires. We are becoming overrun with vampires, right here in Meridian.'

I should have felt more surprised than I did as he told us that, but really he'd just confirmed the destination my intuition had been leading me to. It all made sense. I'd been so insatiably hungry, but then my body had rejected the food I'd put into it; perhaps it wasn't the 'bad trip' that had caused that puking, after all. I also realised my senses seemed to have heightened; I could see all those stars as we lay there in the park, I'd been so goddamned horny and sensual when I was with Ziggy. I'd really struggled to sleep earlier, even though I was absolutely shattered. Was my body beginning the metamorphosis? Was I starting to turn into a blood-sucking vampire?

'Last night we observed you fraternising with a pack of known vampires. Our spies discretely marked you with that symbol so we could identify you if they were to infect you with their disease and they would turn you into creatures like them.'

'Why didn't you kill us then and there if you think we're vampires?' I asked.

'We may be vampire exterminators but we are not murderers. The ink used on your hand has been specially formulated by Vihn Angel experts so that if you were not infected and remained human, then it would naturally fade away in a few days. However, if you are now vampires, the mark will carry with you. Locked in time, as those *things* are.'

'So we just need to wait a few days to see if they fade then, right?' I asked.

'You could,' Kerrish replied. 'But since you came to us, we can find out here and now, if you choose to comply.'

'I don't think we really have a choice, do we? Can I ask though, if we don't pass this test, what will you do with us?'

'If you fail then it means that you will inevitably turn into a vampire... The Vihn Angels are vampire exterminators... Can you do the maths from there, or do you want me to spell it out?'

'Oh my God,' Rachel sobbed. The gravity of all this finally seemed to have dawned on her.

'You'll kill us right away? Here and now?'

'I told you, we are not murderers. We are exterminators. If they have infected you, then you will not be vampires quite yet. We will wait until you have completed your transformation, but that won't be long away.'

'When will we change?' Rachel asked through her tears. I already knew the answer, though.

'Seven forty-three,' I said. 'Sunrise.'

Kerrish nodded approvingly at my astuteness. 'Correct, Melody.' But then his eyes narrowed in suspicion. He glanced at his watch. 'Let's hope we don't have to stay up for another few hours, yes? Let's hope that your luck is in and you've somehow gotten away with it.'

'What did we do with these damned vampires, anyway?' Rachel whined.

Kerrish stood. 'Oh, you know the things that young, carefree people get up to. I'm sure you can use your imagination.'

'What, we shagged them and they gave us vampire AIDS?'

'Well, that's one way of putting it.'

Had I turned into a slut? Jumping into bed with

two different guys on consecutive nights? I wasn't convinced that that's what had happened last night. I can just *tell* the day after if something else has gone in there, you know. But whatever, the fact was that these Vihn Angel spies had spotted us getting up to something, getting too close to some blood suckers, and they deemed us as potentially contaminated.

I wondered why they hadn't killed the vampires they'd seen us with, though. If they were supposed to be exterminating them, why weren't they doing just that, instead of waiting for them to create even more vampires? Why let them keep infecting innocent people like me and Rachel?

'Anyway, ladies, let's not delay the inevitable. Who would like to take the test first?'

'I don't need to piss right now,' Rachel muttered.

'That's not the sample we need from you.'

This was all going so very wrong. My life seemed like it would be over in a matter of hours. I wasn't even out of my teenage years yet. I thought back to Xander's words in the café. Why had he told me to search out these Vihn Angels characters when they were intent on killing me? Sure, he was technically on the right lines when he mentioned about me being *ill*, but why was he so insistent on sending me here? He said these people could help me. Killing me for being turned into a vampire was a twisted way of helping someone!

'What do you want then?' Rachel asked.

'A little blood sample, enough to fill a cup.'

I felt faint already. I hated the sight of blood. Even when I cut my finger open I would come over as though I'd lost an entire limb. Man, I would make the worst vampire. Not that these people would give me the chance to get as far as taking my first bite into someone's neck. Still, if there was a chance of being set free, I had to do this. I had to know the answer to this one, even though deep down inside I already knew it.

Rachel went first. They took her out of the cell, sat her down at the table, and then Snake Hair Donna strapped her arm up before sticking a needle in it, as though she were a nurse and this was some late night Give Blood session, but I didn't see a pack of biscuits and orange squash anywhere for when they'd finished.

My poor friend made no attempt to escape, sitting there in an air of glumness as she let them get on with it. The door to the main room was probably locked, and with presumably more of these Vihn Angel agents in the lounge, it seemed a futile notion to act all Jack Bauer and fight our way out of there. I knew I would behave the same way when it came to my turn.

As I witnessed Rachel's blood pour into the receptacle through my thinned vision, I wondered how they were so sure we were becoming vampires. Drawing someone's blood like that was a fairly serious bodily assault, and then there was the whole kidnapping thing. If it were to turn out that Rachel would pass this test, what were they going to do then? Shrug their shoulders and say *Oh well, shit happens!*? How many times did that ever happen to them?

Once they'd drawn enough blood from her, they ushered her back to our cell and Mantella made a reappearance. He held some conical flask as though he were a mad scientist playing with his chemistry set. Inside it was some thick blue liquid.

'Sit tight, ladies,' Kerrish announced as we came to the most crucial moment of this procedure. 'We will now prove Rachel's infection by demonstrating that her blood has been compromised by the vampire virus. By introducing another strain of virus, something that brings about *sangue debolezza* in vampires, there will be absolutely no mistaking from the reaction you are about to see.'

Mantella cut in over him, probably to blow his own trumpet and steal some of the limelight: 'We've been cultivating our own virus here and are trying to introduce it into the vampire population. Makes those suckers die a slow, horrible death.'

'Indeed,' Kerrish agreed, grabbing the conversational wheel back. 'Along with an additive of colloidal silver we've found the perfect solution to make our test fail-safe.'

'Do you want to...?' Mantella asked, a slight nerdy excitement in his voice that told of no concern for the two young women who were facing certain murder from the positive outcome of this bizarre experiment.

'You do it, Manny,' Kerrish replied as he backed away from the table in anticipation of the reaction that was about to ensue.

Mantella stretched his arm out as far as he could, crouching down too so his head was no higher than the sample of blood before him. He hovered his hand above the cup, ready to pour the blue liquid into it, his other hand already shielding his face.

'Do it!' Kerrish commanded, and with that, Mantella twisted his wrist and the solution poured into the crimson vampire food. His whole body flinched, but nothing else happened. They stood staring at the cup for a moment, a weird gloop of blood and Mantella's magical mixture swirling together in anticlimactic innocuousness. Mantella raised his arms at Kerrish, nonplussed.

'Did you get the right...?' Kerrish began to ask.

'Nothing wrong with the solution,' Mantella interrupted defensively.

Kerrish stood there in silence, eyeing the cup on the table, searching for words to say, quickly readjusting all of his carefully concocted plans after this unexpected twist.

'It seems, Rachel, that you are not infected.'

I looked towards her as she sat huddled in a ball across from me, a solemn look of detachment in her face. For a moment it seemed she hadn't even registered what Kerrish had said.

'You're okay, Rach. You're all clear.'

She peered out into the room curiously, as though she hadn't been watching any of what had just taken place, like she'd gone so far within that her mind was in a completely different place.

'I'm okay?'

I stood up and approached the bars. 'Go on then, let her out of here,' I shrieked at Kerrish.

He, Mantella and Donna all continued to stand

there numbly.

'Come on!'

Eventually Donna stepped towards the cell.

'Wait!' Kerrish shouted. 'We can't let her go.'

'You said you would let us free!'

Donna looked at him, the only one of them feeling compelled to do the right thing and release the innocent prisoner.

'She'll raise the alarm,' Kerrish said. 'She'll bring the fuzz down here to rescue her friend and we'll all be in the shit.'

'But she's not a fucking vampire, Kerrish,' Donna replied. 'Your agents got it wrong.'

He looked so pissed off and I suspected his cohorts who'd stamped us would get a severe ticking off later. But did this mean they'd got it wrong with me as well? Had I done any more than Rachel last night to get infected, or was it all some viral lottery we'd played?

'Let's do the other one first,' Kerrish said as though I was nothing more than some caged rat in his laboratory. 'Drag her out here.'

'I do have a name, you know!'

When it came to it, I wasn't so scared about them drawing blood from me as they took me out of the cell and shoved me down at the table to put me through the same procedure. I was now feeling so angry towards them, and it was that indignation that fuelled me. Whatever the outcome of my test, they had messed up. They weren't the noble vampire killer crusaders they thought they were. They'd now crossed the line and found themselves on the wrong side of their own morality, and Kerrish knew it.

I kept my eyes fixed on him as Donna stuck the needle in me. I'm sure it hurts more if you watch it. I knew Kerrish could feel my stare on him, but he wouldn't look me in the eye. Perhaps my test had become a lot more crucial to him, as a positive result would enable him to salvage some vindication.

With my blood sample taken, she slapped some cotton wool on my arm and ushered me back to the cell. They proceeded in silence as Mantella appeared with another flask of his marvellous mixture. They just wanted to get on with it this time, no building themselves up.

I stood leaning against the bars, hoping beyond hope that another lame chemistry experiment was about to take place, the teacher about to drop a lump of lead into water rather than some potassium, the dud firework about to be lit.

Mantella stretched the flask as far away from his face as before. He shared a look at Kerrish, who stood against the wall, and he nodded back at him. Finally he poured the blue liquid into my blood.

There was a blinding flash, crackling and fizzing as a large cloud of vapour plumed from the cup. I flinched backwards as the mist filled the room, hissing like some giant serpent had just been slain. I heard Donna spluttering and felt the vapour stinging my eyes as I cowered back onto the floor.

'Holy shit!' I heard Mantella call from somewhere in the mist.

I saw a figure appear on the other side of the bars. It was Kerrish.

'Melody, you have failed the test.'

Chapter 11

That was that. My death sentence, announced by the puff of smoke which seemed perfectly apposite for what was about to happen to me. I was soon to be a vampire. My life would be over in around four hours, and my undead afterlife would end very soon after that.

Despite their promise of letting us free should we pass the test, they had not done so with Rachel as they left her in the cell with me. To be fair, she had refused to leave me anyway, as much as I pleaded with her to insist they release her. I guessed they would do that not long after sunrise, after my transmutation was complete and fangs would sprout from my mouth and I faded from the mirror. I just hoped they would take me aside when they killed me. It would totally underline what out-of-touch arseholes they were if Rachel was subjected to witnessing it. Too busy removing the heads from the vampires around them, it seemed they were losing their own heads too.

After scoring positive on my vampire-detection test, Donna opened the only window in the room to diffuse the vapour and I had the tiniest glimpse of the early morning sky. I wondered if, when the daylight crept through it in a few hours, I would burn up in agony. Until then I could only gaze painfully at the fraction of the outside world that I longed to be roaming free in.

Until the sun made its appearance again, I had four measly hours to reflect on my life up to this sad point and wonder what I should do with the smidgeon of time I had left. I felt like I wanted to savour every breath, appreciate every last second. What a total mess I'd made of things, what an abortion I'd made of the chances life had presented me with. I had wonderful parents, warm memories of a loving upbringing, privilege with the chance to go to university to make something of my life. I was born with talents and had dreams, things I wanted to achieve with my music career, but it seemed I'd spurned it all after some drunken night of forgotten frolicking in this strange city of shadows.

I hadn't even wanted to go out that night in the first place! I should have been hating Rachel for tempting me out, for joining the birthday celebrations of someone I didn't even like, but that was so typically me. So weak in the arm. I knew I only had myself to blame, but whilst I was glad my friend was free of this devastating virus I'd contracted, I still envied her pure blood.

Why was I the unlucky one? Is that just the way it went when you played vampire roulette? I at least wanted answers before I got staked and turned to bloody mush. But right now, none of the so-called Vihn Angels were present. They'd left Rachel and me to ourselves as she held a comforting arm around me. I rested my head on her shoulder, breathing in the sweet scent of her exotic-spiced perfume.

'I'm so sorry, Mel. I wish it was me.'

'Thank you for staying with me, Rach.'

'Till the end, sweetie.'

At least all my YouTube videos would live on. I hadn't had the chance to have any children, not that they were part of my plans, but it was some consolation that I'd made some creations to leave something of an impression in this world. That meant more to me than being offered the chance of eternal life through being a supernatural creature. Even that was finite, especially so with these exterminators around. Perhaps I would find posthumous fame, be the next Eva Cassidy. This was probably the best thing that could happen to my music career. So at least there was that. Possibly.

'Why don't you try to fight your way out?' she asked. Her brain had been fixated on ways to get me out of this horrible situation. 'The moment the sun rises, won't you suddenly have vampire strength? Why not fight them?'

'I think they might anticipate that.'

'Or you should turn into a bat and fly away.'

'Jees, Rach, I imagine that might be something of an advanced move. For a three-second-old vampire, I think that would be like asking you to sit down at the piano and play Rachmaninov. And besides... even if I somehow escaped, would you still want to be friends with me? Do I just go back to my life and carry on making performance videos and running to lectures? Knowing these guys are out there wanting to kill me? Hardly a great existence.'

'I'd look after you,' she said. It was such fanciful talk, but Rachel meant it. She really would put herself on the line for me. I raised my head and smiled at her.

'Thanks, Rach.'

I placed my hand on her cheek, and my thumb caressed her. I had only hours left. It made sense to make the most of it, so my lips searched for hers and very soon we were kissing. Such a sweet moment that I could have indulged in until the end of the night. By the way she responded, it could only mean we really had been intimate back at Ziggy's. It seemed her feelings for me were the same as the ones I had for her. Not that this was a thing about possessing each other, I felt. Not about getting serious and dedicated. It's just that I appreciated her beauty and wanted to indulge in it. As she had a sort-of-boyfriend then I figured it was the same thing with her.

Or perhaps I'd completely misunderstood it all. Had she been secretly in love with me the entire time, and her relationships with men were merely for show, to take the attention away from her? Maybe that's why she wanted me around all the time, why she wouldn't leave my side in this dire moment. And maybe my feelings could be explained by my metamorphosis. My blood was simmering, and I yearned to experience all shades of delights of the flesh.

Either way, it didn't matter. Time was short, and I had to enjoy it the best I could, and being left alone with Rachel I wanted nothing more but to keep exploring her body as much as possible.

The sound of the door opening stopped our moment dead. We disconnected, and I turned to see Mantella walking into the room. Bet the guy would have loved to have been watching us a few seconds earlier. He barely offered us a glance though as he walked to his laboratory area, a place I'd spied in better detail when they were taking my blood sample.

He had a large corner desk there that was filled

with computers and screens on one end of it. Perhaps it was some sort of nerve centre where they kept track of the whereabouts of their fellow agents, or used surveillance systems to keep tabs on the vampires. Also stacked on the his workstation were his potions and what I imagined were samples and material taken from vampires or the leftovers of dead ones. I guessed Mantella spent many hours there studying and experimenting. Or hell, for all I knew, the guy probably sat there masturbating at porn all day.

Rachel scooted over towards the bars. 'Yo, Manny, you there?' she shouted over to him. He didn't answer. With none of his buddies around to back him up, he'd become sheepish. 'Hey, Manny. Come talk to me.'

Suddenly he appeared outside our cell. 'You mind keeping quiet? What do you want?'

'Help out a couple of silly little girls, yeah?' Rachel brazenly tried to persuade him. 'Can't you let us out of here? We'll make it look like we escaped, overpowered Mr Manly or whatever, yeah? I mean, come on, if you've got a vampire problem, what's one more vampire out there in this big, bad city going to make a difference?'

'Um no. Kerrish is already pretty pissy tonight. He'd really tear me a new one.' He returned to his desk.

'Well, what could we do to convince you? Come on, you name it. Anything you want. You got two hot chicks locked up here... Use your imagination, Manny!'

'Rachel!' I gasped.

'What?' she said, turning back to me. 'These are desperate times, sweetie.' She pushed her face right up to the bars. 'Come on, Manny. This could be the thrill of your life.'

'I sure ain't touching one of you! Quiet now. I need to get back to work.'

But Rachel was far from done. 'We're taking our clothes off now, Manny. Yep, we are getting completely naked. Got it all on show. That work of yours so important you don't have time to cop a little peep?'

Mantella gave no reply. We listened closely, could practically sense him chewing that temptation round in his brain and trying to resist it, and eventually I heard him getting up out of his seat, magnetised back to us, on the thin chance he may actually now find two stripped off girls in the cell. He was a guy, and a nerdy one at that. He really wasn't going to pass on the opportunity for an unexpected little thrill like this. Except for the fact that we were both still fully clothed. He laughed sarcastically and pointed as though to say *You got me!* At least Rachel was getting into his head.

I decided to try a different tack with him, so I slid my backside over towards him. 'Come on, Manny, sit down and talk to us. I need to understand something. Help put my mind at ease before you kill me.'

He sighed, then grabbed a chair from the middle of the room and sat down. With the prospect of seeing us naked put in his head, perhaps he thought that by humouring me, we might actually end up stripping off for him as reward. It felt like we were starting to get him in our hands.

'What do you want to know?' he asked me.

'I don't understand how I got infected. Is it really like getting an STD?'

'Uh not necessarily. You can contract the virus by a simple kiss from a vampire. Those things are highly infectious.'

'How is it transferred though? Through their blood?'

'Not necessarily. I mean, usually it is. That's where the virus is most concentrated, but the thing is, it's found everywhere throughout them. In their saliva, their tears, their semen.'

'Must have given one a blowie then, hon,' Rachel quipped. 'That's why you should always spit, darling.' I rolled my eyes at her.

'Okay, so I may have kissed a vampire, exchanged a spot of drool with him, and then a day later I'm waking up as one?'

'Once the pathogen has established itself, then yes, you have until the following sunrise.'

'I see. So, I noticed you're a pretty smart guy. Got lots of scientific shit going on in that corner round there. So tell me, do you have an antidote to this virus?'

'Oh, you mean an antibody?'

'Yeah.'

'No,' he replied bluntly. 'Nah, sorry.'

'Guess you would have mentioned it by now if you had. So...' I began on another thought, a question formulating in my brain that wanted to be released as desperately as an orgasm, 'is there any way back once you've been infected? Any way of undoing becoming a vampire?'

'That's so weird. I was talking to Donna about this very idea earlier today.'

'So...?'

'Yeah, I had a bet with her that there absolutely is a means to reverse it,' he nonchalantly replied, completely oblivious to the significance of this for me. 'There's an urban myth within our network about someone reversing it once, and I spoke to a guy who knows a guy who knows a guy whose dad was involved in this case back then, so that confirmed it for me. I think it can be done.'

My spirits elevated immediately like a rush of euphoria, but the annoying sound of his phone soon eclipsed that, rudely interrupting the conversation. He got up and turned away to answer it, leaving me teased in some Rocky Horror anticipation.

'How does his fucking phone work down here and ours don't?' Rachel asked. She held hers up to check it again.

'Did you hear what he said? I can undo this, Rachel!'

'Yeah, right.'

'Didn't you hear him?'

'Well, why aren't they helping us out on that instead of leaving you locked up?'

I shook my head. Did she just want me to die or something? 'Full of fucking joy, aren't you?'

Mantella disappeared from view, wandering back to his work area as he continued to grunt at the person on the other end of the line. I got up and walked to the rear of the cell, peering at those photographs of us still tacked to the wall. Not that I actually wanted to look at them. It was my way of turning my back to Rachel.

She soon got the message though, and I felt her hand on my shoulder. 'I'm going to help you get out of here, Mel. I'm not giving up on you.'

I turned round, my eyes tingling as the tears started to well in them. 'It's not just that. I don't want to be a fucking vampire, Rach. I don't want this virus in me.'

'Have you ever known for vampires to return to being a human? I know there was the whole business of a cure in *Vampire Diaries*, but they were really clutching for storylines by that point...'

'Are we really determining my prospects of staying alive through what we've seen in television shows?'

She buttoned her mouth for a moment. 'Look,' she went on, 'they said this is a virus. We're talking about medical stuff that is beyond our understanding. If there is an antibody, then it's going to be some real specialist medicine that I doubt we'll get on the NHS.'

'But I want to know what the...' I stopped that thought as I suddenly noticed Mantella pacing towards the door. Oh no, he was *not* about to leave me without explaining the rest of this! I darted over to the bars and yelled, 'Do not walk out this room, Manny! Come back here!'

There was no way he hadn't heard me, and yet, he left us alone again. I shook the bars in frustration, wishing that I did have supernatural strength already and could rip them apart. I growled and bashed my head against them. Was this another sign of becoming a vampire, eruptions of aggression like these? I'd never behaved that way before, but then again I'd never been locked up like this and threatened with execution.

I felt like I was a hostage at the mercy of terrorists, my own death looming over me as they taunted me with chopping off my head or ramming a stake into my heart, or whatever they had planned for me. And yet these people thought they were the good guys! Perhaps I could offer myself as a live specimen, stay locked up until the end of time and let them experiment on me. I could be like that zombie in *Day of the Dead*. I could work *with* them. Even though I was the enemy, I was prepared to convert to their ideology. Anything to stay alive!

I was just about to collapse to the floor, a broken person, when the door opened again and in walked Mantella. He had Kerrish with him this time. Mantella sighed as he led him over to his desk, looking like someone fed up with interruptions and needing to get back on with his work. He was about to suffer some more, though.

'Oy, Manny! You didn't finish telling me. How the hell do I undo this?'

He threw me an irritable glance before he disappeared round the corner. 'Forget it, girl. It's not going to happen.'

'Tell me!' I roared at him.

'What is she on about?' Kerrish piped up, pausing to look down at his caged animals.

'Don't worry about it, dude. Shut your trap, girl! We have work to do.'

'No, if you're going to lock us up in your study then I'll do everything I can to annoy the shit out of you.'

'Jesus, Kerrish. I told you I needed somewhere else to work. How can I get anything done when we've got this shit going on?'

Kerrish remained outside the cell, peering through the bars at me. 'What is she on about, Manny? What's yanked her chain?'

'I want to know how I can be human again. I want to know how I can live,' I answered for him.

'You can't. Get over it,' Kerrish replied.

'He said there was a way. Manny, you were about to tell me!'

Kerrish sighed, rubbing his hands over his face as they came together like he was secretly saying a prayer that I would just shut up.

'You told us you recall nothing of last night,' he stated. 'Can't remember where you were or who you were with.'

'Yeah? So?'

'We estimate there's about five thousand vampires

living in this city. You hear me? Five thousand of those things.'

'What are you getting at?' I practically screamed in his face.

'If you wanted to stop your transformation, you would have to find the one who infected you. So, first you have to *get hold of* a vampire, then you have to hope you've got the right one, and as I say, you've got a one in five thousand chance on that. And then when you've found it...'

'Then?' I prompted him.

'You have to kill it. Oh yeah, and you have to do all this before sunrise. Once the sun rises, it's all too late and there's no way back; you're a vampire forever.'

'That's it? I just need to waste the one who made me?'

'Then there's the other factor that we've got you locked up and we're not going to let you free.'

I fell silent in thought, my brain racing too fast for me to keep up with it. There was always the possibility that by some fluke they might have a successful night of slaying and get the very vampire I'd been kissing last night. I had hope. I had a lottery ticket.

'How do you know this?' I eventually asked.

'We actually don't, not for certain,' Mantella called out from round the corner. He joined Kerrish at the bars. I figured this scientific talk was more his thing. 'It was something a fellow agency mentioned to us, our counterparts in Berlin. Apparently it happened to someone once. And that was way back in the eighties. Like I said, an urban myth.'

'Wouldn't you want to find out for certain?' I asked him, desperately hopeful, as ever. 'Wouldn't this be really useful information for you, and your fellow Vihn Angels around the world? Wouldn't it help your quest? Help you unravel the mysteries of this virus?'

For a few seconds I could tell they were actually looking at me as though I had a point, as though contemplating my proposition. It didn't last long. Soon Kerrish was shaking his head.

'I'll help you,' I blurted, to keep their minds in

contemplation mode. 'I'll help you find this vampire, and if we don't, then I promise I won't run away from you. Please.'

'It's more than a five thousand to one shot, Melody,' Kerrish replied. Some part of my brain recognised he'd called me by my name. Mantella had only referred to me as 'girl', as though he was already dehumanising me as he saw me as a blood-sucking creature. But Kerrish acknowledged I was still Melody. Still human. Still had a chance.

'Let me think about it,' he said, staring into space with his hands on his hips.

'Come on, dude,' Mantella grumbled. 'Is she compelling you, or something?' He grabbed Kerrish's arm, but he shoved him away.

'How often do we get this opportunity, Manny? How often do we have a live pre-vampire specimen on our hands?'

'We've got work to do tonight.'

'This *is* our work! It wouldn't take up any more than four hours.'

'But we have no idea which vampire infected her, and even if we did, how the hell are we going to find it?'

'Wait,' Rachel said. 'Maybe we do know which one it was.' She stepped forward, thumbing the screen of her phone until she came to that blurry photo of the mysterious glam rock vampire. 'This was us last night,' she added as she handed it to Kerrish.

Both he and Mantella peered at the screen in fascination.

'That's Wiseau,' Mantella said.

'Indeed, it is. The one and only,' Kerrish confirmed.

'So you know him?' I stated.

'We have a database of vampires that we've identified during our operations. This particular vampire here is one who's evaded us for the past six years, but now you think we can kill him within the next four hours?'

'Please,' I said tearfully. I got down on my knees. Hell, I didn't care how it looked. I was desperate, and I would do anything. I would even go down Rachel's pervy road if it meant I had a chance. 'Please help me.'

Kerrish was silent for a moment, all eyes in the

room eagerly watching as he paced up and down the floor.

'Okay,' he eventually replied. 'Maybe... *maybe* we could give this one a shot.'

Chapter 12

I can't describe how ecstatic I felt when Kerrish opened up our cell and allowed us out. We'd only been in there about an hour but I wondered how my emotions would compare to those of a hostage who'd been held captive for years and against all the odds they'd been set free again and given another chance to live their life. Not that I necessarily had a long road of life ahead of me to drive down, but at least there was hope.

'You're making a big mistake,' Mantella muttered, but even his negativity couldn't kill my buzz. Kerrish was the one in charge. He called the shots on whether or not I should be locked up. It seemed he would ignore him too.

'Oh, hell yes! My phone works now!' Rachel chirped as she stepped into the room.

'Yeah, I fitted the cell with a signal-killer,' Mantella told her, flipping into technical talk. 'You could have stuck your hand out through the bars to get a signal but... I didn't exactly want to tell you that.' I heard Rachel's handset going notification-happy as it spewed a backlog of messages to her.

'Okay, we have to act quickly, Miss Freeman,' Kerrish said, urgency in his voice. He sat down at the table and gestured for us to sit round too, like we were in a war room about to concoct plans. Mantella sulked off to his work area. 'First off, any idea where you met your vampire friend Wiseau last night?'

'No,' I replied.

'Rachel?'

'Huh?' she responded, her face still firmly in her phone.

'We need to find this vampire, Rach!' I said in a deliberately patronising tone. 'What else is so damned important that you can't focus right now?'

'Oh, I'm just writing a tweet. What's a good hashtag for this, do you think?'

'For fuck's sake, Rach! I can't believe you!'

'Well, if I'd done this last night we could have been

following the digital breadcrumbs!'

'Okay, seeing as you didn't, what else can you give us to go on?'

She sat there thinking for a moment. 'What about asking Veronica?'

'She must be asleep by now, Rach.'

'No, she texted about five minutes ago seeing if we wanted to join her at *The Mercury Lounge*.'

'Was this girl with you last night?' Kerrish asked.

'Yeah,' I replied. 'She's... It was her birthday.'

'*The Mercury Lounge* isn't too far from here,' Kerrish carried on. 'Rachel, can you get her to come here? Tell her you need to see her right away.'

'I could say there's an emergency,' she suggested.

'Yeah, something about my life being on the line?' I added with an impish sarcasm it was impossible to contain.

'No... play it cool,' Kerrish advised abruptly. 'But don't *sound* like you're playing it casual.'

'Okay, Captain Solo,' Rachel replied as she started typing a text.

'And how about frickin' call her instead of bloody texting?' I yapped.

'Good idea.' She put her phone to her ear and turned away from us, leaving me and Kerrish in a slightly awkward silence. I caught him looking at me and I smiled stupidly. Perhaps he was trying to read my face to see if he could really trust me, whether I had any secret plot to deceive him and make a run for it now I was out of my cell. He leant back in his chair, putting his fingertips together as he rested them on his lips, his mind a frenetic spinning of cogs and pistons as it worked in overdrive.

It struck me in that moment. A shift of focus, a step back from the immediate situation of being with a vampire killer who had me in his sights, and I could now perceive the observation that Rachel had made. This guy was rather handsome. He had thick locks of dusty hair on his head, stubble on his face making him look a little rugged, yet there remained a boyishness there, like a public schoolboy elegance that had gone wild. There was a faded poshness in his voice, still present enough to sustain a sense of authority.

The guy most probably saw himself as some sort of freedom fighter, full of importance in challenging the invasion of these foreign beings. Did he have time for romance? Or did the nature of this role render him a workaholic and he didn't give women a second thought?

Rachel's call connected, and I could hear the thumping music emanating from the handset. It appeared Veronica was having a swell time of it on the other end, and I listened impatiently as Rachel did her best to steer the conversation and get a drunken Veronica's focus. While she did that, I broke the silence with Kerrish.

'That guy we were talking to back in the bar, before you took us away...'

'David Sherborne?'

'Yeah. Can he help us? What's his bailiwick?'

'I'm not too familiar with him yet. Says he had a partnership with some individual who's a wizard at tracking individuals down. Can't tell you much beyond that.'

I nodded. I didn't know why I kept thinking of him. He was like the only other person I'd talked to at this place. The rest of those people sitting around in that lounge were probably a crack team of exterminators qualified to conduct this operation with the efficiency of the SAS. It was most likely David had gone home to bed by now.

'So how do you do it?' I asked. 'Kill a vampire, I mean.'

Kerrish's blue eyes darted over to mine and I experienced a tingle of excitement as he seemed to penetrate my brain, making me feel strangely vulnerable.

'One way or the other you'll find out soon, won't you, Melody?'

And then he goes ahead and says something like that. I decided to tune myself back into Rachel's conversation.

'Get yourself down here right now, babe! No, never mind them. Just come! We need you! Yep! Okay. Brilliant. See you in five.' She put her phone down and sighed. 'She's on her way.'

Five minutes. That's like no time at all. I could

listen to *Smells Like Teen Spirit* in that time. I could make some porridge, so fast is that five minutes that the manufacturers describe it as 'instant'. I could boil an egg, get halfway to booting up my PC, vacuum my bedroom, yet when you have only a matter of hours to live, a grand total of 240 minutes, then five minutes of that represents quite a significant proportion of it. Not to mention that the person who said she would be five minutes was Veronica, and a drunken one at that, so really you should double that.

Yet, by some miracle, it was only seven minutes later when Rachel announced that Veronica had made it to *The Hooded Claw* and was waiting for us outside.

'You stay here,' Kerrish ordered me. 'Manny, keep an eye on her. Rachel, you come with me. And give me your phone.' He grabbed her arm and led her out of the room.

'Hey, less of the manhandling, Kerrish! I am not your bitch!' she yelled as they disappeared through the door. I turned to see Mantella looking towards me. Although he seemed impatient, as though he was having his night wasted, I didn't doubt his readiness to spring into action should I try anything funny. He certainly didn't look like he wanted to fill the silence with any conversation. What was the point of chitchatting with someone who would be dead soon?

Thankfully, we didn't have too long alone, Kerrish and Rachel returning along with a loudmouthed Veronica hobbling on her high heels.

'Oh hey, Melody,' she said on seeing me. 'Ooh what's this place you're in? Are we in the backroom, or something?'

'Please take a seat, Veronica,' Kerrish said, all of a sudden a delightful charmer.

Veronica's fuzzy eyes opened a fraction more as she noticed the bars to the cell we'd been in. 'Ah this is where you lock up the rowdy lot, isn't it? God, bet you get plenty of them sort in this city.' She sat down on one of the chairs, nearly fell off the side, then quickly righted herself again. Her eyeballs seemed rather bloodshot, her skin pasty, her voice a little louder than it should be. I was very used to seeing her like this as Veronica was forever out on the lash.

She'd always been a bit of a plump lass, which was a shame as she would look so much prettier if she cut the calories. Veronica never seemed to change though, but then she never made any attempts at dieting. It was like she was resigned to being overweight and that's what she would be for the rest of her life.

'Thanks for coming, hon,' I said to her. I was actually really grateful. I'd never been a fan of her before, but when I needed it she'd come through for me. Not that she realised that that was what she was doing, I supposed, but still...

I swallowed hard. 'I'm in trouble...' I felt Kerrish's hand on my arm and I knew that meant I needed to shut up.

'I don't know if you've heard of Project S, Veronica,' Kerrish took over. 'We run a surveillance operation to crack down on predators spiking people's drinks, and I'm afraid that last night Melody had something put in hers.'

Veronica's mouth dropped open melodramatically. 'Oh my God, really? Are you okay?'

Before I had chance to answer, Kerrish kept control of the conversation. 'To cut a long story short, we think we know who did this.'

'You don't think someone touched you, did they?' she asked.

'Please, Veronica, time is of the essence.' He produced Rachel's phone and showed her the screen. 'Do you recognise where these photos were taken?'

She gawped at the phone, a gormless expression on her face, and she was weirdly quiet. After a moment she cleared her throat, and in a hushed voice said, 'That was *Satan's Cellar*.'

'Thanks, Veronica. And this man, do you recognise him? Do you know where he is?' Kerrish showed her the blurry photo. Immediately she leant back in her chair, an odd smile on her lips.

'You think it was him, do you?'

'Yes,' Kerrish replied.

She looked to me, then Rachel, then studied the room some more, scrutinising Mantella who quietly beavered away at his monitors. Suddenly she didn't seem so talkative.

'So, *Satan's Cellar*?' Kerrish asked.

Still she said nothing.

Kerrish turned to me. 'Melody, you said you wanted to know how we do it...'

The next moment seemed to steal the air from my throat as my stomach performed a somersault. Kerrish rose to his feet and from out of nowhere he brandished a wooden stake, sharpened to a brutal point. He raised it high and then swiftly and mercilessly he hammered it straight into Veronica's chest.

Her mouth opened wide, long fangs flicking out from her row of upper teeth. She wailed a horrific shriek in her death cry as she grabbed the stake that stuck out from between her breasts. She looked at each of us in abject disgust, complete shock at our apparent betrayal. Her entire body then convulsed as a deathly grey swept over her face, her veins rushing to the surface of her cheeks as they burst open, her eyes turning red, then black. She juddered herself from side to side, her fading strength vainly trying to remove the stake from her heart, but in another couple of seconds her body suddenly became rigid before it exploded over us in a tsunami of mush.

'Holy fucking shit! What the fuck did you just do?' Rachel roared. She immediately stood up, holding up her arms that were splattered in the liquefied flesh that a few seconds ago was her friend Veronica.

'She was a vampire if you hadn't noticed,' Kerrish calmly replied.

'But... she was my friend!'

'And in case you weren't following the program, Rachel, we are vampire killers!'

'But... but she never told me! How could you do that? I'm fucking covered in this shit!'

I began to scrape the goo off my arms. It had sprayed all over my face, in my hair, everywhere.

Mantella stepped up to us. 'It's okay. The material from dead vampires isn't contagious. You won't get infected. We get this on us all the time.' He then turned to me. 'Not that *you* were worrying, of course.'

I stopped trying to clean myself up when I realised I was just smearing that shit over me, like I was putting on some suntan lotion from hell.

'Oh my God,' Rachel whined again, as though she needed to hammer home the point she was shocked because no one else was capable of understanding how fucked up this moment was. 'Why didn't you tell me you were going to do that to her?'

'Because I didn't realise you were going to bring a vampire here until she turned up!' Kerrish replied.

'But how did you know?'

'We've seen this one a few times before. With Wiseau,' Mantella added.

'And what's the betting Veronica deliberately lured you to him last night?' Kerrish said, putting the pieces together.

'I can't believe she was a vampire,' Rachel exclaimed, as though doing so may help her believe. 'All this time I was friends with her and she was a bloodsucker?'

'She hasn't been one for long,' Mantella replied. 'You can tell she was young. That's how they go, explode in a mush like that.'

'It's fucking disgusting!' Rachel shouted, still holding out her arms as the goo continued to drip from her.

'Here,' Mantella said as he handed her a pack of baby wipes. An essential item for every vampire killer, it seemed.

This wasn't quite making sense to me. Why kill her so abruptly? Shouldn't we have probed her for more information before doing this? I turned to Kerrish for answers. With everything I'd been through tonight, I strangely didn't care about having all this mush over me.

'You didn't want to see what else she had to tell us?'

'Sorry, I had no choice. She was twigging. If she'd got out to her fellow creatures information on the whereabouts of our headquarters, we'd be seriously compromised. I couldn't risk that happening.'

I gazed down at the chair that was covered in a watery mess of dribbling flesh and blood, a defeated mass of mutated DNA that had been corrupted by this horrible virus that swam in my bloodstream. A swift stab in Veronica's heart and that's what it had reduced her to: a puddle. In that moment it really hit me, the gravity of my situation. I felt so hollow, knowing this was the fate that lay in wait for me a short way down the road.

These people had shown no mercy whatsoever. Kerrish had made no hesitation, not thought twice about killing Veronica. I knew he would ensure I went the same way once this virus had transformed me. What chance did I have? Beyond finding the vampire that had given me that fatal kiss, I could perhaps try to escape from the Vihn Angels. Or was a better strategy to make this guy Kerrish fall in love with me and when it came to 7.43 he would find his feelings had gotten in the way and he wouldn't be able to bring himself to do it?

'Clean yourself up,' he ordered me, breaking me out of my forlorn thoughts. He hadn't seemed to get much on him at all. I took some wipes and rubbed them over my exposed skin. My dress was a bit covered in areas, but there wasn't much I could do about that.

Rachel continued to sob and mutter away to herself as she cleaned herself up. Poor girl, she'd come off the worst of all of us. Mantella tried to help her out, but she snapped at him to back off.

'How many vampires do you usually kill in your average night?' she asked them.

'Not enough,' Kerrish replied.

'Since I've evidently given you one vampire tonight, how about seeing that as exchange for Melody?'

'Not a chance.'

'The more there are out there, the more they infect others,' Mantella added. I knew we wouldn't get anywhere with this sort of gentle persuasion, as much as I admired Rachel for trying. Time was ticking.

'What next?' I asked as I threw the last of the wipes on the table. I was far from being immaculate, but it was good enough.

'Time to go hunting,' Kerrish replied. He stepped towards me and grabbed my left wrist. Before I knew what he was doing, he produced a set of handcuffs and wrapped a ring around me before attaching the other to himself.

'Is that so? Or are we about to get kinky, Mr Grey?' I replied, but I could see in his eyes that the comment flickered no desire for any flirtation.

'Just to take away that temptation of doing a runner.'

'You're so considerate.'

'So fucking controlling!' Rachel yapped. 'I suppose I get to be cuffed to Mr Manly, do I?'

Kerrish turned to her. 'No, of course not. I know you won't run away from me, Rachel.'

'Such a cocky sod, aren't you? I could go and get some guys together. I know people.'

'You won't do that, Rachel, because if Melody wants to undo her disease, then it will come down to you.'

'What are you on about?' she asked, as confused as I was.

Kerrish crouched down and picked up the wooden stake from the Veronica-puddle. He handed it to her.

'What the fuck is this?' she asked.

'You'll have to do it, Rachel.'

'What?' she shrieked.

'You're going to have to kill Wiseau.'

'What the hell? No, no, no, no, no!'

'Come on, Kerrish,' I cut in. 'You're the vampire killers, as you've so keenly demonstrated to us. She can't do it. You have to do this.'

'Where we're about to go, I won't even be able to get close to Wiseau. He and his fellow fangs know of me. If they see me, I won't last two minutes.'

'Aren't there any more of you? Isn't there anyone else through there that can do this?' I asked as I pointed towards the lounge.

'No,' he replied.

'Is this all there is of the Vihn Angels? You, Mantella, and Donna?'

'There are others! They have to have nights off though. Besides, I think everyone has gone home by now.'

'Ah Christ,' Rachel sighed. She looked down on the stake that she gripped loosely in her hand. It looked like it

95

was an alien object to her, like she had no idea how it worked. I wasn't sure she even had the strength in her arms to ram it into someone's chest. I couldn't believe they would entrust her with doing this. But then, all they had riding on it was busting some vampire myth. It wasn't their lives on the line.

'What's the plan then?' I asked.

'Give me a moment,' Kerrish replied, pausing to think. 'I'm making this up as I go along.'

'Wear this,' Mantella said as he approached Rachel with an earpiece. 'Kerrish can talk to you over it and feed you instructions.'

'Oh right, and I'm going to be able to hear him on this tiny thing when I'm in the middle of some noisy nightclub?' Rachel put the earpiece on anyway, hiding it under her hair.

'I can guide you to him,' Kerrish resumed. 'I'll have to stay at a distance, but I can point him out to you.'

'And I'm just going to wander in there with this,' Rachel minced as she held up the stake, 'and go "Oh hi there, Mr Wiseau! I've just got to put this in you!"' She mimicked a stabbing motion in a somewhat camp manner as she said this.

'Should we wait till closing time?' Mantella suggested. 'Get him when he's leaving?'

'What time does *Satan's Cellar* close?' I asked, ever-conscious of the time. I looked at my watch and saw that it was about to turn 4am. I didn't know where this place was, even though I'd already been there. Maybe it was closing right now?

No one seemed forthcoming in answering my question. 'Does anyone even know where it is?' I now asked, thirsty for answers. Again, everyone just looked to each other.

'You're the ones who've already been there,' Mantella said.

'You're the ones who prowl the city hunting vampires,' I responded.

'And it's a pretty big city, if you hadn't noticed!'

We weren't getting anywhere. I glanced at Kerrish

who was now gawping at his phone, and I couldn't help but feel irritated that his attention wasn't fully in the room. But then he looked up again and proved me wrong.

'I can't find anything about it on the internet.' I'd obviously been hanging around Rachel too long, automatically assuming that whenever someone was on their phone, they were just texting shit to their friends.

'Maybe your buddies could tell us?' I continued to prompt him. 'Donna perhaps? Is there anyone else in the lounge still here at all?'

'Let's go see,' he replied. He strode towards the door and yanked our attached arms so I would keep up with him, as though I was a mischievous dog. Why did this guy have to be such a dick all the time?

Despite being tethered to a killer, I felt a small degree of relief at having emerged from the backroom they'd restrained me in for the past couple of hours. Since I was last in the lounge, the clientele had indeed thinned out until there was barely anyone left. I spotted one old guy slouching on a couch, and when we got closer to him I saw he was actually asleep. The lights were off at the bar area. However, there were two people sitting there. One of them was Donna. The other person was the man in the mac that we'd been talking to earlier, David Sherborne. For whatever reason, he was still here. I just knew the forces of fate were nudging us onto the same path.

'Donna,' Kerrish called as we rushed over to them. '*Satan's Cellar*. Know where that is?'

She shrugged. 'Under his kitchen? I have no idea,' she replied.

David looked at us curiously, a light going on in his eyes. '*Satan's Cellar*, did you say? That's opposite the old *Rose and Crown*.'

'The one near the strip joints?' Kerrish asked.

'Yes. Sumpton Street. I went there once.' His eyes clouded over and they gazed softly into the ether as though he was reflecting on something more than the simple act of visiting a nightclub, or perhaps he was just tired. 'An important case I was working on.'

'We need to go there,' Kerrish told him. 'Would you

97

mind directing us?'

'What, now? Is this my first operation?'

'Throwing you in at the deep end, Sherborne. Sorry to spring this on you but we need to get there fast.'

'Fast? Well, I have just the thing.'

Chapter 13

I sat in the back of David's car with Kerrish. Rachel sat next to me, while Mantella rode shotgun. David proudly told us all about the spec of his brand new BMW as though he was filming an episode of *Top Gear*. With his crazy crew of people on board, it did actually seem like the setup for another ridiculous piece on that television show. *Let's see how the BMW performs when you're out and about on a vampire hunt!*

I could tell you that this model was M Performance range, and that it had a random number and letter or letters after it, but I really wasn't interested in cars at the best of times. And this? This was absolutely the worst of times, so it was a miracle I had even registered its make. Such information as its horsepower, the size of its cylinders and what particular type of oil the engine took were all offered to me but had as much hope of sticking in my brain as an overweight, tone deaf chicken farmer had of advancing beyond the audition stage of *X-Factor*.

The car was definitely fast though, and David confidently zipped us along the deserted city streets. The early hours of the morning, with no economy vehicles cluttering the roads, were probably the only times that a sports car of this calibre could be operated to its potential. Not that we were at Silverstone. We still had practical laws of the road to abide by. All these fancy expensive cars you see in traffic have to operate within the same speed limits as your average Vauxhall Corsa. I always saw that having a performance vehicle on British roads was as useful as an Olympic athlete using a supermarket aisle to practice their sprinting.

And why did car enthusiasts insist on driving so fast? Doesn't it make more sense to drive at a more leisurely speed, thus maximising your time at the wheel so you could savour even more the process you love so much? Granted, I was incredibly grateful in this particular moment that David was exploiting the potential of his vehicle, but seeing as I was infected with the vampire virus and time was short, then this was an exception to the rule.

A traffic light ahead of us changed to amber and David was clearly far enough away that he wasn't 'committed', but as the beacon turned to red, he zoomed on through.

'Buckle up back there,' he said as he turned round to us. I observed him stealing a glance at the manacle that attached me to Kerrish. He'd noticed we were tethered when we'd first got in the car, but had not questioned it. He seemed a bit like the polite Robin Hood in *Time Bandits* who contrasted with the dubious behaviours of the rabble around him. There certainly was a John Cleese gentlemanliness to him.

'What can you tell us about this place, David?' Kerrish asked him. '*Satan's Cellar.*'

'Something of a secret club, like yours. It became a location of surveillance for me on a certain job, so I researched the place as much as I was able. Found out it's run by...' He paused as he tried to find the right words. 'An individual with particular eccentricities.'

'You've been in there?'

'A few times, yes. I made the acquaintance of one of the bar staff, and he provided me with a wealth of information. I wonder if he still works there...' David appeared to drift off into his memories, but Kerrish was quick to keep his brain on track.

'So what did your contact tell you?'

'Well, he told me about a lot of its secrets. You see, as the name suggests, I found out there are many levels to it, just like hell.'

He fell quiet, and I assumed all the other passengers were waiting for the other to ask what he meant by levels. Instead, it was the impatient Kerrish who asked: 'And what level did you get to?'

'Only the first. The rock 'n roll level. There was a pretty decent band on the first time I went.'

'And what of these other *levels*?' Kerrish asked.

'If you want to carry on down, further into the club, to the good stuff, I heard there are various *tests* to pass before you can proceed to these other areas.'

'But you don't know what they consist of?'

'No. Sorry. Once you've been through them all, once you've proved yourself, then it earns you a pass to this secret, restricted area, which is most probably where your chap resides.'

'You hearing this, Rachel?' Kerrish barked as he turned to her. 'It doesn't sound like a simple case of waltzing in there and finding your target.'

'What exactly is the matter at hand here?' David asked, talking to Rachel and me now. 'If you don't mind me asking. Why do you need to get in there?'

'It's like this,' Rachel replied, 'we've got a bit of a *fangover* situation going on here, and we can't remember where we left our vampire.'

'I see,' David replied politely, although I could tell that he wasn't really following.

Kerrish raised our handcuffed wrists. 'Melody played the tune of twilight last night and became infected. We're trying to find the vampire who got her.'

'Yeah,' Rachel carried on. 'And when we get to breaking dawn it's going to be all over.'

David was blank for a moment. 'Oh, I get it. You're on about Edward Cullen and all that?'

'Please tell me you haven't read that nonsense, David,' Kerrish said.

'Hell no. My daughter was into it. Always watching the films at home. Made me regret retiring.'

'Is that why you're with these vampire slayers now then?' Rachel asked. 'Got a tad bored with retirement and needed another adventure?'

'Something like that, I suppose,' he replied. 'I hope our collaboration can be mutually beneficial, that I can bring something to the table.'

'May well see tonight,' Kerrish said. 'Bit sooner than I'd planned but oh well.'

'Thanks for allowing me access to your database by the way.'

'Did it help?'

'Donna seemed to think that she's made a positive match, so yes, it's been very helpful. Just need to work out my next steps.'

I shared a confused glance with Rachel. It felt like the conversation had suddenly veered into business that was absolutely nothing to do with us, but we couldn't help our intrigue nevertheless.

'Don't worry, David. We'll help you,' Kerrish replied. 'That's what we're here for, after all. We'll figure out what to do once we've dealt with this other little problem on our hands.'

David flipped the indicator and pulled into a parking bay on the side of the street. 'Anyway, we are here. It's just through this alleyway over here.'

We all took a moment to stare out of the side windows towards where this strange establishment was, not that I could quite see it from there. I could definitely tell we'd ended up in a seedy area of the city, tatty posters everywhere advertising 24 hour strip clubs and escort services. A scruffy misfit stood nearby and looked us over before another scrawny fellow approached him. Something was quickly exchanged between them, furtive glances made in various directions before each man darted off on their separate ways.

'Go on then, Rachel!' Kerrish spat as he jabbed his non-tethered hand into her ribs. 'Wasting valuable seconds here.'

Mantella shifted round in the front seat and reached through the gap towards Rachel. They'd given her a jacket to wear, for two reasons: firstly, so she could conceal the wooden stake that she would have to smuggle in there with no one noticing. Secondly, the jacket was apparently also fitted with a spy camera on its lapel, and gadget man Mantella now switched it on. On the journey here he'd been connecting his equipment to the vehicle's built-in monitor.

'Camera on,' he announced. 'And you've already got your earpiece.'

She pushed back a curtain of hair to reveal the device wrapped around her ear.

'And how am I going to hear you over the music?' she asked.

Mantella put his wrist to his mouth as he spoke into

a microphone. 'How's this?'

Rachel winced as the sound of Mantella's voice whistled through her earpiece. It was more like a speaker, loud and clear for everyone in the car.

'Maybe turn it down a little?' she pleaded.

'There's a dial on it.'

She reached behind her long blond hair to adjust it.

'Come on, Rachel,' Kerrish continued to bark. 'Time is ticking here.'

'Okay!' She grabbed the door handle, but before she left, I placed my hand on her leg.

'Good luck, chick,' I whispered to her.

She turned to look at me but she said nothing, just nodded, a little gesture within a swamp of emotions. I could see it in her eyes, the doubt she was feeling towards the grave task at hand, but she would not dampen the thin amount of hope that I was clinging to. She would never give up on me.

She hobbled out onto the pavement littered with fast food wrappings and the dropped chips of drunken revellers who'd been feeling those alcohol-induced hunger pangs. Closing the door behind her, she wandered across to the alleyway David had pointed out a moment ago. I gazed on as she disappeared into the darkness.

'Budge over,' Kerrish ordered as he nudged me along. He wanted to take the middle seat to get a better view of the monitor. I peered beyond David's headrest to look at it too, a nightvision of green defined shapes on display.

'Are you really going to let her go in there on her own?' David asked, concern laden in his voice.

'If she wants to help her friend, then she has no choice.'

'But she's a young woman on her own. This isn't Euro Disney she's off to. You really think she's got the strength in her slender wrists to put that stake through one of those creatures?'

'There's no other option, David,' Kerrish continued to explain. 'The vampire she's going after is an old enemy. I can't risk him seeing us and being trapped in an unfamiliar place, especially if it's as arcane as you make out.'

'Well, what about if we all go in there together?'

Kerrish was quiet for a moment, which suggested that he was giving the idea some contemplation. 'It's too risky,' he eventually replied.

'What about me, then? They don't know me. Perhaps I could talk to my contact in there, if he's on tonight.'

'It's your call, David.'

The old investigator gazed towards Rachel again, but already she was out of view. He sighed, then undid his seatbelt.

'Can't let her go on her own.' He exited the car and hurried up the alleyway like Dick Tracy in hot pursuit looking to save the day again. Once he too was swallowed by the murk of this mysterious corner of Meridian, we all eagerly turned to the BMW's dashboard monitor.

Chapter 14

The three of us sat there quietly as we watched the proceeding drama unfold. It was like we were watching one of those found footage films such as *Cloverfield*, where the characters create all the visuals themselves on their mobile phone cameras. Except what we were seeing was actually a live film taking place right in our vicinity, with characters we knew personally, one of whom I cared about deeply. And this was a film I so desperately needed to have a happy ever after, for it was the outcome of this narrative that dictated whether I got to live or die, so despite there being no A-list actors or Oscar-winning directors involved, I was completely gripped by the action, my heart thumping away in my chest, pumping my infected blood throughout my compromised body.

I longed to be so absorbed by this movie that its point of view nature would draw me in so much and by some real movie magic it would actually be me who was Rachel, the girl who'd passed the vampire detection test. Not that I would want her to trade places with me and see her suffer this position, but I couldn't ignore the thought that I would much rather be in the role of trying to save someone's life than having a very probable death sentence that lay in wait only a matter of hours away.

Pressing the side of my face against the front seat's headrest to get closer to the monitor, I saw that Rachel had arrived at the entrance of *Satan's Cellar*. Its name was emblazoned across a board above the doorway in some chaotic scrawl of a font. Impish demons poked their head above the boarding surrounding the lord of all darkness himself, the horned Satan holding a fork with one hand as his other hand beckoned people to enter his domain. I saw a flight of stairs immediately beyond leading down into his cellar. Our heroine was about to take a step towards them when we heard the off-mic voice of David calling her.

The frame panned round and there he appeared, running up to her with his mac streaming behind him.

'Young lady!' he called. 'Rachel, isn't it?' Her lapel

camera framed him badly, his black tie dominating the shot as his chin just about edged into the top of the screen.

'What are you doing here?' she asked, her voice much louder and clearer.

'Come on, let me lead the way.' He stepped ahead of her but then turned round again as his tie filled the monitor even more than before. 'You need to keep casual and don't get too close to this guy, okay?'

'Okay.'

'Good luck. Let's go get our vampire.'

The visuals were frustratingly obscured for an interminable amount of time, pretty much just David's back in view as he presumably led Rachel down the staircase into the bowels of the club. I searched the far edges of the screen hoping to see something else, hungrily looking for any other visual information so I could understand better the environment they were heading into. But all that filled the shot was a grainy image that was the fabric of David's mac.

I looked at the clock on the dashboard. It was rapidly approaching half past four. 4.28 to be precise. If you were to ask anyone else what the time was at this exact moment, then they'd inevitably round it up and tell you it was half past four. But it wasn't half past the hour to me. There were still two minutes till that milestone, and those 120 seconds were valuable seconds that I would cling to and not throw away through a lazy lack of precision. They could find that vampire Wiseau in that time. They might even kill him before the clock reached 4.30. My ordeal could already be over and my life saved in the time that someone would dismiss those two minutes to give a satisfyingly even answer.

Still staring at the clock as I was lost in my thoughts, it now turned to 4.29. Another minute gone. Thankfully Rachel and David reached the foot of the stairs as they entered *Satan's Cellar*, the supporting investigator moving from shot and unveiling the club to us.

Late night revellers infested the room, and a live band was still performing. The camera rested on a guitarist on the stage. He wore a tattered sleeveless t-shirt as his head rotated to the crunching of the heavy riffs, his long purple hair spinning round like some shaggy Catherine wheel.

'Oh, I think these are The Crystal Misfits!' I heard Rachel say. 'I hope you're seeing this, Mel. This is that band I was telling you about.'

I rubbed my eyes. 'For fuck's sake.' *Just get on with it, girl!* I willed her.

'Where is David?' Mantella spoke into his microphone.

Rachel evidently heard him as the camera began panning left to right to the turning of her body. Suddenly the investigator emerged from the throngs of club-goers as he walked up to her.

'My friend is here,' David said. 'The guy behind the bar...' His chest filled the screen again as he leant towards Rachel, presumably so he could speak closer to the microphone on the covert camera for the benefit of those watching the footage back in his car. 'I'm going to have a word with him, see if he'll tell me where we need to go to advance to the secret areas of this place.'

'Give me the mic a sec,' Kerrish ordered Mantella. He passed it over to him. 'Rachel, tell David to ask for a Wiseau. That's the vampire we're looking for.'

'They say to ask for someone called Wiseau,' Rachel relayed the message to the investigator. 'Oh wait, I have a photo on my phone you can show him.'

'Great,' David replied.

We watched as Rachel flipped through her photos trying to find the one of the glam rock vampire. I don't think she was quite tuned in to the fact that we were seeing all this too back in the car as she swiped past various personal photographs she'd taken of herself with Ziggy. Eventually she came to the all-important image of Wiseau and handed the phone to David.

'Just don't swipe!' she advised him.

'Got it. Wait here. I'll be right back.' He turned away from her and we watched him walking towards the bar area. After a couple of moments though, the camera drifted back to the stage where The Crystal Misfits continued to perform their raucous show.

'Rachel, stay on David, please!' Kerrish shouted into the microphone.

'Jesus, who made you dungeon master?' she whined as she eventually followed the action. By now David was leaning across the bar conversing with some shifty-looking bearded guy, talking with an urgency that I was so thankful for. I could see the glow of Rachel's phone screen as David now showed this barman the photograph of Wiseau. The barman stood there taking it all in. Maybe he nodded softly. Maybe the expression on his face portrayed understanding towards David, concern for the pressing issue being relayed to him. It was possible this new character was acting as the sympathetic ally, willing to help the investigator on his quest, someone who was essentially a stranger to me himself. On this tiny monitor though, and at this distant angle, I could tell none of these things, only what I wanted to project onto this narrative, my own selfish hopes.

Occasionally the screen would flicker black. I presumed it was Rachel's arm blocking the lens as she swept her hair out of her face. No doubt she liked the look of this brutish barman.

'Oh shit,' Mantella muttered. 'This doesn't look good.'

As he was closest to the monitor, he was the first to make out two burly figures approaching David from behind, the camera framing them right on the very edge such that a film director would generate unease in her audience at their stealthy appearance. The camera tracked towards them as Rachel also noticed their arrival, moving closer to get a better view, the tension of the drama building further as our central character worked out what the hell was transpiring.

'What's going on?' Rachel cried to us through the microphone.

The two burly characters grabbed David and ushered him away, the poor investigator looking worriedly around himself as they carted him out of sight before he knew what had hit him.

'Oh shit-sticks, Rachel whined.

'Fuck!' Kerrish spat so loudly next to me it made me

jump.

'Where are they taking him?' Rachel continued to whine pitifully through the microphone as though Kerrish might give her a reassuring answer. She darted between revellers up to the bar where David had been standing one moment ago, looking to see where they'd taken him, but there was no sign of him anywhere. We all noticed the barman glaring Rachel's way, a character who we now knew to be yet another foe. The camera panned away as she presumably tried to melt into the crowd.

'Well, she's on her own again,' Kerrish announced. He grabbed the microphone. 'Stick with the programme, Rachel. You need to find Wiseau.'

'But... David...' Rachel began. 'He's got my phone!'

'You don't need it,' Kerrish replied to her.

'That's a fucking iPhone X! Do you know how much those things cost?'

He was about to say something into the microphone but then sighed as he lowered his hand, his hope disintegrating. It was so late. It had been such a long night already and Kerrish looked like a man who just wanted to give up and go home.

'We can't leave her in there on her own,' I said. 'We have to go in and help her.'

'Not happening, Melody,' Kerrish replied.

'She can't do this! She's a fucking Drama student, not Jack bloody Bauer!'

'Well, she's the only hope you've got, vampire lover, so you better find some way to motivate her,' Kerrish roared as he shoved the microphone in my face.

'What do I do?' Rachel's voice bleated through the monitor. 'I don't know where to go.'

'Hey Rach, it's me,' I spoke into the microphone. 'You're doing really well.' It was all I could think of to say. It was naff and she would surely see through it, but I was losing my words and my will too. 'Just keep looking for Wiseau. Please, hon.'

'They'll probably come for me too any second,' she cried. 'And what do I tell them when I've got this sharpened two foot lump of wood under my jacket?'

I put the microphone down. 'Please. Why can't we just go in there?'

'You want to drag even more people down into the shit you've created?' Kerrish spat back at me. 'They're probably beating David fifty shades to shit right now and you want to bring me and Mantella into that too?'

'But... I don't want to die!' I started to cry, putting my head in my hands. Hopelessness wasn't my overriding emotion right at that moment, and the tears had to be somewhat forced, but I hoped that having some teary woman on his arm would help break him.

'What about it, Kerrish?' Mantella pondered. Was I perhaps winning the sidekick over?

Kerrish opened his mouth to reply when my phone interrupted with a notification. Who the hell would be messaging me at half four in the morning? I swiftly fumbled it out of my purse and read the name on the screen.

'It's from Rachel.'

'Rachel?' Mantella replied in confusion.

'Shit, it's from David!' I cried. 'He got a message away.'

'Give it to me,' Kerrish snapped as he grabbed it out of my hands and held it close to his eyes. I peered over his shoulder and could see the communication was very brief, its subtext suggesting that David had made a subtle tapping of the minimum of words to get his message across before his captives noticed what he was doing. 'Last cubicle gents.'

'What?' Mantella puzzled. 'They took him for a piss?'

'No! Don't you see?' I cried.

He continued to look at me blankly.

'David said there were other levels to this place, other areas beyond this mosh pit. He's telling us where to go.'

'Or they chained him up in the bogs and he wants us to rescue him?' Kerrish argued back as he finished tapping a reply and hit send.

'Well... *that* then! So are you just going to leave him there? He tells you where he is and you leave an apprehended man to your enemies?' I was pleased with myself. That was a really smart reply, and Kerrish didn't have a comeback to that one.

'Come on, man,' his buddy Mantella reasoned with him. 'I think she's right. We've got to go in there.'

Kerrish continued to gaze at the screen of my phone, vainly hoping for more communication from the captive to help him decide what to do. He looked like he was chewing on an invisible bone for a moment, his teeth grinding together before he spat out another, 'Fuck!' which essentially translated to: *Okay, my friend, I know you're right on this and we have no choice but to go in there.*

'Come on, then!' I shouted at him as I grabbed his shoulder and attempted to shake him into action. He instantly flung me away. He was actually pretty strong, and I made a mental note that I shouldn't piss him off too much.

Throwing open the door, he immediately stepped onto the road and I lurched forward as he dragged me along by the handcuffs.

'Hey wait!' I cried as I tried to find my footing, spilling out of the car. I landed on the floor, but he yanked me up to my feet like I was some mischievous puppy dog on a leash. 'You're such a dick sometimes, Kerrish!'

'Oh. Well, I'm glad you think it's only *sometimes*.'

'Do you think I could have my phone back?'

'No.' He slipped it into his pocket.

'Bastard.'

Mantella got out of the car too. He'd retrieved the keys from the ignition and locked up, or perhaps this fancy car locked itself all on its own.

'Let's do this.'

Chapter 15

The three of us marched up the alleyway towards the action zone. No longer were we the passive audience sitting in front of the movie screen. Now we were the Last Action Heroes jumping into the drama.

'Hold my hand,' Kerrish ordered me. 'Don't want to draw attention to ourselves, being chained to you like this.'

'What, you don't want people knowing you're some sort of Christian Grey? We'll probably fit right in with the eccentrics of this place.' I did as I was told and offered him my hand, and he interlocked his fingers with mine. He pissed me off so much, but even in a dire moment such as this, I still felt a tingle of excitement walking side by side with him like late night lovers.

'More likely they'll think I'm a copper.'

'Why don't you just remove it then? You don't still think I'll run away, do you?'

'No chance. Besides, I left the key at *The Claw.*'

Behind us I heard the voice of Mantella, evidently speaking to Rachel through his microphone. 'Just keep searching the area. We'll be with you very soon. Coming your way now.'

I had a weird sense of déjà vu as we approached the entrance to *Satan's Cellar*, gazing up at the sign in glorious full colour three dimensional reality instead of the filter of some nightvision display. Kerrish and I descended the stairs in step with one another. The walls were caked in layers of old posters advertising bands that had played in the club down the years, and blended within all that was years-old graffiti.

By the time we reached the bottom of the staircase, the stale smell of sweat and beer hit my nostrils. The club was still buzzing with the activity of drunks and druggies riding and fuelling their highs. It was quite likely this was the only place in the city still open at this time of day, or maybe it was a 24 hour party zone where revellers could endlessly frolic with satanic abandon, and the lively energy of a punk band headbanging at silly o'clock was two fingers up to society and its structure of work-play-rest. Here you could play forever until you burned up.

Still hand in hand, Kerrish and I weaved between the moshers like the innocent lovers Adam and Eve being tempted into the earthly delights of this electrifying realm. I searched the crowd for Rachel, hoping that in the time it had taken for us to walk from the car to here she hadn't been abducted by any of the resident demons.

Eventually I spotted her across the room, the ill-fitting jacket smothering her slender frame. She looked so hopelessly lost, dwarfed by the magnitude of the situation she was in, but her eyes soon found mine and they lit up. She darted over to us and threw her arms around me, and I hugged her back with my free arm. I imagined she was sobbing in relief, although I couldn't properly hear it over the clamorous music that penetrated my ear holes.

'You okay, Rach?' I asked her.

'Better now you're here.'

Kerrish yanked his wrist and broke us apart. 'Come on, ladies. Let's not get all touchy-feely right now.'

'Bogs are over there,' Mantella stated as he appeared next to Kerrish. He pointed towards a dingy nook and I imagined beyond the door of the gents' toilets, junkies were swimming in the sludge and stench of absolute filth.

'Let's move,' Kerrish barked as he began the march over there. I attempted to explain to Rachel the significance of us all going en masse to the little boys' room, that it wasn't because we'd all been glugging gallons of water while we were sitting in the car, but that we were investigating the mysterious message that David had got away on her phone.

'Great,' Rachel replied. 'Let's hope our vampire is in there as he sure as hell isn't rocking it to The Crystal Misfits.'

They were words of encouragement but it just made it clear to me the utterly anorexic thread we were following, that perhaps in some unknown and out-the-way corner of this weird nightclub some vampire was chilling away, and this would be the very creature that had infected me last night. For all we knew, this Wiseau character may have actually stayed in tonight watching *The Lost Boys* on DVD, sipping from a straw dipped into a stolen blood bag.

Mantella reached the door first and pushed it open. We filed inside, wading through a pool of festering piss-water as a buzzing light flickered on and off. To our right was a line of three toilet cubicles. The doors to the first two were wide open, and we soon gathered that they were vacant, but the third one, the significant last one that David had messaged us about, was closed, as though someone was in there taking a dump or having his cock sucked by some chick... Hell, for all I knew with this place, it may well have been both.

Walking ahead, Mantella crouched down to peer under the cubicle door to see if anyone was inside. He wasn't able to get down very low without placing a knee or hand on this yucky floor, so instead he jumped up and clung to the edge of the door as he peered beyond it.

'It's clear,' he announced.

Kerrish kicked it, and it flung open.

'Oh sweet Jesus on roller skates,' Rachel spluttered as she grimaced at the lovely sight he'd revealed. 'Yeah, that's really clear.'

The seat was up, of course, and the bowl and rim were completely covered in a mousse-like showering of shit, as though the toilet were some monster and had just vomited all the detritus that this evening's, or perhaps the whole week's, revellers had deposited within it. It was all up the walls, all over the floor.

'Yep,' Mantella announced. 'We found the worst toilet in Meridian.'

'Oh my fucking God,' Rachel said. 'Did David do that?' All three of us turned in unison to throw her raised eyebrows. 'We get him abducted, so he gets his revenge by leading us here, to this? That's nasty,' she went on.

Mantella shrugged. 'Did the excitement get too much for him?'

'Jesus,' Rachel whined. 'Does he want us to rate it or something?'

'Look!' Kerrish said, cutting through the inane conversation. He pointed above the toilet.

'It's a doorway,' Mantella replied. It was some small

wooden hatch about three feet high like it was the front door to some lost resident of Hobbiton.

'You first,' Rachel prompted him.

Hesitantly, Mantella stepped inside the cubicle, moving steadily so he wouldn't come into contact with any of the yuckiness. He reached forward for the handle to this little door before thinking twice about putting his skin to it. He checked the toilet paper dispenser. As if there would really be anything in that!

'Anyone got a tissue?' he asked. Rachel was already on it, as though she'd read his thought before it had entered his brain.

'Here,' she said as she handed him one from her purse.

With that, he twisted the handle and pulled the hatch open. He then used the tissue to put the toilet seat down, which was now going to be the step to this strange passageway. I couldn't actually see much inside. That was until Mantella brought out a little LED torch that he shone into the darkness. It looked like the corridor was about ten feet in length and at the far end was another wooden doorway.

'Who wants to go first?' Mantella asked, an over-enthusiasm masking the fact that he really didn't want to have that privilege bestowed upon him.

'Rachel?' Kerrish prompted.

'Yeah?' she replied.

'You're the one with the stake.'

'Here, you take it. You're the alleged expert vampire killers.'

'You think Wiseau's through there?' I asked hopefully.

'Who knows?' Kerrish replied dismissively. 'For all I know we'll end up in friggin' Narnia.'

'Come on,' I said, taking the initiative. I really didn't have time to stand around hesitating. We needed to keep moving, keep making progress through this house of fun. I skipped up onto the toilet. The top of the seat had thankfully avoided any soiling. Once I'd steadied myself, I then yanked Kerrish over towards me, a bit of perverse satisfaction coming through that I was getting to pull him along for a change.

He stepped up on there with me then put a hand on my waist as he tried to usher me into the secret passageway.

'Hey! Hands off.'

It was awkward trying to manoeuvre myself in there, being handcuffed to someone. I approached it sideways, pivoting myself above the cistern with my knee, leaving my tethered arm dangling from the opening so Kerrish could climb in there after me. Claustrophobia came over me once he'd joined me in the passageway, his body blocking the strained light from the toilets. I had no choice but to carry on into the darkness.

I hobbled forwards in a crouched position, Kerrish silently following me, his breath like a draft on my hair. Before I knew it, I'd reached the door at the other end. I didn't know what was beyond it. Perhaps there would be a pack of vampires lying in wait for any prey to fall into their trap and they would instantly pounce on us and feed on our blood until we were nothing but a bundle of bones in a sack of skin.

'Kick it,' Kerrish told me.

I ignored him, instead grabbing the handle and gently pushing the door open. I'd already braced myself for whatever surprise I was about to reveal, but to my relief an army of fangs did not ambush me.

Perhaps I should have hoped for that outcome, that Wiseau had greeted me and we'd swiftly see to him and put an end to this.

Instead, I had the sense that we had a much longer journey to make.

Chapter 16

I again had the sense of déjà vu as I examined the scene before me. We appeared to have found some quiet lounge area. There were plush-looking sofas around the room, tasteful paintings adorning the walls, a lush grey carpet. It was all in complete contrast to the intensity of *Satan's Cellar* and indeed the literal shithole we'd just stepped out of. Hissy old-time music played at a gentle volume, an affected voice singing a song I recognised, *A Nightingale Sang in Berkeley Square*, making me feel like I'd suddenly travelled back in time to a cabaret club.

In the corner of the room was another bar and behind that was a man in a white shirt and black bow tie. The guy was bald and had massive, beady eyes that never seemed to blink.

'More visitors!' he announced as he saw us poking out of the hatch in the wall. 'Please, come and join me in the Foyer of Fortune!'

'Ooookay,' Kerrish muttered in my ear.

I stepped down onto the table and I noticed that this friendly bartender wasn't the only person present. There were three punters dotted around: one was lying on a sofa in the foetal position with his eyes closed, one sat at the bar, and another next to him doubled over. They all looked pretty worse for wear, not that there was anything surprising about that.

Kerrish and I jumped off the table, venturing farther into the room as we took in our surroundings. Trailing us, I could hear Rachel bickering with Mantella as they entered the lounge through the narrow passageway.

As we reached the bar, I twigged why this place felt familiar. Behind the beaming bartender were lines of label-less bottles hanging like potions in some mad scientist's lab. This was the place I'd seen in some of the photographs on our phones. We were getting somewhere.

'We were here,' I said to Kerrish. I turned to the bartender. 'Excuse me, do you recognise me?'

His head pivoted round like the head on a

ventriloquist's dummy and he continued to gawp at me with the same creepy grin on his face. 'I'm sorry, miss, I do not.'

'Me and my friend Rachel were in here last night.'

'I was in another department.'

'Hey, I know this place,' Rachel said as she caught up with us, the environment triggering recognition in her too. 'Ooh, what's in all these bottles?'

The inebriated guy with his head hunched into his knees suddenly made an almighty retch and we heard the glorious sound of vomit splattering. I dared to look his way out of the corner of my eye and noticed he had a bucket between his legs. I shut my eyes tight again as I realised it was nearly full of puke.

'Think he's had a little too much to drink,' I remarked.

'Not so much *too much* to drink,' the bizarre bartender told us. 'More the *wrong* drink.'

'Right, well we won't have what he's having then,' Kerrish said. He turned away from the bar and continued scrutinising the strange room we were in. 'What is this place?' he demanded from the bartender. 'How do we get out of here? We're looking for someone and we need to crack on.'

'You search for the other levels?' the bartender asked.

'I guess.'

'To proceed from one to the other you must take the challenge first.'

'Okay, so... What do we do?'

'It's a simple drinking game in the Foyer of Fortune.'

'I see. And this is where these guys struck misfortune?' Kerrish asked as he pointed at the puking people. The poor guy sitting at the bar clutched his stomach as he belched. I took a step away from him to avoid being in the firing range of a rainbow shower.

The bartender shrugged. 'Do you wish to play?'

'Look, we don't have time for this nonsense,' Kerrish went on. 'Can you just tell us where we need to go?'

'Nah uh uh!' the bartender trilled, wagging a finger

at us like some vaudeville ringmaster. 'First you must play the game.'

Kerrish rubbed his eyes. 'Okay. What is it?'

Our host gestured towards a table in the corner next to the bar. Shot glasses were arranged on it, about a hundred of them, all filled with purple liquid.

'Come and take a seat over here.'

We all stepped over to him and sat around on the cushioned seats. The bartender stood before us like a casino croupier and placed his fingertips on the table. With a sweep of his hand, the tabletop twirled before us like you get in Chinese restaurants. I watched the shot glasses spinning round me like they were the numbers on the Wheel of Fortune board game and with my mind racing ahead, I guessed that the *fortune* the wheel may bring me might be my stomach being bankrupted of its stock like the poor pukers over there.

'To play this game is simple,' the bartender announced. 'All you have to do is pick one of the glasses of drink before you and swallow the contents whole.'

I was confused. A game? Would I have played this last night when we were fraternising with Wiseau and his fellow vampires? That thought didn't seem to ring true with me, despite the void in my memory.

'What's in these?' Kerrish asked as he peered at the glasses, his eyebrows furrowing in suspicion.

'Seventy-five percent of them are filled with an innocuous but delicious fruity beverage that will have no side effect on you at all. The other twenty-five percent, however, are laced with ipecac.'

'Ah Christ,' Kerrish muttered.

'What the hell is ipecac?' Rachel asked, her voice laden with worry.

'He wants us to play ipecac roulette,' Mantella stated matter-of-factly. 'I saw some guys doing this on a YouTube video.'

'It's an emetic,' Kerrish told her. 'Makes you puke. Hence the Spewie Lewies over there.'

'Oh, I see,' Rachel replied. 'How long does it take to work?'

'Not long at all,' the bartender advised.

'Well, a seventy-five percent chance is pretty good,' she conceded.

'But it means that one of us is going to get the puke bullet most likely,' Mantella said. 'Since there are four of us and...'

'Yeah, I can do the maths,' Rachel snapped back. 'Well, fuck it. As far as I'm concerned, if the night hasn't involved puking somewhere along the line then you haven't had a proper night, and that's one thing I haven't done yet.'

With that she grabbed a glass at random and completely devoid of any hesitation she swiftly knocked the drink down her throat. She slammed the glass down on the table, and we all sat there in quiet anticipation.

It never ceased to amaze me how some people could have no qualms whatsoever about throwing up. Rachel was one of those sorts who would throw caution to the wind with whatever she ate (or drank) and who had that *if you're gonna be ill then you're gonna be ill* attitude that I could not relate to in the slightest. I was the complete opposite, taking all measures to make sure I avoided it. I hated it. Absolutely hated it, and it was an experience I'd already endured on this messed up evening. If you were poorly and needed the comforting hand of a friend to lift your hair as you puked your guts up into the toilet, then I was *not* the person to do that. You were on your own with that shit, I'm afraid. I was already subconsciously edging away from her in case she might erupt.

Seconds passed, and we continued to stare at Rachel as she sat there smiling cheerfully. Suddenly, however, the smile disappeared, a frown forming. She turned to me, beckoning with her hand one of those *pass the bucket quickly* gestures. As I bunched up against Kerrish, she moved her head closer to mine and her mouth snapped open.

'Bleuuuurrrggghhhh!' she exploded in my face, but it was only her breath I felt on my skin in wicked mocking of our apprehension. 'Yeah, it looks like I'm fine.'

'Well played, miss,' the bartender said. 'It appears you chose a dud.'

It was great for Rachel, but it meant with her choosing successfully, the odds for the rest of us had shortened.

'Me next,' I said. I really didn't want to throw up, but I had no choice. I needed to get on with this. Besides, the threat of puking again paled in significance when you had the threat of imminent death on your shoulders.

My hand searched for a shot glass, but then I hesitated as it hovered above them. Were some of them a different shade of purple to the others? Would I be able to spot the ipecac drinks?

'What did it taste like?' Mantella asked.

'Fruity,' Rachel replied.

'I bet it was Vimto. Right?' Mantella chirped with self-satisfaction, digging for some recognition from us of the brilliant point he was making. 'Yeah? Because you know what Vimto is an anagram of, right?'

Rachel sat there blankly. 'Motive?'

'Where's the e?' Mantella replied in exasperation. 'And you're a university student? Jesus!'

I would have to do this the Rachel way. Just stop thinking about it. Pick one, knock it back, and to hell with it. My eyes rested on the particular glass that was closest to me, interpreting this as a friendly gesture from the universe that from the spinning of the vomit roulette table, fate had kindly presented the drink I was supposed to drink by putting it right in front of me.

I grabbed it, put the glass to my lips and emptied it. I swallowed hard, then closed my eyes tight as I waited for the inevitable to happen.

'Mel?' Rachel asked, nudging my arm. 'You okay, hon?'

For a moment I thought the nerves would make me puke naturally. The flesh in my throat felt like it was crawling, my stomach spinning around like a washing machine. The seconds continued to pass, and I dared to open my eyes again, dared to believe that I too had chosen well. I began to register the taste this drink had left on my tongue. It was actually quite fruity. Perhaps it was merely Vimto after all.

'I think I'm okay,' I said.

'Halfway there,' the bartender spoke. 'Now which one of you brave gentlemen will take their turn first?'

'I really don't see why the hell I should have to do this,' Kerrish moaned before turning to me and adding: 'This is not my mess.'

'Well, maybe he'll let me and Rachel go through on our own then. We'll leave you two cowards here.'

'I have a *thing* about throwing up,' Kerrish muttered to me like he was making a little confession. By a 'thing' I knew he meant that he too found it a deeply unpleasant prospect, not that it was some perverse *2 Girls 1 Cup* thing.

'Please,' I said, trying to make my eyes as puppy dog-like as I could. 'I'm running out of time. Do it for me.'

'You choose,' he said, his eyes closed.

'What?'

'You pick which glass.'

'Um... okay.' I looked around the table. Do I pick the one that fell closest to him? Had the universe engineered this all so neatly and conveniently for us that I just needed to go by the same rationale? Or did I actually care whether or not he would puke? Picking an ipecac-laced drink might provide me with a satisfying moment of schadenfreude by seeing Kerrish suffer.

'Pick a wrong one and it'll just be another reason for me to hate you more,' he said.

With that I didn't even look as my hand picked up any old glass. 'Here.'

He breathed in deeply for a moment. 'And for the record, I'll make sure to get it over you,' he added as he lifted the drink and knocked back the mystery potion.

Again we all stared at him as he sat there stone-faced. After a few moments, he shrugged.

'Great,' Mantella said. 'So you guys all get duds and so the law of averages mean I'm going to be in that twenty-five percent.'

'No, Manny,' Kerrish reassured him. 'It's the same probability for you.'

'Except it's slightly less as you've taken three of the

good glasses away. I can't believe this. Why did I have to gorge on pizza and fries tonight?'

'Come on, Mantella,' I prompted him. It felt like we'd been sitting around this table for far too long now.

'Yeah, come on, Manny,' Kerrish added. 'Just take a drink. We all did it. We need to get moving.'

The man remained hesitant, though. These were vital seconds he was wasting here. Kerrish sighed. Even he was getting impatient. Eventually Mantella picked out a glass, but then he put it down again.

'Manny!'

'I don't know if I want to do this.'

Rachel jutted her head towards him. 'Hey, Manny. Do this and I'll give you a blow job.'

I could see his eyes practically light up as though expunging a 12 inch Hawaiian pizza with extra cheese from his stomach was a small price to pay for being able to put his knob in Rachel's mouth, a 'no brainer', as they say.

He picked up the drink again and swallowed it in one. 'You got yourself a deal, Miss Rachel.'

'Well, look forward to that, *Dickfloss*,' I muttered to her so quietly that only she would hear me.

'Come on, get up,' Kerrish barked at us all, yanking the handcuffs as he manipulated me to my feet. Was there a touch of jealousy there? 'Okay, we did your stupid challenge,' he said as he approached the bartender. 'Now take us to the next level.'

I heard Mantella groaning as he still sat at the table. 'Oh no,' he moaned. I immediately closed my eyes but my ears painted a vivid picture in my head: Mantella rushing to his feet, darting over to the bar, grabbing the ice bucket and violently filling it with the chunder of bile and pizza from his stomach. Once that horror show abated, he was practically crying.

'Well done, my friends,' the bartender announced. 'You have all taken the challenge and are eligible for the next level. Follow me... if you can!' He walked over towards the fireplace in the middle of the lounge.

'Move it, Manny,' Kerrish said. 'Bring the ice bucket with you.'

We followed the bartender, but I'd only taken a couple of steps before the guy sitting at the bar stopped me, putting a hand on my arm. He leaned in close and muttered: 'Don't think it gets any better,' before letting me go again.

'This way,' our guide said as he beckoned us over. 'That's right, over here.'

Kerrish and I joined him, wondering what the hell would happen next. Rachel was a step behind, looking back with concern at poor Mantella who continued to sit on a bar stool hunched over the bucket.

'I want to go home,' he moaned.

'Get your arse over here,' Kerrish shouted.

I noticed by the fireplace there was a tall grandfather clock, its pendulum swinging back and forth. I saw the little hand was heading towards the five and wondered how many of these challenges we would have to go through, how many more levels of this hellish place we would have to navigate ourselves through. I now had less than three hours till sunrise. The rate we were going, I would make my transformation right here in *Satan's Cellar*.

Perhaps my best chance of survival, though, was by continuing through this house of tricks and letting it wear down my captives as had happened with Mantella. Another couple more of these tests and maybe Kerrish would be moaning too that he wanted to give up and go home. Even if that transpired though, I was sure they would come looking for me again, once they'd had time to regroup. At best I probably only had another day or so before they would find me and terminate me as they had made overwhelmingly clear to me. They knew my name, knew I was a student. Kerrish even had my phone. But was that scenario a better prospect than trying to hunt down this vampire and killing him within the next three hours?

'Why don't we go on without him?' I suggested to Kerrish. If we were down to three, then the number of our captors was halved. It was two against one. Granted, one of those two was Rachel, and granted I remained handcuffed to my captor and unable to do a runner, but still. The multitude of different possibilities swarmed throughout my brain, and I was desperately trying to cling onto anything to get me out of this horrible situation.

'Manny, would you get over here now!' he shouted. Of course, he was having none of my suggestion. Groaning, Mantella slid off his stool, holding the ice bucket like a frightened kid clutching his teddy bear.

'Go and help him,' I said to Rachel.

'I don't want to get puke on me,' she protested, although she soon relented and attended to him. She stopped short of lending him an arm, but she gave him some gentle words of encouragement, or maybe she was just reminding him about the special reward she'd promised him a moment ago. He gingerly followed her as he hobbled over to us. Finally, all four of us stood with the peculiar bartender around the fireplace.

'All ready? Great. Onwards you shall go. Good luck with the rest of your journey!'

He stepped backwards and then turned to a bookcase, searching out a hardback. I'd seen them do this in the movies before, or it may have been in an episode of *Batman*, the old Adam West series. I knew what would happen next. It made me wonder just what crazy crackpot had put this place together.

'Wait,' I said to the bartender. 'Are there many more rooms? How many of these stupid challenges do we have to take?'

'Only one way to find out.' He pulled back a book and the ground at our feet trembled as hidden mechanics clunked into motion. And with that, everything started spinning, and I watched the beaming barman gawping in what was probably sadistic pleasure with the thought of us continuing on to even more perverse torture. We were taken from the Foyer or Fortune and whooshed into the next level. There we were immersed in darkness.

Chapter 17

'Oh God. I think I'm going to throw up again,' I heard Mantella say. A few seconds later he indeed confirmed that particular suspicion. I felt the tug of the handcuffs as Kerrish stepped away from him and any splatter.

'Can anyone see anything?' Rachel asked. 'Manny, where's your torch?'

After a few moments, though, my eyes adjusted to the darkness and I could make out we were in some sort of bricked chamber. Turning around, I was faced with another passageway.

'Look over there,' I said, but Kerrish was already marching towards it, and a moment later I had no choice but to do likewise. Behind us I heard Rachel continuing to attend to the poorly Mantella, coaxing him along. The ground seemed strange and our steps became increasingly tentative. There was a sponginess beneath our feet, as though we were treading over a sea of cockroaches and beetles. Even if I had a torch, I preferred to remain ignorant to what the soles of my shoes were coming into contact with.

Besides, we were too distracted by the tassels of material that hung from the ceiling like cobwebs and which we had to weave ourselves through. It reminded me of walking through a ghost train, or some haunted house attraction at an amusement park.

Eerie music played in the background over speakers: some tuneless, improvised organ playing that meandered nowhere. On the walls I could faintly make out there were various pictures hanging, vintage black and white photographs where no one smiled. I remembered reading on the internet once about a fashion back in the Victorian era where people would have their portraits taken with recently deceased loved ones. I glanced momentarily at a family photograph as I trailed through and wondered which members might be dead and which were still living. None of the people in it were smiling. Hell, maybe they were all dead.

Eventually we reached a T-junction in the corridor. On the wall were two signs, each in the shape of a grisly skeleton's hand pointing in either direction. 'The easy way' one announced, and 'the hard way' the other.

'I'm all for an easy life,' Kerrish said. 'Let's go that way.'

Down either corridor there were doors, so we had no idea as to the complexity beyond them. I seriously doubted that 'the easy way' would do as it described and be as breezy as a river cruise, but then was it a double bluff? Either way, I didn't have time to dwell on it.

'Try it,' I replied.

He stepped towards it and grabbed the handle. Wisely he opened the door just far enough for him to peep through the crack to examine what was beyond it. Immediately he pushed it shut and double-backed.

'That'll be a nope.'

'What?' a curious Rachel asked as she appeared behind us. 'What was through there?'

'Come on, Rach,' I encouraged her. If it had taken Kerrish half a second to determine we shouldn't go that way, then there was no point wasting our time satisfying our curiosity as to what he had seen.

'It was a dead end,' he stated, and if he'd left it there, that would have been enough to leave it be, but then he had to add: 'Quite literally.'

Rachel turned to me, a 'huh' expression distorting her face. She shook her head and stepped over to the door, grabbed the handle and pulled it wide open.

My ear holes bristled as she screamed, two corpses popping out from the doorway as they hung there with their dead-eyed stares right in Rachel's face. She stumbled backwards and fell onto her arse, the corpses staring at us grimly, their mouths agape, or perhaps they were supposed to be grinning. Gradually Rachel's screaming eased as she realised they weren't really dead bodies, just dummies. The one on the right had a bald patch on his head crowned by erect golden hair.

'Oh, I think he's Donald Trump,' Rachel calmly mused in sudden contrast to her melodramatic scream. She was probably right, but I couldn't afford this any deliberation. It was the same silly trick found in fairground ghost trains, two corpses hidden in a little closet that would pop out when the door opened.

'So who's the other guy?' Kerrish asked.

'Uh... Vladimir Putin?'

'He's too fat to be Putin,' Mantella added unexpectedly.

'Kim Jong Un then?' she replied. 'Is this some lame political statement or something? Because it's kind of a weird place to be making it.'

'I don't know,' I said. 'But how about we leave Donald and his undetermined friend alone and go the other way until we can get Robert Peston down here to clarify what it's all about?'

'I wonder if it's James Corden,' Rachel pondered as she got to her feet.

'Why the hell would he be in there with Donald Trump?' Mantella couldn't help but ask.

I tuned myself out of their pointless conversation as I turned to the other door, bracing myself for more bizarre waxwork models lunging out from 'the hard way'. I quickly threw it open and there we discovered an empty passageway.

Onwards we marched. I didn't even glance round to see if Rachel and Mantella were following. I just needed them to keep up, and if they weren't doing that, then they could give up and go home. Ahead of us was a chamber, a large fountain in the middle of it, ornately carved with imps and gargoyles that crawled around a spurting of red water from its centre. As we emerged into the chamber and walked round the fountain, I noticed the pool beneath it was full of coins.

I wondered why the previous voyagers of *Satan's Cellar* had taken a moment here to remove a coin from their wallet and throw it into the pool. Perhaps it was a natural compulsion to do so on seeing a fountain like you might in a shopping mall, or perhaps they just needed a wish to come true when they reached this particular point.

Or perhaps they'd been using that coin to work out

which way to go next; as we continued to take in our surroundings, we soon worked out we now had three options available. In the middle of the far wall were the doors to a lift. On the left of this lift was an entrance to a chute, like a slide on a helter-skelter. To the right, there was a staircase that spiralled down.

'Which way do we go now?' I asked.

'Look!' Kerrish replied as he pointed up at the ceiling. I arched back my head and saw there were instructions painted on it.

I heard Rachel's voice echoing behind me as she read them. 'For *pleasure* travel the slide, for *pain* ride the elevator, for *glory* take the stairs.'

We all looked at each other as though one of us might have the insight to answer, but all I could hear was the soft trickling of water. I don't think it really mattered which way we would pick; they'd all be as bad as each other. What worried me most of all was how labyrinthine this place was turning out to be, especially now we were faced with this *choose your own adventure* crossroad. How long was it going to take to get to this secret VIP area that David spoke of? And how did we even know that Wiseau would be there, anyway? Or maybe we'd stumble on him somewhere along the way, somewhere on one of these many trails.

'There are three routes,' Mantella began, 'and since the four of us split three ways, why don't we take one each?'

It sounded logical, but the plan didn't sit right in my mind. Surely we were best off sticking together? This fork in the road was probably another silly trick. Perhaps all options just ended up in the same place.

'I'm not going to be left on my own again,' Rachel replied defiantly, which was enough for us to dismiss Mantella's idea.

'So, we've already had fortune,' Kerrish said. 'Time now for glory?' It seemed as good a suggestion as anything. I didn't fancy getting into a lift that might turn out to be as crazy as Willy Wonka's glass elevator, or going down a slide where it would be difficult to stop ourselves once we realised we were about to land in a massive pool of shit.

'Fortune and glory, kid,' I replied. 'The stairs it is.'

Neither Rachel nor Mantella had any objection to that, so we quickly began descending the steps. It soon felt like a never-ending spiral that was taking us down to the centre of the earth. I think it was even longer than the steps at Covent Garden tube station.

I had a sinking suspicion these stairs were another stunt, that we would get all the way to the bottom only to realise it was a dead end, and then we'd have to climb all the way back up again. The way this place was influencing my brain, I bet I could have come up with a twisted theme park of my own.

Fortunately though, it would not turn out we were about to be greeted by a brick wall or a Mr Blobby holding a Gotcha award down there, but by the time we reached the bottom, my head was spinning. I felt sorry for poor Mantella, as the dizzying spiral induced yet another round of vomiting, although it didn't last too long this time. I doubted the poor guy had any of that pizza left in his stomach now.

Down here we were in a featureless chamber, and we paused to get our bearings. Lights went on ahead, a chain of bulbs lighting a panel like the lights on a fairground ride. It looked like there was writing on this panel, but I couldn't read it from there. I knew that this placard would give us further instruction on our next challenge, and I just hoped it wouldn't be as sadistic as the last one in the Foyer of Fortune.

With my nerves continuing to spiral down into a hopeless pit, we marched over towards our next ordeal.

Chapter 18

As Kerrish and I arrived at the illuminated placard, I could see it was inscribed with another chaotic, jagged font. It was attached to what looked like a rock face, as though we had now gone so far underground we were mining into the earth's core. It felt like we were the Fellowship and had reached the Walls of Moria where we had to solve the riddle at the gateway before we were allowed to enter. Hopefully, it would be as simple as saying the word 'friend'.

'Welcome to the Grotto of Glory,' Kerrish read.

'Are we about to meet Santa?' I asked him. 'Because you know what *that* is an anagram of.'

He turned back to the placard. 'Slide yourself into the grotto and glory shall be found when you ring the correct bell.'

'Doesn't sound so complicated,' I suggested, some pitiful attempt to reassure myself.

Next to the placard was a slit in the rock face, a cave-like passageway that I couldn't help but notice had a certain 'yonic' quality to it. This was the opening we were supposed to penetrate, and I guessed that would make us a bunch of dicks for heading on in there.

'Okay,' Kerrish said. 'Looks like it's time for some spelunking.'

'Ring the right bell, huh?' Rachel muttered. She and Mantella had caught up with us, although I presumed her companion wasn't as mentally up to speed as her.

'Don't all stand around then,' I said, ever-conscious of the time that was slipping by too quickly. 'Come on.'

Normally I would not have led the way into some dark cave in some mysterious hellhole, but that is what I did as I dragged Kerrish inside the opening, pushing all thoughts of claustrophobia out of my mind. It was amazing how the ultimate fear totally eclipsed such trivial fears as that. I had to angle my body through the gap, but as it slanted away to the left, I saw light ahead. We soon arrived at a bigger chamber shaped like a dome. It was dingy in there, feeble red lights shining down on us as though we were in a photographer's darkroom. At least there was no one in there, no gormless bartender about to witness any further misfortune of our fellowship.

'There's the doorway,' Kerrish announced. I followed his pointing finger and sure enough there was a door there. He darted over to it and tried the handle, but with no surprise at all it was locked shut. I sensed we wouldn't be able to break it down with a forceful kick. It seemed like a solid door to a bank vault.

'I don't see no doorbell,' I said. 'Look around, everyone. See if you can find any bells anywhere.'

Rachel did so, and after an irritating moment of attempting to move in opposite directions, Kerrish and I circled the dome in unison as we quickly scoured the walls. As for Mantella, he simply slumped down on the ground with his bucket.

'Wait,' Kerrish said. 'What are all these holes? There's one here, and I saw another one over there.'

I spotted what he was looking at, a neat, circular perforation about the width of a tennis ball. Maybe inside one we would find a buzzer, a doorbell to press.

'Want me to reach inside?' I asked.

'There's a few more holes this side,' Rachel told us. 'What, do you reckon there's about ten of them?'

'Yeah,' Kerrish replied, 'which makes me worry what's going to happen each time we ring the wrong bell.'

'You never know. We might get lucky first time,' I suggested. 'Shall I pick which one?'

'Go ahead.'

But I didn't get as far as reaching my hand into any of the holes, for it was in the very next moment that it became blatantly apparent what their true purpose was.

'Ohhhhh,' Rachel gasped. 'They mean *that* kind of bell.'

From each of the holes something started protruding, firm fleshy rods all pointing towards us. I'd never actually seen that many dicks before in my life, not all at once. Immediately I had that embarrassed feeling of not knowing where to look, and so averted my gaze by looking at poor Mantella who continued to sit slumped against the wall. That was until he became aware of what horror was now occurring, stealing a glance above his head as he saw a massive erect penis hanging directly over him. He scooted himself away from it as though it was an alien creature that was slithering into the chamber and about to spit its venom over him. I don't think the poor guy could look any more disturbed and his stomach would have surely been turning if it wasn't already.

'Right,' Rachel calmly announced. 'I get it. Grotto of *Glory*. We are in a massive glory hole.'

'Just a regular Friday night, eh, Rach?' I mocked. 'Drinking games, then pleasuring some random strangers.'

'Who do you reckon these people are?' she mused. 'Do you think one of them is that creepo bartender guy?'

She stood there unfazed, peering up at this army of cocks as though she was gazing up at the nighttime stars, pondering the mysteries of the universe. It was like each of these one-eyed trouser snakes was staring back at us, willing us to get started on our challenge. I needed to fast forward this. Rachel may have found herself in the uppermost level of heaven, but I couldn't let us all stand around like a bunch of schoolboys in a brothel.

'Okay, so look, we're supposed to *ring the bells*, and when we've rung the right one, the door will open and we can carry on.'

'So you're saying that we need to pleasure these dicks?' Rachel asked as though she was checking the instructions on something much more mundane, like we were working out a new microwave. 'And when the right one has found his happy ending he'll open the door for us?'

'That's my understanding of this one, yes, Rachel.'

'All right.'

Kerrish had been standing next to me in total silence and devoid of any expression on his face, but at that moment he made a point of clearing his throat. 'I don't know whether this even needs saying at this particular juncture, but just so everyone's absolutely clear here... You two girls are totally on your own on this one.'

'Oh God, I don't even know where to start,' Rachel said, as though it was a given that she would be helping me

133

out on this challenge. 'This whole place is like a totally fucked up version of *The Crystal Maze*.'

Like a willing workhorse, Rachel got to work on one of the dongs, grabbing it firmly and working it with a deft touch. Both Kerrish and Mantella stared at her as she did this, and as I was trying to comprehend the surrealness of our situation, I could not help but stand there dumbly as well.

'I take it it doesn't matter what method we use, right?' Rachel asked. 'Hand jobs are fine, yeah? We don't need to use anything else?' We all continued to gawp in disbelief, or possibly in the case of the two guys they were just enjoying the live porn show going on in front of them and were secretly projecting themselves onto this unidentified gentleman on the other side of the glory hole whom Rachel continued to masturbate. Already Mantella was starting to look better. You put the sight of a sexy young girl performing a sexual act in front of a sick man and it would work true miracles on him, much more than any faith healer on those God channels could achieve. *The power of Jesus will make you walk again!* Nah, just give the guy a wank and in those sixty seconds he'll forget he was ill.

'Are you pervs just going to stand there and watch?' she scolded us all. Sheepishly, they both turned away.

'Are you okay doing this one-handed?' Kerrish asked me. 'If you use your left hand, it might put you off your stride as we're handcuffed.'

'Don't worry,' I replied. 'Good job I'm right-handed, isn't it?'

I realised I needed to get on with it. I considered the dick closest to me but noticed it wasn't quite as rigid as the rest. I thought that one would need a lot of work, although it would just be my luck that that was the 'bell' I needed to pick. I looked for the proudest one; I didn't want to burn myself out and waste my energy on any duds. I suspected the reality was that we'd have to go through the whole lot before that door opened.

As I wrapped my fingers around this cock, I was sure I could hear the guy's gasp escaping through the hole.

As my hand slid up and down his shaft, horrible images formed in my mind of who this particular gentlemen could be. It could have been one of my university professors. What if it was one of Ziggy's fire breather friends? Oh God. Maybe it was my dad!

I figured I was much better off not knowing. It was actually something I *never* wanted to know, if I were to make it out of this night alive. I could go the rest of my life in ignorance of whose penis I was working to orgasm at this particular moment.

'Oh oh oh!' Rachel exclaimed. 'Ladies and gentlemen, this dynamite is about to explode.'

I continued to work mine as I glanced over just in time to see Rachel ring out a stream of ejaculate from hers. She stood back and examined her hands, grimacing slightly as she wiped them on the wall. The anonymous penis withdrew from the hole. One down.

'So do we have ourselves a winner?' she asked as she looked towards the door, hoping it would fling open. I shook my head as it remained motionless.

'Come on,' I called over to her. 'Let's just assume we'll have to settle them all.' With that, she sighed.

'You know, it makes a lot of sense if you two chaps were to help us out here,' she pleaded with our male companions. 'Close your eyes and think of England.'

'Not really the type to fiddle with other guys' junk, Miss Rachel,' Kerrish shouted back.

'She has a point, Kerrish,' I added. 'Go on, that one there is within your reach.'

He ignored me, but, strangely, Mantella now got to his feet.

'Just playing devil's advocate here, if you'd ever had any curiosity to touch some other guy's dick, then this particular occasion would be the least gay opportunity to do that.'

'Not selling it, Mantella,' Kerrish retorted.

I saw Rachel grab another one, working it with enthusiastic vigour as she continued to rant at the male representatives of our party.

'Besides, you two should be the most qualified here

to handle penises. I mean, you're definitely the biggest pair of wankers I've ever met.'

Mantella smiled in amusement at her banter. I had to be fair to the guy. He took it well, appreciating her wit rather than acting all personally offended.

'Come on, Kerrish,' Mantella said. 'You're a single man now.'

I felt my ears pricking, if that was the right word for such a moment as this. Why was I so interested to learn that Kerrish was single? *Yeah, Melody, why not start flirting with him? I mean, surely this is a great moment when you're wanking off some stranger's dick right in front of him.*

'Well, *technically*, anyway,' Mantella went on. Technically? What the hell did he mean by *that*? I watched as he approached one of the dicks and prodded it with his fingertip. 'Maybe you need to get yourself back out there. Experiment a little.'

'Mantella, please don't grab anything in here,' Kerrish told him. 'I really don't want to make this situation any more disturbing than it already is.'

His buddy grinned as he wrapped his hand around the penis nearest to him, beaming back at Kerrish to tease repulsion out of him.

'Jesus,' Kerrish muttered. 'Someone give him some more ipecac.'

'Ah, I'm feeling good now. I'm feeling clean inside,' Mantella went on, evidently in some sort of post-vomit euphoria, continuing to stroke the stranger's penis with an enthusiasm that no one had seen coming. 'Hey, Kerrish, I bet if you stand right next to it you can almost imagine it's your own.'

Kerrish closed his eyes and bowed his head with a long sigh. Right then I felt something wet splashing up my arm. I looked towards the hole and could definitely hear some moaning going on on the other side of the wall that time. I held my hand up to the light to see he'd made a right silky mess. There was no point in cleaning myself up though. We still had a bunch more to get through.

'Looks like I have the magic touch,' Mantella

bragged. I turned to see that he had already brought his guy to orgasm. Well, he was a guy himself. As Rachel pointed out, he should really be an expert in handling this piece of equipment. I noticed Kerrish open his eyes and sneer at him.

'Well done,' he said, shaking his head. 'Where do your talents end?'

I looked around, wondering which one to work on next. Should I go straight for that flaccid one? Or should I leave that little challenge to Mantella, the rate he was going? Or maybe I didn't need to worry anymore...

A loud clunk reverberated throughout the dome. We all stared towards the door and after a further few thuds, the thick portal swung open. He'd done it. Mantella had done it.

'Yes!' I gasped. 'Come on!' I darted over there, towards the entrance of our next challenge, Kerrish in tow. As I reached the door, I turned round.

'Hey, Rach, you can stop doing that now. We did it!'

'Yeah, I'm nearly there.'

'Rachel! For fuck's sake, you don't need to do that anymore!'

'But I can tell he's...' She sighed, then released her grip in clear disappointment. 'I'm so sorry, mister, but I have to go now.'

She hopped over to me, and we left this twisted grotto behind us.

Chapter 19

I marched along the dingy corridor eagerly, even though I knew some other sick challenge awaited us up ahead. So far I'd risked being poisoned by drinking some mysterious concoction; how stupid of me was it to do that? And then I'd had to jerk myself out of the glory hole. I rubbed my hand on my dress as I walked, trying to wipe off that stranger's semen. But despite what we'd already been through, I just wanted to get on with the next thing.

We had no idea how many more of these levels there were to navigate. I imagined how this was like a certain old computer game that my dad would nostalgically play sometimes; maybe I was living some sort of *Jet Set Willy* type scenario where we would endlessly search through these rooms of debauchery and nightmares and we would never get to accomplish what we were ultimately trying to achieve. That was quite possibly the ultimate joke here. This was a thing that could never be completed and we might as well flush ourselves down the toilet right now. Already it felt like my pride and dignity were well on their way to the sewer.

Up ahead, down the other end of the corridor, I spotted a figure. He stood there motionless beside an entrance, dressed in a tuxedo. As we got closer, I noticed he was holding a gun and pointing it straight towards us. Still we marched on though. Something about it just didn't seem right, wasn't quickening my pulse, and as we reached him, I realised why: it was merely a cardboard cut-out.

We all knew the guy. It was James Bond, the incarnation of the licence to kill spy played by Sean Connery. He looked like he was guarding the entrance to a theatre hall. A billboard style sign above the doorway informed us this was The Hall of Harmony. Sounded perfectly serene. I hated how this place lulled you into a false sense of security like this. Multi-coloured lights lined the doorway, and as we stepped through it, we discovered a room covered with vintage movie posters and headshots of movie stars, like we were in the foyer of some olde worlde cinema.

It seemed such a comforting environment, certainly compared to the last place we were in. We trod on a burgundy carpet with art deco patterns decorating it, and the air was redolent with the cosy smell of popcorn. In fact, there was a counter across the room that was made out of a vat filled with the stuff.

Music permeated the air as the four of us stood there taking it all in. It was the unmistakable tune of *Für Elise*, and for a moment I could believe it was being played live by the Invisible Man, for on the other side of the room there was a grand Wurlitzer organ and I observed the keys magically depress by themselves. We cautiously approached it. I could only assume it was somehow rigged up to something to make it play like that, like a band organ being fed a perforated sequence of pleated cardboard into its barrel.

I'd once been to a cinema that still had a Wurlitzer. During the intermission, a trapdoor on the stage would open and the organ would rise from below, an octopus-like organist dancing away on it with his hands and feet as he played an old music hall tune. I felt magnetised to this instrument, not just because of my musical proclivity. I sensed it was the key to advancing to the next stage of this infernal labyrinth.

'So what do you think this room is about?' Rachel asked. 'What's the challenge here?'

'They're playing the *50 Shades of Grey* trilogy,' Mantella suggested. 'And they want us to sit through it all.'

'Sweet.'

'Here, look!' I told them as I pointed to a book on the Wurlitzer's music stand. It didn't have the sheet music to *Für Elise* on it, however. These were instructions.

Kerrish peered down to read it. 'Welcome to the Hall of Harmony. Here you must play the tune note for note, and a successful performance will unlock the right door. Break the melody and you will open the wrong door...'

Flanking the organ, there were indeed two doors. We knew we wouldn't be able to open them by our own physical efforts and so none of us even bothered to try.

Unsurprisingly, I think we were all getting tired at this point.

'So...' Rachel muttered. 'No vomit this time. No dicks. We just sit and play a keyboard? This place is losing its touch.'

'Yeah, but you see when we open the wrong door,' Mantella continued to drone on. 'The Incredible Hulk will come out of there and piss in your face.'

Rachel shrugged. 'You know what? I'm game for that shit.'

'Okay,' Kerrish cut in to silence the banter. 'Anyone here got any musical talent?'

'Yeah!' Rachel replied. 'Melody has. She's a musical genius in the making. Only pissing here will be her pissing all over this challenge.'

'Melody? Is that right? You can play the keyboard?'

'Yeah. I can play *Für Elise*.' There was no delusional wishful thinking to it. It was one of the first things I'd learnt. It was one of the first things that every piano player learns. I could play it in my sleep. In fact, I'd most probably even done that.

'You were born for this moment, darling,' Rachel chirped, cheerleading me on.

'So is Melody your real name or your stage name?' Kerrish asked.

I opened my mouth to answer, but then closed it again. Why give him a reply? The bastard wanted to kill me in a couple of hours, less than that actually, as another check of my watch confirmed. Or maybe I should tell him as much of myself as I could. Humanise myself. Make him see me as a young woman with hopes and dreams, perhaps make him realise that somewhere deep down inside I was a person with a soul, even though I'd seemed to have lost sight of that of late.

'It's my real name,' I admitted.

'I just hope you're as good as your BFF says you are.'

'We'll see, won't we?' I snapped at him as I peered down at the Wurlitzer. There were several rows of keys and various switches all around them. All I was used to was a simple keyboard with one pedal. The pedals on this thing looked like a keyboard in themselves. Surely they weren't expecting me to turn into some virtuoso.

'Are you ready?' Kerrish asked. He pointed at a big red button above the organ with the word 'Start' printed on it.

I psyched myself up for a moment, then quickly realised I should sit at the instrument properly rather than standing over it. That meant Kerrish sitting next to me too and giving me slack on my arm so I could recite the tune.

'I need to sit.'

He complied as I settled into the seat.

'Want me to punch it?'

I breathed in deeply. 'Go for it.'

He hit the button.

'Good luck, Mel,' I heard Rachel say behind me.

I wasn't precisely sure how the game would play out, but it soon became apparent. Right after Kerrish pressed the button, one of the keys on the keyboard, an E, depressed by itself and a note sounded. I knew that I had to repeat the key-press myself, to follow the tune. After that another note sounded, a D sharp, and again I echoed it. This continued for the next few notes, and in my brain I tried separating the pre-echoed tune so I could feel the thread of Beethoven's arrangement.

It was easy. Rachel could have done it. You didn't need any musical competence to do this. You simply had to watch closely to see which key went down and repeat it.

But it soon got harder. Suddenly it played a few notes in succession, and although I was still able to repeat the sequence, I began to fathom how this task could quickly get complicated. It was like that electronic memory game I had as a kid, Simon, just with many more buttons and many more combinations. But I would be okay, surely. I knew how to play *Für Elise* without the guide of the organ playing it for me. I didn't have to remember the notes being played because I'd performed that damned tune so many times before in my piano practice that I'd practically embedded it into my own DNA. But what if I lost track of the sequence and 'did a Mozart' by playing too many notes?

The doubt creeping into my brain was destroying my razor sharp concentration. *Don't think you'll go wrong because then you will go wrong!* That's what my piano teacher always used to say to me. Conceiving an error in your play was the first step to manifesting it, and my talent had improved so much when I thought positively, when I imagined myself playing nothing but a sublime performance.

But these weren't the ideal conditions to produce a perfect musical performance. I was tired. It felt like my body had been through a war, what with everything I had been through on this one night. And this was on top of a hangover from the night before when I'd been going through even more exertions and partying.

'You're doing really well, Mel,' Rachel whispered as she put a hand on my shoulder. I'd paused to take a moment, the Wurlitzer eagerly waiting for my response to its guide track.

'How much longer is this going to go on?' I sighed. Crap. Where the hell was I? My hand hovered over the keys as I tried to find the rhythm of the tune again. Nervously I jabbed my forefinger down on one of them, and then followed this with a quick flurry of further notes.

Neither of the doors had opened. At least I hadn't gone wrong, not yet. *Stop thinking you're going to go wrong, Melody Freeman!* It would be typical of me though. A lifetime of preparation to get me through this challenge, the ideal candidate for the task, yet with the stars having aligned to give me this platform for glory it would just be me to go ahead and mess it right up.

'Melody?' Kerrish prompted me. 'Why do you keep stopping?'

'I'm sorry.' I shook my head, trying to shake the doubt out of my brain. 'I lost track.'

'That one.' He pointed to a white key. He'd been watching it all too, keeping up with the sequence of notes rather than sitting back and enjoying my Wurlitzer show.

'Um... that one?' I asked as I pointed at it.

'Yes! Just press it.'

'Weren't we up to the bit where it goes dah da dah

da dah,' I said, attempting to vocalise the tune.

'Press the key, Melody!'

'It's not that one.'

'It is!'

'Just let me do this, Kerrish! I didn't know you were Elton fucking John!'

He shook his head at me. Pissed off, I jabbed at a key, a different one from the one he'd told me to press.

It turned out I'd hit the wrong note.

Suddenly the Wurlitzer sounded a deafening chord, much more apocalyptic and oppressive than the final chord in The Beatles' *A Day in the Life*. It was like the full power of Bach's Fugue in D Minor all in one, and I felt my stomach sink as though I was hearing the opening strand of a march for my own funeral.

I didn't wish for the ground to open up and swallow me away in my abject failure. Yet, bizarrely, that was exactly what happened. Much like the end of the cinema organist's performance when he disappears back into the stage trapdoor, our stool angled down into the abyss and Kerrish and I tumbled helplessly into the unknown.

'Melody!' Rachel called from up in the Hall of Harmony. Her screaming face got smaller and smaller as we slid deeper into this chute like we were garbage, and as we continued to tumble, I saw the trapdoor close up again and Rachel and Mantella were both gone. It was just me and Kerrish, surely falling into a realm of fire and brimstone that was certainly befitting of the failed lost soul that I was.

Chapter 20

We landed in a pool of gunk. I had no idea what the knee-height slop was and to be honest, I really didn't want to know. It was almost devoid of light where we were, so it was difficult at first to see what we were swimming in. It smelt foul, like rotten vegetables. As I brought myself upright and examined my slathered fingers, I had the impression we were in a food waste repository. Thrown away as though we were pigswill.

'Great,' Kerrish muttered. 'That's just fucking great! Why didn't you listen to me?'

'I'm sorry,' was all I could say.

I realised that I'd completely failed. All my hope of surviving my hellish predicament was lost. I'd flunked the challenges of *Satan's Cellar* and this is where I would complete my transmutation into a vampire, in a little over one hundred minutes now, the duration of two halves of a football match. No time for extra time or penalties (and that was definitely assuming there was no VAR either). Just certain victory for Kerrish at the end of it all when he would kill me. I sobbed. All he did was yank the cuffs.

'Come on, we need to find a way out of this,' he barked at me.

'Forget it,' I said. 'It's over, Kerrish. I'm not going to make it.'

He stood there silently for a moment, realising I was a defeated person. 'Well, I don't have a death sentence. I don't want to spend the rest of my life in this dump. I've got much longer to live!'

'Why are you such a heartless bastard?' I roared at him, my words reverberating off the walls. It didn't matter what I said anymore. He could kill me that very minute for all I now cared. I had no more mind games or ploys to work with him. Might as well go out in a bitchfest blaze. Give him a proper gob-full, fuelled by all my resentment towards him.

'No wonder you're single. She must have found out what a total selfish cunt you are!'

I sat in the detritus of that dump waiting for a spiky retort from him, expecting him to pull me to pieces, but he said nothing, just slumped down too.

'Or did her leaving you turn you into some woman-hater and you take it out on people like me?'

'I don't hate women.'

'Could have fooled me.'

'Vampires. I hate vampires, Melody. That's all. It's not my fault you're soon about to be one of those things, a blood-sucking monster. So stop playing the sexist card.' He turned his head away and muttered, 'Why do women always do that?'

What a dick.

'So why are you so self-righteously anti-vampire?' I goaded him. 'Why is it so personal for you?'

'Because it *is* personal,' he barked back in my face.

'Go on then. Why?' I didn't care if I was prying and I was asking questions I shouldn't be asking. Being remembered by this guy as an inquisitive bitch was the least of my troubles right now.

'None of your business.'

'Well, what does it matter? You're going to kill me soon. What will it matter then?'

'Exactly. Why waste my time opening up to you when you'll be a pile of mush by dawn?'

I shook my head and muttered, 'Bastard.' I don't know why I said it so quietly.

He stood up again, peering into the rafters as he inspected our dingy chamber, presumably working out how we might escape, but I had no motivation to help. The cockbag would have to carry me if he wanted to manoeuvre around. He twitched his hand trying to get me to budge, but he soon fathomed the extent of my stubbornness. With a sharp huff, he collapsed into the pool of slush.

'I was married, Melody. About to start a family. We'd known each other since we were at primary school. Childhood sweethearts.' He looked away from me as he spoke. His voice had taken on a soft tone.

'What happened to her?' I asked. I already knew the answer would revolve around vampires somehow, but the devil was always in the details. '*They* killed her?'

'She was studying them. Not like Mantella studies them, I don't mean. She was a writer. Wrote vampire novels. Like any good writer she wanted to really understand her subject, and unfortunately she got a little too close to them.'

'Well, for what it's worth, Kerrish, I'm sorry you lost her.'

'Thanks,' he muttered, his face still angled away from me.

'Did you ever find the vampire that got her?'

'No.'

'So you just want to kill each and every one? Get your revenge on them all.'

'Right on.'

'Do you think that's what she would have wanted though? She'd want you to be all *Kill Bill*, always an angry butcher like this?'

'Of course not.'

'I bet you were a much different person before she died. I daresay, Kerrish, you were possibly something resembling likeable.'

He turned and smiled wryly at me. 'Yeah? Maybe you'll have to ask her.'

Before I could ask what the hell he meant by that last comment, he stiffened up again. 'Not that you'll have the chance.'

'Wait... What do you...?'

'She's not quite dead, is she, Melody?' he lectured. 'She's still walking around, still essentially looks like the same beautiful woman I once married. Except inside her, her heart is no longer beating like a normal human being.'

'She's a vampire.'

'And my child, still locked within her for eternity. A dead foetus? An undead foetus? A little vampire baby feeding off its vampire mother? Who the hell knows?' He shouted all this out, as though he was at war with the monstrous thoughts inside his head. It was an eruption of the rage that fuelled him, that fuelled his purpose.

'I'm sorry,' I said, trying to soothe him. But he'd

146

already worked himself up, jutting his limbs around like a boxer waiting for the fight, kicking some of the debris away before even more debris swarmed to his knees.

'And who the hell knows how to get out of this fucking dump?' he roared.

I had another question on my mind, but I didn't dare voice it right at this moment. His seething anger threatened to overflow, and I feared he would wrap the handcuffs around my throat and choke me so I would ask no more difficult questions ever again.

Instead, I found myself standing up, and put a hand on his arm, soothing the rage. He responded to my touch, hanging his head as he attempted to harness the emotions. For a moment I could have forgotten I was his enemy, that I was his captive awaiting execution. I could imagine he was the dashing hero trying to free the world of this plague that had infected me. In another dimension perhaps we'd crossed paths some other way, and I was his faithful sidekick. A tiny looping of metal on our wrists was the only detail that undermined that narrative. I gazed down at our conjoined wrists and in the gloom I found another detail, another hoop of metal, around one of his fingers, indicating the other lost soul that he'd formed a union with.

'What's her name?' I asked, trying to calm him. Perhaps I should have phrased that question in the past tense.

'I think I've told you enough about her.'

'Okay.' I wasn't going to push it with him. I didn't want to prod that rage out of him again. Didn't want to shorten my life even more. 'Do you still have my phone?' I asked him, putting our minds onto something else.

'You're not having it.'

'How about using it to call for help, yeah?'

'Thanks, yeah, I can't do that with my own phone, of course.'

'Well, whatever! Maybe do something useful or just stand here being a clever dick?'

'You're right,' he said. He proceeded to get his phone out and put it straight to his ear. 'Oh hi Mom, can you come and help me? I'm in some nightclub and I'm trapped in a garbage dump with some crazy bitch.'

What the hell had gotten into him? I tried wrestling the phone from him, but it soon turned into a scuffling slanging match as we traded increasingly crude insults at each other. In the end, I resorted to leaning my entire weight into him to topple us both into the slop. Served the idiot right.

Over the sloshing, we heard something, a metallic screeching sound like a door being opened. Light crept into the chamber and we both gazed up to see a head peering at us from a hatch in the wall.

'Oh, my goodness. It smells awful in here,' the stranger said.

'David?' Kerrish called out. 'Is that you?'

The head shifted to the edge of the opening and the creeping light illuminated his face as I saw that it was indeed David Sherborne. Thank Christ.

'I heard voices. You know, you two sound rather loud when you're angry. Anyway, do you need a hand?' He sounded so casual as he asked us this.

We both shot up and waded over. The hatch was a few feet above our heads and already my mind was sizing up how we would get up to it.

'I don't suppose you have a rope up there, David?' Kerrish called out.

'Even if he did,' I quickly countered, 'how are we both going to climb it at once with these handcuffs on? Think it's time you took them off?'

'I told you, I don't have the key.'

'Well, break them off then.'

'With what?' he spat back. 'Think I brought some bolt cutters with me?'

'Hey, I have an idea,' David cut in. 'Why don't you lift Melody upside down? I'll grab her legs and pull her up.'

'Great idea,' Kerrish replied.

Yeah, great. Nice view of my arse you're going to have there, David, especially when my dress starts to ride, I thought. When I compared it to everything else I'd been through tonight, I doubted that would be the overriding headline of the night, however.

148

'All right. Let's do this,' I said. I took a moment, standing there facing Kerrish, both of us wondering how we would pull off this manoeuvre exactly. I grabbed his hands.

'Okay, hold my weight.' I leant into him and pivoted my body so my legs could clumsily hoof against the wall. As though I was now a circus performer, I positioned myself so I was upside down, Kerrish supporting me as I slid my straightened legs up the wall towards David.

I couldn't see how far they were sliding, but I soon felt David grab me and lift me out of this rotten chamber. Half dangling out of the hatch, I looked down on Kerrish as his tethered hand reached up towards me. For a moment there seemed to be a shade of vulnerability in his face, a fear that our handcuffs might unexpectedly snap, and I would break free and slam that hatch shut and leave him to rot within that stinking slop. How could I even afford a modicum of sorrow for him?

'Hold her,' he advised David. I felt the investigator grab my shoulder with one hand while he reached forward with his other. Kerrish pulled himself up against my weight, the handcuffs digging painfully into my skin, but he quickly grabbed David's hand and with that we both hauled him up to our sanctuary.

Chapter 21

'What happened to you, David?' Kerrish asked. 'We were worried they would lock you up in their dungeon and torture you.'

I examined the room he'd lifted us into. It looked to be a storage area, or rather a place to dump stuff. There were racks and racks of dusty stage lights, large bottles of what was probably dry ice. Right next to me was a table full of junk. Lying on top of it all was a tatty black balaclava, a full face one like the type bank robbers wear. I presumed it must have belonged to one of the many wild performers who'd graced the *Satan's Cellar* stage.

'Ah, well they locked me up for a little while, but I soon escaped. Did you get my text?'

'Yes, you told us to go to the toilet cubicle. That's how we ultimately ended up here. We were going through the levels, playing the games when Melody fucked up and we fell into that dump you just dragged us out of.'

'I sent you some more after that one.'

'You did?' Kerrish looked sheepish for a moment and avoided my eyes.

'See? Told you to look at my phone!' I slapped him on the arm. I wasn't really the type to do that sort of thing, but I was so pissed off with him. He was such a bigheaded prick who would rather haughtily arse around than listen to me.

Kerrish got my phone out and quietly checked the messages. A few seconds later his eyes lit up, his head slowly rising.

'So he's here?'
David nodded.
'Wait. Who?' I asked.
'Can you take us to him?'
'Who, for fuck's sake?' I demanded.
'Your fangy friend! Wiseau!'
'He came and probed me with questions while they had me imprisoned,' David informed us. 'Don't worry. He has no idea I was trying to lead a band of vampire hunters

to him.'

He was here. My maker. I'd fallen so flat inside, resigned to my fate, but this revelation sparked the hope again. Would we really be able to do this? Had the little episode in the garbage chamber just been the low moment in the journey when all hope seemed lost, but then some serendipitous development occurred against all odds and the hero went on from there to succeed? Or was this just another false dawn, another cruel trick before we were about to be ambushed by a pack of vampires who made us their breakfast?

'So where is he?' Kerrish asked.

'When I got out of my hold, I stalked the place out,' David told us. 'I roamed around all the back corridors, discovered some rather strange corners.'

'Wait...' I stopped him, an uncomfortable thought in my head. 'You didn't happen to come by the Grotto of Glory by any chance?' Kerrish arrogantly put his hand over my mouth to hush me, but David was already pondering the question.

'I don't think so. Anyway, I found some area that appears to be their private quarters. I'm thinking that's where he might be.'

'Private quarters?' I asked.

'The place was full of coffins.'

Kerrish shook his head. 'It's still nighttime. They wouldn't have turned in yet.'

'Why don't we check it out, anyway?'

He looked at me as though I were a silly schoolgirl who'd just made some daft suggestion.

'We can't just run into a room that's potentially swarming with vampires, not without a plan.'

'Do you have a stake on you?' David asked.

Kerrish immediately produced a sharpened spike of wood from his jacket, something he'd kept secret until now. Not that it surprised me. Surely it was a standard item to have on him at all times, like a Jedi and his lightsaber.

'We could do with Mantella,' he pondered.

David continued to stare at the wooden weapon. 'So you literally just jab that thing into their heart and they fall down and die?'

'Hmm not quite,' I replied. 'I mean, the first bit is right. But after that it can get really messy.'

'Sounds intriguing,' David said. 'Can't wait to get stuck into this.'

'Great choice of phrase,' Kerrish muttered.

'So where are your companions?' David asked.

'We left them up in the Hall of Harmony right before Melody sent us down the garbage chute.'

'The Hall of...' David began to ask.

'It looked like some cinema foyer.'

'Ah yes. That was one of the first few levels. Is that only as far as you'd got?'

'How many more are there?' Kerrish asked before I could get the same words off my tongue.

'You know, I think it's just as well you fell off the rollercoaster. You had lots more rooms to navigate through.'

'What is the point of this place, anyway?' I asked. I wondered why anyone would put themselves through all this horror and humiliation. What was at the end of it all for them? A pot of gold or something?

'Good question, young Melody,' David said. 'When I was holed up, I asked my captor the same thing. It seems that those who make it through the many levels of *Satan's Cellar* earns themselves a free pass to hang out in the Sphere of Sins.'

'Man, they love their alliteration in this place,' I muttered.

'And what's that?' Kerrish asked.

'A series of rooms based on sins. You pick whichever one you want, go in there and indulge to your heart's sinful content. There are seven of them, inspired, of course, by the seven deadly sins.'

'Right,' Kerrish pondered. 'So I get how the Gluttony Room or the Lust Room might work, but... the Envy Room?'

'Well, for you there's a guy in there with a three and a half inch penis,' I told him.

He didn't even hear any of that, instead just staring

into space, lost in his thoughts. I hoped his brain was forming a plan, that he was solving this whole thing and very soon he would lead us to success.

'I think that's where we need to head if we can, to this Sphere of Sins. That must be where Wiseau is.'

It all seemed to make sense. Why else would a pack of vampires want to hang out in this place, if it wasn't to satiate their desires? I imagined the crackpot architect of *Satan's Cellar* would be interested in catering for them, where they could indulge in their carnal sin of lust, or gluttonously feed on the blood of the poor souls who wound up here, as had apparently been the case with me last night. He even had beds for them here.

I was prepared to run into Wiseau again, willing to face these undead adversaries. One person I hoped we would not encounter though was the masterbrain behind this diabolical establishment. I shuddered as I imagined what such a screwball would be like in the flesh, more fucked up than the Wanky Shit Demon in that crazy YouTube animation where that poor clay character was taunted with wonderful promises, only to suffer the torment of dreams made out of wank and shit. It was kind of like how my night had gone so far, really.

The more I pondered on it though, the more it rang true that the establishment's architect was a vampire himself, and perhaps this whole Sphere of Sins area was just some mirage to entice people into a trap, take them down the rabbit hole where they'd become vampire food. Whatever he was, I could have done with giving him a miss till another day. *If* I should ever see another day beyond this one.

I looked at my watch and immediately I felt the adrenaline surging through my blood like I'd just taken some speed. It had just gone a quarter past six.

'Wherever we're going, we need to move,' I said to them, almost ordered them.

'Come on, John McClane,' Kerrish said to David. 'Show us the right air vent or whatever we need to scoot down.'

'Okay. Listen to me though; be careful...' the

investigator began. It seemed like he had much more to say, more advice regarding how to navigate through the backrooms of *Satan's Cellar*, but something interrupted him; there was a knock at the door.

'Shit,' Kerrish muttered. 'I think we're in trouble.'

'Stay behind me,' David advised us. He then glanced at the opening from which we'd escaped the garbage dump. 'Maybe get ready to jump back in there.'

He then turned to the door and crossed the room. I braced myself for what he was about to reveal, ready for an onslaught of vampires bursting inside and dragging us all away. I had nothing to defend myself. Would they recognise that I was different from regular uninfected humans? Might they sense that I was a vampire in the making, and would leave me be? Maybe this was about to be my *rescue*.

David grabbed the handle and swiftly pulled the door open. There stood a figure with a shocking growth of hair splaying out from his head like a lion's mane. Wiseau. He grinned at us all as though he'd found a trio of mice, and with his large fangs, he was the predator that was about to devour us.

'Not alone then after all, Sherborne.' He stepped towards us. 'And what do we have here? None other than my archenemy Paul Kerrish.' As he spoke, further vampires filed into the room, two more of the things.

Surely this was the moment when Kerrish would demonstrate his heroism. Surely he'd be spinning around the air like Neo from *The Matrix* and stabbing each of those vampires in the heart as blood sprayed out from all of them before they rained down on the floor in a splatter of dead vampire mush. Instead, he just stood there, holding the stake in his hand like he was holding a plastic toy.

That was it. The game was over. But somewhere in that moment, I felt it, that selfish thought that the game wasn't over for all over us. Just for Kerrish, and, most probably, David as well. I was one of these creatures. They weren't about to kill me. These were my saviours. This was all a case of mistaken perception, this whole evening.

This Wiseau vampire was really the antihero. He was the character with a tortuous tale to tell, who would always endure whatever scrapes and predicaments he found himself in. He was one of the Salvatore brothers, or Bill Compton, or even that soppy Edward Cullen, a bloodsucking monster who'd killed many people or at the very least fed off them, and yet he was the one we all rooted for. And Kerrish was just another bland character that no one cared about, who no one would miss if he were to be sauced right now.

This was just the start of the flipping of my perspective, something that would undoubtedly be completed when I reached 7.43. This was the moment where I stepped over to the dark side, where I abandoned my humanity as they exterminated my fellow humans, and Wiseau would take me away to begin my new life, my undead life.

As the antihero vampire stood there, I observed how handsome he was with his square jaw and his thick eyebrows above his dark eyes. His skin had a slight plastic-like quality to it, free of blemish, free of wrinkles and worry lines and crows' feet. This was the life for me now, an undead eternity where together we could indulge in a hedonistic pursuit of pleasure and flesh and blood, and we would both be forever beautiful.

As he smiled softly, I had a thought quietly entering my brain, something that normally I would have pushed away or denied, but given all the circumstances of this crazy night, on this occasion I had no will to resist it: this beautiful creature before me was someone I could easily fall in love with.

Wiseau suddenly howled, a piercing shriek that for one moment I presumed was some sort of victory call. His mouth opened so wide, his head angling up towards the ceiling as he held his hands in front of them, rubbing them together in delight. They were gripping something, something that oozed blood. His entire body trembled as a froth formed at his lips.

Behind him, I saw David brace himself. The other vampires looked on at their master in horror as he began spewing the bloody froth into the air as it showered down on us. Wiseau fell to his knees and his arms dangled limply

155

from his body. That was when I saw it, the stake protruding from his chest. David had rammed it in hard through his back, penetrating Wiseau's heart, and now the vampire who'd probably lived centuries and centuries of adventure and inequity, a long narrative that we would never now know about, turned a grey colour as his undead life came to its conclusion. Millions of teenage fans would have been weeping at his demise, but all I felt was a weirdly numb kind of euphoria.

David kicked over the kneeling corpse and Wiseau fell to the ground as his body slowly continued to turn to mush, like a retired waxwork model of a faded star being melted down so it could be turned into the latest popstar sensation.

I stood there passively as Kerrish now rammed his stake into one of the vampire henchmen. David removed the stake from Wiseau's melting heart and swiftly stabbed it into the last of the vampires and again the room was filled with a cacophony of howling as the two other monsters went through their death throes. With that, the howling then turned to gurgling. It was apparent these two were much younger specimens, the way they went. It was more like how Veronica had gone, a spraying of yucky mush splattering us all as the gurgling dwindled into a soft popping sound like bubbles in a bubble bath, before that died down to a soothing silence.

'I forgot to mention,' David panted. 'After I broke free, I also made myself a wooden stake.'

I was too numb to say anything, and so, it seemed, was Kerrish. He stepped over towards Wiseau's melting corpse and slowly crouched down, staring down at the increasingly shapeless mess as though his brain was trying to process what had just happened, that one of his biggest enemies had suddenly been destroyed.

I squatted down there with him. I was still too numb to work out what I was feeling. Had I felt a sudden change within me? Would I notice anything were my maker to be killed before I completed my transformation? What effect had the death of Wiseau suddenly made to the virus that had infiltrated my body last night?

'That's it then,' I said. 'I'm free. It's over.' Kerrish didn't move. David put his hand on my shoulder.

'I'm so happy for you, young Melody. Thank goodness we were able to rescue you from this nightmare.'

I looked up at the kindly investigator, tears forming in my eyes.

'Thank you, David.' I turned back to Kerrish. 'And well over an hour to spare. Never in any doubt eh?' I attempted to quip with him, light-hearted banter that was surely earned after going through such a tense ordeal.

Kerrish suddenly stood up. 'We need to find Mantella.' I guessed he wasn't quite in tune with the emotion I was currently experiencing, wasn't bothered about taking a moment to revel in our glory. I supposed we were still in danger, still lost within this horrible place, more potential dangers and misfortune in wait for us before we got the hell out of there.

Yes, it made sense to find Rachel and Mantella first, make sure they were both safe, and then we could work our way out of this nightmare once and for all and return to our lives. I felt such a weight off my shoulders, such an oppressive mass of angst dispersing from my brain, and the cleansing of all this now brought a deluge of tears.

David cleared his throat. 'So, I know this is probably not at the forefront of your minds at this precise moment, but it's something that's been really worrying me... I don't suppose you know if anyone thought to grab my car keys?'

Chapter 22

'Why isn't he picking up?' Kerrish whined. 'The phone is ringing. What are they up to?'

We remained in the storage room, figuring it made more sense if we got the message to Mantella and Rachel to play the game back up in the Hall of Harmony, deliberately mess it up (which Rachel would most probably do on the very first note), and then they'd fall through the trapdoor into the garbage chamber.

'Since they got themselves a bit of alone time, she might be keeping good on her promise to Mantella,' I suggested.

'Wait, it's connected. Manny? Hello?' Kerrish called into his phone. I watched on anxiously, hoping our friends would be on the other end of the line. After a moment his body eased up. 'Yes, it's me. We're okay, bud...'

David and I shared a knowing glance as we sensed that things were okay. Kerrish then explained the plan to Mantella.

'It's fine, Manny. We just fell into this chute, you know, like at the swimming pool? And then we dropped into this...'

'Into a big room filled with marshmallows,' I quickly interrupted him. Kerrish looked up at me blankly for a moment and I half-expected him to bite my head off.

'Did you get that? Yeah, you land in these marshmallows,' he muttered, not even believing himself that he was selling this. 'It's great. Just like you got Willy Wonka's golden ticket... Okay... We'll see you down there.' He hung up, then turned to us. 'They're on their way. I think.'

The three of us stood there quietly for a moment, but it wasn't long at all before we heard Rachel scream. We darted over to the hatch and peered down.

'What the fuck is all this shit?' she yelled. 'Oh God. These aren't fucking marshmallows! You bastards!'

I smiled, not at some perverse delight in seeing her gunked up, but because I was so happy to see her again.

'Over here, babe!' I called to her, waving excitedly.

For a good few moments she stood there in disbelief, her hands aloft, unwilling to deal with this mess, not wanting any more of her situation of having landed in a pile of yuck, but eventually we got her to wade through that filth and head towards us. We pulled Mantella up into the storage room first, and after plenty of coaxing, Rachel was in reaching distance too and we lifted her from the slop.

'I am *never* going to forgive you, Melody Freeman!' Despite her protestations, I threw my arms around her. 'Don't come near me. I smell like a tramp's arsehole.'

'That makes two of us,' I reassured her. 'We did it, Rach. We found Wiseau.'

'Oh my God, what?' she said, suddenly breaking out of her melodrama.

'He's dead, Rach. We killed him.'

She looked beyond me and got with the picture, realising that the room was decorated with the remains of three slain vampires.

'Man, I missed it?' She held her stake in her hand limply, as though it was now just an old bit of wood she'd picked up on a woodland walk rather than a magical weapon that was her ticket to glory. 'At least I can get my phone back now.'

Mantella was already crouching down at Wiseau's remains, examining it with fascination. I noticed him even producing some sort of petri dish and scraping some of the goo into it. *Whatever turns you on, pal.*

With his specimen collected he approached me, switching on his little torch and shining it into my eyes. I had no idea what he was specifically looking for, but I assumed he was trying to detect if there was any noticeable change in me now that we'd destroyed my maker vampire. I blinked, dazzled by the light.

'We need to get her back to *The Claw*,' he stated.

'Yes,' I replied, facing Kerrish as I raised my tethered hand, puppeteering him in the process. 'Unlock this thing at last.'

'We need to run the test again,' Mantella added.

'Right,' I muttered. 'Do what you've got to do, Mr

Big Bang Theory. Can we just get out of here now?'

We all subconsciously turned to Kerrish for instructions, but he seemed somewhat subdued, perched on a table and staring into space. I suspected it was all catching up with him. I again yanked the cuffs and his hand wafted around in the air, but his brain didn't register it at all.

'Kerrish?' I prompted him. 'Time to go home?'

He slowly raised his head to me and I could see in his eyes that his mind had been elsewhere, in another universe. Suddenly they flickered into focus, though. He stood upright and turned to David.

'Can you lead us out of here, Sherborne?'

The investigator nodded.

'Stakes at the ready, everyone,' Kerrish instructed us, the captain back on deck. I felt somewhat reassured by that. 'Let's get the hell out of here.'

'Before we set off,' David began, 'I still need my car keys.'

'Right here, Sherborne,' Mantella replied as he instantly threw a set of keys towards him.

David caught them, and he smiled. 'Follow me.'

We nervously stepped out of the storage room. Rachel gripped her stake tightly and held it in front of her like she was holding a microphone, ready to stab it down on anything sinister that was to pop out of the shadows. At first we entered a darkened corridor. David, leading the way, looked up and down, before pointing the direction for us to tread. We all trailed after him silently, my breathing shallow, my blood thumping through my head.

Surely this place had security cameras. Surely we were being observed this very moment by more vampires who were waiting to ambush us. That must have been how Wiseau had found us in the storage room, by tracking David there. They'd been watching his every move, much like we'd been watching the visuals of Rachel's covert camera when she'd first stepped into *Satan's Cellar*. The tables had turned and now we were under surveillance and about to fall into their trap.

We steadily made our way down the corridor and

then David pointed to the right to indicate our next steps. I held my breath as we turned the corner, expecting to discover a scene of blood and horror that lay in wait for us, a grinning vampire about to lunge his fangs into us. However, to my relief, it was empty. We carried on down there.

I felt like running. I just wanted to get out of there as soon as I could. That panicked sensation of claustrophobia hummed in my bones, as though this entire building seemed to have wrapped itself around me and I was trapped within it, unable to escape. David had talked of the coffins he'd found in one of the rooms. For me right now the whole place was one big coffin and all of my fingers were curled round as though I was trying to scrape my way out of it.

Strangely, it turned out that Kerrish was thinking of those coffins too.

'Are we anywhere near the vampires' sleeping quarters, David?' he whispered.

The investigator paused, and we clustered behind him.

'It's back the other way.'

'Come on, Kerrish,' Mantella added. 'Let's go now. We can come back another time.'

Kerrish didn't reply, just staring over his shoulder towards the way we'd come as though mentally reaching out to that room of coffins for some reason that I knew he wouldn't divulge.

Mantella put a hand on his shoulder. 'Another time. Let's get back to base.'

Wasn't he satisfied with what we'd accomplished already tonight? We'd exterminated three vampires, and one of them was one of the top guys. Surely right now wasn't the time to get greedy and go pick off more of the suckers by staking them in their sleep. He'd said they wouldn't have gone to bed – gone to coffin – yet, anyway. Or maybe there was some logic in it, some sort of insurance. There was always the off chance a different vampire had infected me here last night. Maybe by killing as many of them as possible we'd make it even more certain, strengthen our odds even further that we'd got the right one. However, that plan could very easily backfire.

I tugged at the handcuffs, breaking him out of his thoughts. With that, he turned back around and we all set off again towards our escape. We still needed to get back to their headquarters so that Mantella could run his vampire test once more, give them the undeniable proof and validate the myth, that they could stop the metamorphosis process. I would not contemplate any other outcome to this experiment. I felt that I deserved this now, after everything we'd been through.

And besides, I was essentially out of time now. As we continued to work our way out of the labyrinth, through endless corridors and access ways and staircases, I kept looking at my watch, waiting for the precise moment we got to 6.43. One hour to go till sunrise, till I would become a vampire. Except that we'd stopped that now, of course, hadn't we? What was there time to do in this remaining hour? One way or the other, this operation was over. I just wished I was no longer in this horrible establishment.

We all came to a stop again as David paused. It looked like we roamed the corridor of some eerie hotel, doorways dotted along the walls hiding a multitude of rooms I did not have the stomach to comprehend. Ahead of us I could imagine the butchered remains of twin girls decorating the angular-patterned carpet, but this was not *The Overlook Hotel* we had somehow slipped into.

'How much farther is it, David?' I couldn't help but ask, like the impatient kid in the back of the car. He didn't answer me though, just stood there staring at something.

'What is it?' Kerrish asked him.

It was dark in that corridor, but I could see the look of apprehension on David's face, the grimace that his mouth was etched in, the fear in his eyes. What had he seen? Or maybe he'd heard something going on beyond one of those doors.

'I hadn't noticed that when I came this way earlier,' he muttered.

'Noticed what?' Kerrish asked.

David stepped towards one of the rooms. There was

no number on it, no do-not-disturb sign, merely a plain wooden door painted white. On it was some graffiti, a symbol. It looked like a giant A within a circle, rather like the Anarchy symbol. It had been slapped on there in a deep red colour. For all I knew it was blood.

I wouldn't have been surprised if some anarchist dwelled beyond that door. This whole place was an establishment built on utter anarchy, so it was just like finding a joker in a pack of jokers. But it was obvious this symbol meant something to the old investigator.

'I'm sorry. I have to take a look in there,' he announced.

'Why?' Rachel asked, cocking her head.

'Come on, David,' Kerrish said, the voice of reason. 'Let's not get distracted. We still need to get out of here.'

'I won't be long.' He stepped forward and turned the handle. The door opened a fraction. 'Wait here.'

He slid through the gap into the grim room. A light went on but before I got a glimpse of what was inside, the door closed again, seemingly by itself. Kerrish immediately stepped up to it, sensing trouble. He tried the handle, but now it would not open.

'What the hell?' he muttered. 'Why would he do this?' He banged his fist a couple of times and called David's name as loud as he dared shout.

We could only imagine what he'd discovered in there. Perhaps this was like the dangerously haunted Room 237 in *The Shining*, and the guy was about to make an interesting discovery as he saw a beautiful naked woman emerge from a bathtub. If David was familiar with the twisted trap that poor Jack Torrance had fallen into as he'd proceeded to seduce the hottie that then turned into a hideous old hag, perhaps he was now weighing up whether an initial few seconds of smooching a sexy lady was worth it for what horror the moment would descend into.

Whatever he'd discovered in there, I did not have a good feeling about it at all. I sensed much more than anarchy beyond that door. Inside that room was complete hopelessness, the collapse and degeneration of humanity, a black hole of pure evil. Why the hell would he walk straight into that?

'Mantella, help me break this door down,' Kerrish said.

'Crap, let's just leave him there. Let's find our own way out. We don't know what's in there.' Poor Mantella sounded perturbed too, trepidation dripping from his words. I knew it was selfish of me, but I kind of agreed with him. I was petrified and had a stomach-churning instinct that if any of us went into that room we would not be coming out again.

All four of us jumped at the sound of the deafening thud. It sounded like David's body had been spat against the other side of the door.

'Holy shit!' Rachel cried.

Kerrish tried the handle again, and this time it opened. The light had gone off and so I could see nothing through the crack. Slowly he pushed the door open but even with my keen eyesight, no suggestion of any shape started to emerge from the blackness.

'Don't go in there, Kerrish,' I said. It was out of concern that I'd spoken those words, forgetting for one moment that I was still tethered to him, and that Kerrish entering this unnatural chamber inevitably meant that I would be dragged in there too. I just feared that if he were to step inside that blackness we would never see him again.

'David?' he instead called into the room. 'David, are you there?'

There was no answer, a void of sound like he was vainly calling into the vacuum of space, and perhaps our friend was now as lost as a spaceman who'd been blasted into the nether corners of the universe.

'What the crap happened to him?' Rachel cried.

Suddenly a form appeared in the doorway, someone gasping for breath like his lungs had been crushed. He collapsed onto his face in the corridor and instantly I recognised the beige Macintosh. David.

Kerrish and I crouched down to him as the poor man writhed on the ground.

'Are you okay, mate?' he asked as he placed his free hand on the investigator's shoulder.

The poor chap continued to draw in some deep gulps, attempting to harness his breath. He muttered something, but none of us could make out what he was saying. We all looked to each other in confusion.

Eventually the investigator sat up and pointed towards the room. 'Close the door,' he wheezed.

Instantly Mantella was on it, planting the sole of his boot on it and kicking it shut. Of all the devilish places we'd experienced in this funhouse tonight, this was the one room that I absolutely would not go anywhere near again. It was like we'd discovered the very beating heart of *Satan's Cellar* and witnessed the hub of malevolence that fuelled the whole thing.

'What the hell did you discover in there, David?' Kerrish asked.

'I'm sorry... I couldn't help myself...' He paused as he drew in more breaths. It seemed like he was gathering his composure once more, thankfully. 'It's an old nightmare of mine... a ghost from the past. Sorry. Curiosity got the better of me.' Wearily he rose to his feet. The way his back hunched over, he looked like he'd come out of that room ten years older.

'Old habits die hard, huh?' Kerrish said.

'I should bring my friend down here and see what he makes of it,' David replied, his eyes gazing into space.

'Please,' Kerrish prompted him. 'We must carry on.'

'Ah yes. Yes, it's not far at all now, actually.'

I was so pleased to hear him say those words. I really needed out of there. If I would spend another minute in there, I feared its spirit of anarchy would send me insane.

He neatened up his splaying hair again, then staggered on down the corridor, away from that creepy room. At the end of the hall he made a left. In front of us was another spiral staircase and I just hoped that it would not be as long and winding as the previous one we'd gone down.

We twisted round on ourselves only a few times, however, and before any time at all we reached the bottom and emerged into a small access room.

'After you,' David said as he pressed his hand down

on the release bar of a fire escape. The door swung open and I saw the wonderful sight of a grimy Meridian side street before us. I felt the smoggy city air brush over my face as I breathed in our freedom. I darted outside, dragging Kerrish along with me. At last my body began to relax, my shoulders easing, the fire of the adrenaline in my bloodstream cooling down once more.

'Aha, and there's my car,' David announced as he pointed up the street. Suddenly the guy seemed so much happier, the haunted spectre melting from his face.

We stepped along the pavement swiftly, each of us leaving our personal horrors behind us.

Chapter 23

We all took our same seats in the car: me between Kerrish and Rachel in the rear, Mantella in the front passenger seat. David again drove at least ten miles over the speed limit as we headed back to *The Hooded Claw*. Fortunately, we encountered no cop cars on the return journey. Perhaps the police were too busy attending to all the lunatics and murderers in this city, and speeding BMWs were the least of their worries.

There was a silence in the car as we rode, and so David turned on the radio. The coda of an ELO song blared out, so he adjusted the volume to a suitable level. Soon the early morning news would be on. A new day starting, not that we were quite done with our night yet. I turned to Kerrish to ask him something, but I noticed he'd nodded off. I thought about rummaging through his coat pocket and trying to find the key for our handcuffs that he'd told me he didn't have on him. Chances were he was lying about that.

As the car zipped through the empty streets, Kerrish's head rocked forward. He swayed for a moment before he came to a rest on my shoulder. I really should have flexed it and jolted him awake so he would get off me, but somehow, against all logic and my own self-respect, I guess I didn't mind him using me as a pillow. Sure the guy had wanted to kill me and treated me as though I was subhuman, which I suppose I was from his point of view, but still I couldn't deny something. If we'd met in some other way, in better circumstances, I would have looked at him in a different way. Rachel was right. He was cute. Especially so when he wasn't being a dick.

'Jeez, get a room, you two,' she said under her breath. 'First you go around everywhere with your kinky sex gear, and now he's all over you.'

I rolled my eyes at her. 'Shut it, girl.'

'Can't wait to get home and take a long, hot shower. I smell so bad I can practically hear it humming off me.'

I nodded softly. We weren't quite there yet, though. I wasn't exactly free, not about to start planning my day or thinking about what I would have for breakfast, as much as I longed for these sorts of easy-going thoughts to be occupying my mind.

'What did you do when we got separated?' I asked her.

'Panicked. Had a meltdown. Cried my heart out. Made out with Mantella, then sucked him dry.'

'I knew it.' We both chuckled.

'Nah, we went looking for you. And we sort of talked a bit.' She looked over towards Mantella, perhaps to detect whether he was listening in on our girl talk. Maybe he was and was only pretending not to hear.

'Kerrish opened up a little too,' I told her. 'Said his wife was turned into a vampire, but she's still out there somewhere.'

'So I heard. The one that got away.'

'What do you mean?'

'Mantella said he and Kerrish have run into her a few times since she turned. Several opportunities he's had now to kill her, but every time he bottled it.'

'It's his wife.'

'And he's a vampire killer! You think he always did this? You think that was his line of work all along? He used to run his own business, some tame new media agency. Nothing to do with slaying creatures of the night. But now it's all a personal vendetta for him. He wants to wipe them all out. But of course, that will never happen. No one will ever stop the spread.'

'Is that what happens when you become a vampire? You abandon your old life and all your friends?'

'Hard to live a normal life when you're a blood-drinking monster, I guess. They form new loyalties, don't they? Feel bonds with their own, especially with the one who made them. And I don't think vampirism exactly fits the lifestyle of being married. Apparently they're always screwing each other. Screw anything that moves.'

'Wow, Rach, it's amazing you've never been mistaken for one.'

'Yeah? Didn't see you complaining.'

Out of the corner of my eye I looked down at

Kerrish, still asleep against my shoulder. So there was a soft side to him after all. Not quite the uncompromising killer he made himself out to be. A man with feelings that he allowed to get in the way of his noble quest of destroying monsters.

If this whole operation was to prove to be one big epic fail, then I had no doubt that, in the brief time I'd known him, Kerrish would not have developed any remote amount of feeling for me, that he would not bottle it again when my transformation came about. I knew he wouldn't hesitate. I would go the same way as the other vampires I'd seen him dispatch with on this long and twisting night.

And, my goodness, how painful it had appeared for those staked creatures when they were dying. It looked like absolute torture, and it seemed to have gone on a really long time. I bet it felt like your whole body was on fire. I felt sick just contemplating it.

I had to derail my train of thought. Why was I still worried about this? I'd killed my maker, undone the infection. I had to believe this. All I needed to do now was to go through the formality of taking the test and getting the all clear. And beyond that? It wasn't like I would say to Kerrish, *'Say, now that all this vampire nonsense has blown over, do you fancy going for a drink tomorrow evening?'* I wasn't trying to make some updated, Meridian-centric equivalent to Craig David's song here. *'He locked me in his cell on Monday. Took him to a glory hole on Tuesday. We were hunting vampires by Wednesday, and Thursday and Friday and Saturday. We killed on Sunday.'* Not that it had taken me a whole seven days to do all that. Did it all in one night.

Fuck it. Why submit to them and go back and do this stupid test? I had a chance to escape. I had to take it.

'Give me one of your hair clips,' I whispered to Rachel.

'What?'

'Just fucking do it!' I muttered as loudly as I could. She shrugged and pulled a metal strand out of her blonde locks. I'd seen people do this in films. You merely had to wiggle a little rod around in the keyhole to a pair of handcuffs and it would magically unlock them. Easy.

'What are you doing?' she asked.

'Making sure.'

'Of what?'

'That I'm going to live to see the start of *Saturday Kitchen*!'

'What are you on about? You're just going to take his stupid test again and then we can go home.'

'But what if we messed up, Rach? What if we didn't get the right one?'

'He was in the photo, the one you killed, yeah? I didn't notice any other vampires in our drunken photoshoot last night.'

'I know, but...'

'Come on, Mel. It's over. We won. Relax, girl.'

I kept waggling the hair clip around frantically, but it wasn't doing anything. Why do we always go along with all those bullshit myths we see in the cinema? I gave up.

Pips sounded on the radio. The seven o'clock news was beginning. The newsreader delivered the headlines about another suspected terrorist operation involving a shooting somewhere on the continent, the usual Trump and Brexit bollocks, and there was talk of blizzard conditions coming which would probably equate to a few spots of sleet. It suddenly hit me how I'd forgotten about the entire outside world. All of this depression-inducing drama had been going on, and the personal dramas of Melody Freeman and her student friend Rachel Dickfloss was a little story that would never be known to the mainstream. Unless I wrote a song about it one day or Rachel made a film about it.

I was listening to the news reports, momentarily escaping from the troubles I'd been living, when the car slowed and the Chapman Hall Business Centre loomed through the side window.

Kerrish suddenly woke with a jolt, instantly sitting bolt upright as he realised he'd left himself vulnerable. He raised his hand to check the handcuffs were still perfectly locked to my arm and then eased up.

'We're here,' David announced. Mantella was finishing gathering up the wires and stuff he'd been setting up in the front. Kerrish rubbed his bloodshot eyes. They may have been vampire hunters, but I doubted they did all-nighters like this on a typical shift.

'Thank you for everything, David,' he said. 'Sorry we dragged you onto the front line tonight, but at least you've got the perfect insight on what we do now.'

'Happy to be of service,' he replied. 'I hope you can involve me more.'

'Let me call you later on today and we'll talk more. We'll see what we can do with that little problem of yours.'

'Absolutely. That would be a big weight off my mind.'

I willed them to get the hell on with their conversation. I had no idea what problem David was going through, and selfishly my mind didn't have any room right now to afford him any concern of my own. Even though David had helped us tonight, too. The guy could be dying for all I knew, or maybe there were other lives at risk, but all I seemed to care about at this moment was my own. What a selfish cow I was.

'I'll talk to my *occasional sidekick* too,' David went on. 'Really think he can bring some valuable skills to the table for you as well. You will be quite amazed.'

'I look forward to meeting him.'

David nodded. 'I'll do my best to get him involved. He often goes off the radar. Bit of a mysterious fellow at times.'

I cleared my throat deliberately. 'It was nice meeting you, David.'

'And you,' he replied.

Rachel patted him on the shoulder. 'Wait till we tell Samantha about all this,' she chirped. She opened the door and stepped out. I nudged Kerrish to get him moving. I didn't want to admit it to myself, but I still had that gnawing sense of urgency.

'See you again,' David called as we got out the car.

Will you, David? Do you promise you'll see me again? I smiled back at him as I closed the door. He waved and then the BMW zoomed off down the street, the growl of the engine gradually fading from our ears.

I was sad to watch him go. It was like the safety net had been taken away. Without him I was purely at the mercy of Kerrish the fearsome vampire hunter and his other Vihn Angels, no influential voice on his shoulder questioning his actions. David was a rookie to this organisation. He wasn't hardened and uncompromising to the vampire threat. He could have offered me more naïve sympathy on the off chance this test wouldn't come out the way I wanted it to. Not that that was about to happen. Surely no one could be *that* unlucky, right?

Chapter 24

We all marched across the square to *The Hooded Claw*, albeit with different motivations. I wanted to prove that I was now clean, Mantella wanted to be the one to make a breakthrough in vampire virology. Donna was lurking around at the front door when we arrived. She seemed to be expecting us, so I figured that Mantella had texted her ahead. There was absolutely no one else still there though, all the lights off at the bar, the tables cleared, the chess pieces put away.

We trailed through the lounge towards the operations room. Mantella made a beeline for his desk and began his preparations. Kerrish reached into his jacket pocket and produced a small key.

'Bastard,' I hissed. 'I knew you had that all along.' He unlocked the cuffs, but before I could free my wrist, he shoved me back into the cell we'd been locked in earlier, and cuffed me to the bars. 'What the hell?' I shouted.

'You're not free yet, Miss Freeman,' he spat at me. 'Let's not start slapping ourselves on the back just yet. You're still vampire scum to me until we can prove otherwise.'

'Well! Someone's a right cranky bastard when they've just woken up.'

'Would have been in bed hours ago if it wasn't for you.'

'Hope you've got your stake ready to kill me then,' I shouted at him, 'coz that's clearly what you want to do.'

He sneered at me before turning away.

'At least give me my phone back,' I pleaded.

He casually took it out of his jacket pocket and looked down on it, wondering if he should hand it back to me or whether he should be a cock and keep on to it. He glanced my way, and that was his mistake. Rachel quickly reached over like a ninja and whipped it out of his hand before he could react.

'Here you go, Mel,' she said as she skipped over to me. Kerrish shrugged his shoulders, then sat down at the table and yawned.

Before I had a chance to have a proper look at my phone (all I took account of was the time on the screensaver) the door opened and in walked Donna.

'Okay, blood sample time again.'

Ah crap. I didn't know why, but I hadn't thought about having to open my veins yet again. If I was going to fail this test, they would have one very thirsty vampire on their hands in thirty-seven minutes' time.

'Don't worry, Mel,' Rachel encouraged me as Donna dug the needle into my arm. She kept talking to take my mind off it. 'We'll very soon be out of here, and we'll never have to see any of these freaks again. And if there's one thing we've learnt, it's that we'll have to make sure we never go into town without our wooden stakes again, eh?'

I fixed my gaze on her until the cup was full. Donna handed it to Kerrish and he held up as though a waitress had handed him a cocktail. It was ironic. These people were vampire hunters and yet they were the only ones who'd been draining me of my blood tonight. He continued to sit there staring at me sternly, his other hand drumming annoyingly on the table in his over-tiredness, unaware of how irritating it was to everyone else in the room.

I could see the hatred in his eyes. I represented the enemy that had taken away his wife. Having the opportunity to kill another vampire would add to his sense of vengeance, but also, as it turned out, it would help to paper over the cracks in his fortitude. He hadn't been able to bring himself to waste one particular vampire, the one he'd been in love with. Killing me would mean he could tell himself he was the uncompromising hard guy. I'd never had any chance with him. I was never going to be able to appeal to his good nature, melt his heart, and talk him out of destroying me. The guy was as fifty shades of fucked up as Christian Grey, just without all the fun stuff.

'All right, I'm ready,' Mantella announced. My stomach fired with static as I heard these simple words. He emerged from his corner and approached with his flask of blue potion. Kerrish stood up and grabbed it off him, pulling rank as he took control of the experiment. The three of them stood round the table, eyes open wide in anticipation.

'Stand back, everyone,' Kerrish advised them. 'Just in case.'

Mantella didn't take his advice though, not until Kerrish glared at him and he backed away. Donna walked over to the door. I noticed her locking it. *Like I'm going to make a run for it, chick!*

Rachel held my free hand. 'It's going to be okay, babe,' she whispered.

'Good luck, Miss Freeman,' Kerrish said, insincerity like a stench in his voice. We watched him raise the flask of potion and there he left it hovering in the air, the same sort of dramatic pause we're used to seeing with talent shows where the presenter is announcing who is going out of the competition this week, or who gets to fight to see another day. I wasn't hanging on the flick of his wrist for a shot at fame and another shitty hit single here, though; this was the rest of my life he held in his hand. I'd never known such nerves before. My entire body trembled, sweat oozed from all of my pores, the membrane of my brain vibrating.

People talk about their lives flashing through their mind in such moments of acute tension as this. For me, so much of my life indeed fought for attention in my brain and triggered such overwhelming regret: for all that I should have done differently, for all the potential I may have wasted, for all the music I may have created but would be lost. All because of one night of drunken debauchery and a dance with some demon with big teeth.

I realised that what this quest to kill Wiseau had offered me was another chance. These guys had rescued me from the jaws of destruction, cheated my own undeath, and I knew that after today I would have to make my life mean something. I would really have to focus from now on, channel my energies into constructive pursuits, push my music. Practice my instruments. Go to lectures. Spend as little time as possible in the wasteland of hangovers. Already I perceived my new life before me, all that I could achieve. Perhaps one day I would even be on one of those talent shows, waiting for the presenter to announce my name as the winner, instead of being locked up in the backroom of this secret club in the shadows of Meridian.

I felt Rachel's heavy breath gushing on my shoulder. Her grip on my hand tightened. She couldn't take it any more than I could.

'Just do it!' she called out.

Kerrish raised his eyes, and I saw him softly nod. Right then I noticed something: he was standing this time. Last time he'd crouched by the table as he'd poured the potion onto our blood samples, anticipating the cloud of smoke that had appeared on my test. But this time he stood in the line of the potential blast of vapour. What did that mean? That he was expecting a successful outcome here? That he was *hoping* for one?

I saw his hand start to tilt. I saw the blue mixture emerge from the mouth of the flask, rushing forth to mix with my blood. It was like my brain was now a high shutter speed camera that caught every detail of the motion: the mixture forming into a large tear as it now dripped from the flask towards my blood...

I heard it. The thundering crackle. The blinding light stinging my eyes. The devilish hiss as though we'd opened a portal to hell. The cloud of vapour mushroomed from the cup just as all our worlds crumbled in an explosion of failure.

My brain could not compute what it had just experienced. I felt as though madness had overtaken me in a sleep deprivation-induced hallucination. Rachel screamed in my ear hole.

'What the shit was that?' she roared. 'Why did it do that? What's going on?'

Nobody seemed willing to answer the question. I couldn't even see them anyway for a good few moments, until the vapour dispersed to reveal the static figure of Kerrish standing by the table solemnly, a hand shielding his eyes from the explosion.

'I don't fucking believe it,' Mantella cried.

'You did it wrong,' Rachel continued to protest. 'Do the experiment again!'

Kerrish languidly shook his head in resignation

before he erupted, throwing the flask against the wall as it smashed into a thousand pieces, then kicking a chair across the floor.

'We went through all that just to prove this doesn't work?' Mantella ranted. 'I don't believe it!'

'Or maybe you killed the wrong vampire?' Donna suggested from the other side of the room. 'It's not like you knew for certain it was Wiseau. Come on, guys, it could have been anyone.'

I knew we should have stayed longer, should have used the time we had available to continue searching throughout that place and killing as many of those things as possible. Why hadn't I said that back then when I'd thought of it? When Kerrish was most probably thinking the same thing too! Now there was no time left. By the time we got back to *Satan's Cellar* again and made our way through those sadistic challenges, I would be making my transformation.

I couldn't believe it. Why would fate offer me this chance, give me hope, and then cruelly crush it in its hands like this? It was like with those horrible stories you heard of those poor hostages. They'd spend months or years locked up by terrorists, and then one day the cruel bastards would tell them they would be freed, but they wouldn't be taking them somewhere to hand them over. They'd just take them out to the desert and hack their heads off.

'So you're saying she's still infected?' Rachel cried, unwilling to accept what was plainly obvious to us all. 'You're saying she's still going to turn into a vampire?'

'Wow. I don't know why you went to Meridian University, blondie,' Donna said. 'You really should have gone to Cambridge.'

'But you killed him! You said she would be all right if we killed him!' she continued to yell. I hugged her, trying to console her as she now sobbed.

Kerrish approached me. 'I'm sorry, Melody. We failed.'

'So I'm still on Death Row?' I calmly asked him.

'We tried. We did all that we could. Trust me, no one has ever had this chance before.'

'I suppose a false hope was better than nothing.'

'So how long has she got?' Donna asked. She sounded impatient, as though she wanted nothing more but to get on with it so she could get off home to bed.

Kerrish glanced at his watch, then shook his head. 'Half an hour.'

'Time for a coffee,' she muttered as she left the room.

Chapter 25

Minutes later we were back where we started, locked up in the cell. Or at least I was. They'd left Rachel on the other side of the bars this time, the three Vihn Angels leaving us on our own. I didn't think Rachel would attempt a runner and alert someone to come and rescue me, and I guess neither did they. The game was up. There was no fight left in either of us now.

I presumed the overriding reason for keeping us separated was so she wouldn't be trapped in the cell when a new vampire was born. Often in television shows, virgin blood-drinkers were characterised as having little self-restraint, and so presumably I would instantly see the prey before me and get carried away gorging on Rachel's blood until she exsanguinated.

It could have been worse, reduced to spending the whole night locked up. I realised I was clutching at straws in this pitiful situation, but at least I'd had a final taste of freedom, felt some sense of purpose as we'd gone on that crazy adventure in *Satan's Cellar*. It was better than counting your last hours in a dingy cell.

All I could do as I lay on the cold floor in my final moments as a human was to reflect on all the missed opportunities I'd had on this night. I should have seen the opportunity of being outside as a chance to escape from the Vihn Angels. I should have looked for the key to our handcuffs when Kerrish had fallen asleep on the car journey back here. All along I'd had the feeling he'd been lying to me, and I was right! Why hadn't I at least tried? What would he have done if he'd woken up and found me going through his pockets? Kill me?

'They won't do it, Mel. They won't kill you. Not after all we've been through,' Rachel said, but it sounded like she was trying to fool herself. I knew I had no hope. 'They'll have to get through me first. I promise you.'

'Thanks, Rach,' I humoured her. I somehow doubted Kerrish would actually be the one to do it. I couldn't even see Mantella doing it. Couldn't picture him killing any vampire if I was honest. No, I suspected the one to be the Jihadi John would be Donna. A nagging sense told me it would be her. Perhaps my supernatural hearing was already kicking in and I could subconsciously hear them in the other room discussing how they would do this.

My thoughts turned to practical matters. I had only minutes left to live. I had to use them wisely.

'Nice dream,' I said to Rachel. 'That's in brackets as well. The N is a capital.'

'The hell you on about, darling?'

'Open bracket, nice dream, closed bracket. Capital N. Will you remember that?'

'Why?'

'That's my password. Works for Facebook and YouTube. Instagram and Twitter is GF in a coma, but I'm not as bothered about those.'

She sighed. This was not the defeatist talk she wanted to hear.

'I still had plenty of videos to upload to YouTube,' I told her. 'You'll find them on my laptop. I want you to keep uploading them, keep my career going a little longer. Hell, just keep uploading anything you find. There were loads of demos I'd recorded. You could put them to photographs or make shitty lyric videos to them.'

'Why are you saying this, Mel?'

'Because it's my way of living on. Please promise me you'll do this for me.'

'You can do it yourself!'

'On my laptop, if you go into *My Documents* you'll find a folder called *Screaming Butterfly*. That was supposed to be magnum opus...'

'Your what?'

'My *Bohemian Rhapsody*, my *Stairway to Heaven*, my signature song. I put a lot of it down, but I never got to finish it. Something I'd been working on since I was about thirteen. If there's any chance you can complete it, I would be grateful. I was almost there with it. Just kept putting it off. All the song needed was a guitar solo and a bit of polish.'

'Do I look like Phil fucking Spector to you?'

'Well, obviously you'll have to get some help with it, girl! Talk to Olly.'

'Your old flame?'

'He was helping me record it.'

'Right. I'll tell him he was the love of your life too and he was the best you'd ever had.'

'If nothing else, please upload that one song,' I carried on, ignoring her. 'Put it on Spotify or whatever. You can have all the royalties and hopefully in three years you'll have made enough to buy yourself a cup of coffee. Can you do that for me?' She didn't reply, not right away. It wasn't because she didn't want the burden, more that she didn't want to accept that I wouldn't be around to finish the song myself. Reluctantly, she conceded.

'You got it, babe.'

'Thanks.'

'Anything else you need me to take care of?' she asked. 'Like, do you need your browsing history deleted or anything? Any lewd pictures stored anywhere?'

'No,' was my knee-jerk reply, but then I thought about it for a moment. 'You know what? You may as well run CCleaner just to be on the safe side. And uh... actually yeah, it might be best if you wiped my phone while you're at it.' I started flicking through the photos on it, remembering some I'd taken for a guy a couple of years back. Yeah, it would definitely be a good idea if they were deleted.

'No problem. No questions asked,' she said with a wry smile and a wink. 'God, I really hope no one goes through my laptop when I peg it. I should do a bit of spring cleaning myself...'

'Ah save it for when your acting career is on the wane. That stuff might be valuable one day.'

'Knowing my luck, if I ever get famous, some spotty-faced freakazoid in Russia will hack my phone and release it all himself, and I tell you, that Fappening day is going to be like nothing the world has ever seen before.'

I chuckled, even in a moment as bleak as this. 'I don't doubt that one bit, Rachel. You're really going to make millions of teenage boys very happy one day.'

'What an inspiring thought.'

'Oh, wait!' I shouted, my eyes open wide in the eureka. 'There is one thing you absolutely have to do first, Miss Dickfloss!'

'What?'

I reached into my bra and felt for the little piece of plastic that had been pressing into my breast during this whole adventure. I'm sure if I'd taken my clothes off right now I would have found a flash card shaped imprint on my tit, and yet the discomfort of having it there had not registered in my mind once.

'The card we got from Ziggy's camera,' I announced as I held it up for her, suddenly remembering the pervy session we'd had with him earlier. It felt like that whole escapade was a lifetime ago. 'Please, whatever you do, promise me you smash this under your heel, set fire to it, piss on it, then go on an Atlantic cruise and throw it into the sea somewhere near the *Titanic*. But not too close to the *Titanic*. I don't want some salvage crew accidentally finding it while they're out looking for shipwreck artefacts and then discovering they were able to retrieve the data off it. Because, judging by how tonight has gone, that would be just my luck.'

'Shit, I totally forgot about this,' she replied as she took the card off me, her eyes twinkling with curiosity. 'But I'm not going to promise you I won't watch it before I destroy it.'

'Knock yourself out, babe.' I didn't care if she watched it. She was part of that sex video, to be fair. 'I guess I would have watched it myself if I had the chance,' I conceded.

'Well, why don't you now?'

'How?'

'Put the card in your phone,' she said as she handed it back to me.

'You really think it'll be that simple? It'll just happen to be the right sort of card, the right size to slot in? And my phone will be able to read the particular video file format? Nothing's that easy! And honestly, Rachel, even if it did work, by the time I got it going it would be sunrise.'

'My gawd, why do you always talk yourself out of

everything?'

'I've got like twenty minutes of my life left, and I'm going to spend it watching myself in a sex tape?'

'Yeah?' she asked, as though she didn't understand where I was coming from.

'I could actually spend this time making another video, recording a heartfelt message for my parents, apologising for being a fuckup, but no, porn it is?'

She looked at me blankly.

'All right, sod it.' I picked up my phone and dug my nails into the thin cleft along its side to pull the casing apart. I found the existing memory card in it and removed it. By some miracle it was the same type as the one from the camera. I slotted Ziggy's card in there and put the casing back together. I then thumbed away on the screen as I tried to find the particular file in question. 'Right, let's see if this works.'

'Fast forward the boring bits,' Rachel said. 'You know, as we're pressed for time.'

'I haven't even found it yet! Oh wait, this could be it.' On the screen was a tiny thumbnail of a blurry image of someone's thigh or something, not that I could tell whose it was. It certainly had that dodgy vibe that instantly suggested sauciness.

'Hit play then,' she said eagerly. I slumped against the bars of my cell and held the phone between them so we both had a decent view.

'Sitting comfortably? Let's go.' I breathed in through my teeth dramatically, then punched it.

I had no memory of Ziggy's bedroom being anything other than a fancy palace boudoir in my drug-induced hallucination, so it was somewhat jarring to see the reality of the scene of our self porn, that it was a *typical guy's* bedroom. Not that he was any old guy that I'd been screwing there. This was Rachel's boyfriend. Well, her sort-of-boyfriend.

'I didn't realise Ziggy's shag pit was so... dated,' I said. He really could have done with some new wallpaper. I didn't know what century that current décor was from, but it looked rather old.

'Oh look, there's you,' Rachel said as I came into shot. I was absolutely naked, of course. That bit I remembered. What I'd imagined though was that I was sitting at an expensive grand piano when in fact it was just some crappy electronic keyboard I was playing. Continuing the sobering *reality vs expectation* theme was the realisation that my musical performance in this video was less Chopin and more Les Dawson.

'Looking sexy,' she added, followed by a cheesy wolf whistle. She evidently had no sense of jealousy whatsoever, that I was about to be seduced by her boyfriend.

'How long have you and Ziggy been going out?' I asked.

'Jees, going out? I'm not sure that's what you'd call it. He's just a fuck-buddy, babe.'

'So how long have you been fuck-buddying?'

'Off and on a year, maybe?' I was about to ask her if she'd ever thought about getting herself tested, but I suspected her ears would be deaf and I may as well save my breath. It didn't matter for me, of course, if I'd caught anything from him, but I shuddered to think what that guy was probably carrying.

I settled on offering her a casual, 'Make sure you get him to wrap it.'

'He didn't with you.'

'Yeah, I thought you were watching, perv. I guess we'll never know if he gave me any sexual souvenir.'

The footage suddenly went still. This was the moment Ziggy had placed the camera down and changed his role from cameraman to performer. His naked form stepped into shot and he walked behind me as I continued to play the piano. I watched his hands caressing my breasts before they slid down my waist. It was almost comical, the duff notes I was hitting while he was fondling me. That was a whole sketch that Les Dawson never thought up. Not that seeing Les Dawson being fondled would be a classic.

'You have to admit,' Rachel said. 'He's pretty good with his hands.' I supposed she was right. I'd give him that; the guy knew what he was doing. Not that I would go back for seconds even if I had the opportunity. He was one gentleman I was happy to never see again for the rest of my life.

'How did you meet him?' I asked.

'Well, he was... I can't quite remember now. He's always been *there*, you know what I mean?'

'Like a bad penny.' Ziggy now appeared in shot as he leant down to kiss my neck. 'Oh, look at him smelling me, the hound.'

Rachel mimicked him by pressing her head against the bars as she now smelt me. 'Think you need a shower, babe.'

'Yeah, I ain't the only one, princess.'

I watched as I cocked my head to offer my neck to Ziggy, and he continued to caress me, then run his tongue down my flesh. And then we saw it.

'Holy. Fucking. Shit!'

'Pause it, pause it! Let me see that!' Rachel cried. 'Zoom in closer. Is that for real?'

It absolutely was. Ziggy's dark secret, hidden in our drugged-up haze. I paused the video, and not that I needed to, I enlarged the freeze frame on his face, his mouth open in delight and those elongated fangs protruding from his top row of teeth as he resisted the urge to sink them into my neck.

'He's a fucking vampire,' I cried.

'The bastard. He never told me that!'

'Oh my God, Rachel. You don't think... You don't think that... it was *him*, do you?'

She stared back at me, frantically trying to put the pieces together. 'Ziggy infected you?'

'Did we see him the night of Veronica's birthday?' I asked.

'I told you, I don't... Oh shit. Oh shit,' she said, which I understood to mean that, at last, Rachel had somehow remembered that yes, we did in fact see him that night. *NOW? Now you decide to remember that particular piece of information, girl!?*

'But why have I never been infected if I've been fucking him all this time?' she asked.

'Because you're just a jammy cow, Rachel!'

'Why did he infect you though?'

'I don't know. He wanted me in his brood? He wanted to keep you under his compulsion because he's been feeding off you this whole time? Your blood is champagne, and mine is just piss? But he liked my body, so he figured he would turn me and I would forever be bonded to him?'

'Oh my God. What time is it?'

I looked at the clock in the corner of my phone screen. 'I've got nineteen minutes, Rach.'

'There's still time!' She rushed to her feet and darted over to the locked door. 'Hey!' she roared at the top of her lungs as she smacked both of her palms against the door. 'Open up! Open up! Manny! Kerrish! Bring your arses over here!'

Already I began mentally calculating this one. My God, this would be tight. So, so tight. It had taken us about fifteen minutes to get from Ziggy's house to here in the taxi. It was now Saturday morning, so the roads would not be clogged up with commuting traffic. If we drove like Mr Wolf, we could easily be there in ten minutes, probably less. How many minutes would we need to convince Kerrish to go out again on a vampire hunt after the complete disaster that this night had been? Maybe I'd need a whole hour for that one.

I knew it though. I knew it was Ziggy who'd infected me. I just sensed it, could feel my tummy buzzing, as though some long dormant intuition had finally been given a platform to make its voice heard.

'Somebody come in here now!' Rachel continued to roar. We didn't hear the door unlock under her shouting, but she quickly stepped backwards as it opened. Kerrish burst in.

'What the fuck is going on in here?' Behind him, Mantella and Donna had also come to see what all the fuss was about.

'We worked out who the vampire is,' Rachel told them.

Kerrish sighed and hung his head. I didn't think he would be too receptive to our revelation.

'Look at this, Kerrish,' Rachel went on. 'This is

something that happened right before we first came here. We were with my... boyfriend, and he shot this video. I stole the memory card off him and we were just watching it back and...'

'Shit, yeah, I see some fangs there,' Mantella said. He'd stepped over to me and was peering down at my phone as I held it out. He took it off me. 'What the hell is he doing?' At that point it was clearly apparent with his eyes widening that he'd returned the freeze frame to its original resolution to give himself the full context of the shot. 'Wait, you're kind of a bit naked there, Melody.'

Kerrish opened his eyes. 'Let me see.' He stormed over to him and grabbed the phone from him, analysing the image, although I don't think it was the vampire he wanted to study. 'Who the fuck is this guy?'

'He's called Ziggy.'

'He your boyfriend?'

'Not quite. Rachel's actually.' He threw me a funny luck. 'It's a long story.'

He handed me back the phone. 'Well, yeah he's definitely a vampire.'

'He's the one, Kerrish,' I pleaded.

'Clearly. When's the wedding?'

'I mean it! He's the one who infected me. I know it.'

His shoulders drooped, unable to summon any more energy for yet another vampire-hunting quest.

'Please, I can take you to him right now. He's not that far away,' Rachel now protested. 'Just stop thinking about this. The more time you stand here faffing is time we're wasting. What's another twenty minutes of gallivanting when this is another vampire we can take out, and one we can hopefully stop from arising in the first place?'

'Fuck it. I'm game,' Mantella said. But Donna's standpoint was much different.

'Kerrish, come on, you already tried this. Don't waste any more time on these girls.'

'Shut the fuck up, bitch!' Rachel yelled at her.

'Where is he?' Kerrish asked.

'Molko Road,' Rachel replied. 'I can show you the

way.'

'I know where it is. All right, shit, we have to go right now. Get her out.'

'Yes!' Rachel cried.

Mantella dug out his keys to unlock my cell. 'Here we go again,' he said to me.

Kerrish was over in the nerve centre, rummaging through the crap on the desks.

'What are you looking for?' Rachel asked him.

'I need the cuffs.'

'Oh, for fuck's sake, Kerrish!' I cried at him. Already Mantella had opened my cell door, and I'd stepped outside. He could see I wasn't about to do a runner. 'Let's just move.' With that, Kerrish stormed up to me and clamped his hand around my wrist.

'Let's go,' he said, and the four of us ran as fast as we could.

Chapter 26

They formed their plan as we ran. Without David's BMW at our immediate disposal, they decided to head to Mantella's car which sat in a private parking area a short distance from the club, although first Kerrish made him assure him there was enough fuel in it. Within about ninety seconds we were there. Another significant chunk of my time gone. I hated that feeling of time running out. I didn't know of anything else that could twist the nerves or generate the stress as much as the sense that you don't have enough time left to do what needed to be done. And when it was your life at stake on that matter? Panic seemed too pale a word.

The car was some crappy old Fiesta, no doors to the backseats so Kerrish had to lift the front passenger seat forward before he bundled me in. After he'd jumped in beside me and restored the seat to its position, Rachel had to waste another few seconds clearing it of all the junk of McDonald's wrappings, frantically scooping it out onto the ground as she whined in frustration.

Mantella got behind the wheel and fumbled for his key. This would surely be the moment the engine wouldn't start, and this whole mission would be defeated by the time it took us all to push the car down the street to get it going. But maybe the fates were finally smiling down on me; the rust bucket started first time and a loud blast of the last CD Mantella had been listening to blared over the speakers. I recognised the unmistakable Green Day song but my brain could spare no more power to recall its title.

After turning down Billie Joe's voice, he crunched it into reverse before taking off. This was definitely not the occasion for driving defensively, and Mantella took risks as he drove straight over junctions and ignored traffic lights. I glanced at the clock on the dashboard and it told me it was now 7.33. Ten minutes left. They seemed to be slipping away too quickly.

As though reading my thoughts, Mantella said, 'I set my clock two minutes late. Helps me get to places on time.' It felt like he'd tricked the universe into giving me a precious extra two minutes of my life.

Up ahead, the city rose over the horizon, the Leech Tower standing taller than all the inferior skyscrapers around it as they enviously looked up on its magnificence. Behind the buildings was a cloudless morning sky, a faint orange hue that announced the imminent arrival of the sun as the ever-turning world would spin out of the darkness, the meridian of the sun's illumination brushing closer to our Meridian.

I willed the car to move faster. I felt trapped within the back of it, almost claustrophobic, as though this metal casing were my coffin and the game was already up. Ahead of us I spotted a speed camera, and it seemed a small victory as Mantella ignored it, taking three points and a fine for the team as he zoomed on through. I just hoped there were no cops around and that this wouldn't turn into a high-speed pursuit and we would all be arrested or shot down before we could go knock on Ziggy's door.

'How much farther is it, Rach?' I asked, not that I expected her to give me anything of a useful answer.

'We're getting there,' she replied. So it wasn't quite an 'almost there' but definitely not a 'still a fair bit to go', so perhaps we were halfway there? I glanced at the clock again. It said it was now 7.35 which meant that it was 7.33. What was the point in setting your clock two minutes fast if all you would do is mentally take it off again?

I closed my eyes, since my mental concentration could do nothing to make that car go faster. Right then I noticed Kerrish no longer had a manacle grip around my wrist, but rather was holding my hand. I had no idea how we'd ended up like this, whether he'd taken my hand or I'd taken his.

'Next right,' Rachel said. I opened my eyes again and I could swear the world suddenly seemed a notch or two brighter.

'Are you sure? Don't we need to go down Rice Street?' Mantella replied.

'Rach...' I muttered, extending the syllable. I didn't want her to fuck this up by sending us down the wrong road. A decision like that and this whole thing would be messed up.

'Trust me. It's a shortcut.' But Mantella wasn't slowing down for the upcoming junction.

'Are you sure?' he roared.

'Yes. Do it!'

With that, he yanked the steering wheel, and we arched across the lanes. Fortunately, there was nothing coming the other way. Rachel continued to navigate but as we traversed deeper and deeper into her shortcut, I couldn't help the trepidation as we became more and more lost within a concrete jungle. I pictured us coming to a stop down some dead end, the car no longer able to move because all the tyres had blown out from the stinger trap we'd sped over. And then Ziggy and his fire breather friends would ambush us and kill our fellow vampire hunters as they waited a further few minutes for me to become one of them. And if *that* were the case, the first thing I would be doing was feeding off the blonde bitch who'd led us here!

'Where the fuck are we, Rach?' I didn't recognise the area. The surrounding buildings didn't even look like the terraced houses of Ziggy's residence. 'Where are you taking us?'

'We're nearly there, all right!?' she shot back at me, her voice almost hysterical. 'Now take this left here.'

Our driver complied. At last it looked as though we were in a residential area, but to my horror it was apparent we were advancing down a cul-de-sac. Mantella eased off the accelerator as he realised it too.

'Down here?' he asked her.

'Yes! Foot down, Manny!'

'But it's a dead end!'

'Just keep going!'

He floored it, and the sound of the revs echoed off the buildings as an annoyed neighbourhood was probably dragged prematurely out of their Saturday morning slumber, cursing at another dickhead boy racer. There were no more junctions along this road, a line of bollards denoting the end of the street as they guarded a common. Was this the park we'd sat in earlier after escaping Ziggy's house?

My eyes flicked to the clock again and I saw it turn 7.40. I had just three minutes to go plus Mantella's bonus two minutes. Had this really been a shortcut? Or would Rachel prove to be the reason for my downfall? Of course, nothing that I had done before in my life would now be the cause of this disaster, merely what Rachel had chosen to do in my final few minutes. As though some football team losing 1-0 would blame their defeat on the striker who blasted the ball over the bar in the 95th minute, rather than all the shit play the whole team had produced before that moment. That was the curse of the present. It always carried the most significance. But as the Fiesta skidded to a stop by the bollards, this whole car journey was now history.

'Grab your stakes, guys. Ziggy's house is just the other side of that field.'

The two in the front spilled out of the doors, Rachel fumbling to turn the lever so we could escape from the back, before Kerrish growled at her and did it himself. Still holding my hand, he led me out of there, and the four of us ran like hell.

I didn't need any fitness levels, any stamina for this. I was fuelled by pure adrenaline, and being free of that car I now felt high on the chemical, as though I were Wonder Woman and had superheroic abilities. Or perhaps these were my supernatural abilities starting to emerge as the amber skies glowed an even brighter orange. I ran my tongue over my teeth, half expecting my fangs to start growing forth. I looked down to check if my feet were still pounding across the grass or whether I was flying over it.

A yell rang in my ears, and the grip on my hand released. I paused to see Kerrish on the ground grimacing. There were divots in the turf, possibly rabbit holes? I was free of him. Rachel and Mantella were still yards behind. I could have taken this moment to flee, to escape the vampire hunters and accept the supernatural fate that was about to emerge. But I had to stick to the program. I needed to finish this.

Kerrish looked up at me and an entire conversation passed unspoken between us, purely through the looks on our faces. He handed me his stake. I reached forward and grabbed it like this was a relay race, carrying on running as fast as I could with much more than a gold medal as incentive, sprinting far ahead of the rest of the uninjured party. I'd probably have to pause beyond the common as I waited for Rachel to tell me where to run next, or maybe I'd work it out without her.

Glancing back I saw my companions were veering off to the right and Rachel was frantically trying to point towards where I needed to go. I adjusted my course and there I could see it: an alleyway leading into a housing estate.

I was there within seconds, springing over an upturned shopping trolley as I landed with a crunch on broken cider bottles and flattened beer cans. Onwards I sprinted down the dog shit covered path, overgrown shrubs from people's back yards tangling in my hair as I darted through.

As I reached the housing estate, I paused to get my bearings. Another glance at the time. I no longer had the buffer of Mantella's two minutes bonus time, not with my watch. I hadn't specifically set it with atomic precision, hadn't previously synchronised it to the bongs of Big Ben or anything. All I knew was that it was just *generally* right, as accurate as it needed to be to get me by. It wasn't like I'd ever arrived at a lecture late by seven seconds and then lost my life because of it. My watch told me it was 7.40 and my eyes now looked for a further detail: the third hand. It was 7.40 and twenty-seven seconds... twenty-eight seconds... twenty-nine seconds...

Two and a half minutes to go and I didn't know which way to run. I peered up and down the street, desperately looking for some feature that I might recognise. Some early bird with his dog sauntered past and wished me a good morning. Even if I was bothered about being polite in a desperate moment like this, I was panting too heavily to get any words out of my lungs.

Fuck fuck fuck! How far away was Rachel? Should I just guess on which direction I went next?

Another voice came to my ears. I edged back to the

alleyway and saw that Rachel was now entering it, pointing and calling to me: 'Go left!'

Immediately I ran, pumping my arms and legs as fast as they would go, hoping it would become apparent to me as I flew along where Ziggy's house was. I was surrounded by rows of homologous houses. I didn't know what number Ziggy lived at, didn't even know if I was on his street yet.

The seconds continued to tick, my heartbeat racing even faster, my breathing almost at hyperventilating levels, the air now emitting in whimpers. I reached a junction and then I saw a sign opposite: Molko Road. Ziggy's street! I sped on, ignoring the mucky white van coming down the road as I darted in front of it, and I imagined how the Green Cross Code Man would surely be frowning on me at my stupidity, how this moment could make the perfect public information film on how idiots cross the road. The van braked to a halt and in the corner of my eye I noticed the driver gesticulating as he hit the horn. Onwards I ran.

All I remembered was that he lived somewhere in the middle of the street. I saw on one side the row of garages and then I suddenly recalled that Ziggy and his mates used those carports to store the vehicles they worked on. His house was directly opposite them, but I couldn't remember which particular one it was. They all seemed the same.

I arrived at the first of the carports and paused as I studied the houses. Which one was his? What colour was his front door? Do I knock on all of them? This whole place looked so different in the emerging dawn!

My eyes came to a rest on a walkway tunnelling between two of the residences, and it suddenly occurred to me this was where Rachel and I had escaped through hours earlier. I mentally retraced those steps and remembered we'd jumped from Ziggy's back garden into the garden of the house to his right, and then we'd found the walkway. So Ziggy's house was just one along to the left!

Instantly I sprang across the road and flung myself forwards as I smacked my palms against the door. I yelled, I bashed the knocker down, and I even tried the doorbell, not that there was any hope of it working, but I jabbed that button and continued doing so over and over as I shouted at the top of my lungs. There was no way he would not hear me. The whole street surely could, the way my voice was echoing along the terrace. I paused for a moment, the thought coming to my brain to try the handle in case the door was unlocked. No such luck.

The time on my watch caught my eye. Shit! The second hand was six flicks away from 7.43. Zero hour.

'Ziggy! Open this door now!' I roared as loud as I'd ever shouted before in my life, producing a timbre in my voice I'd never heard before.

Another check of the time. 7.43. Sunrise. I was now going into overtime. I now clung to the hope that either my watch was set fractionally slow, or that the precise moment of sunrise was a few seconds on from 7.43. Or that sunrise arrived in Meridian slightly later than whatever place it was actually measured to when we'd looked it up on Google. Or maybe supernatural transitions had a fractional delay?

I spastically rammed my fists against the panels and then I heard a bolt sliding. I paused. The door creaked open and there stood Ziggy in his dressing gown holding a tumbler of whisky.

'What the...?' he began, before his eyes focussed on me and suddenly twinkled with recognition. 'Milady!'

'Fuck you!' I spat in his face as I raised my weapon up high with both hands. In one swift and powerful motion I lunged it straight into his heart with all the force I could muster from my exhausted body.

His eyes opened wide, his lips curling back in terror as he dropped the glass of spirit from his hand. He clutched the fatal stake as he glared at me in absolute disgust, the fangs in his mouth now betraying his secret as they revealed his true nature. He staggered a few feet backwards and fell to his knees. He wasn't quite dead yet, so I followed him inside, and perhaps for me it was a pitiful attempt to escape the rising sun as it came to transform the infected. We'd surely hit the magic moment by now.

Ziggy's face turned grey, his eyes slowly revolving in his skull. Desperately I lunged forward and kicked the wooden shaft deeper into his heart as he collapsed to the ground.

'Hurry up and die, you bastard!' I shouted at him. Still he continued to wheeze as he made a pathetic attempt to remove the wooden stake with his waning strength.

Behind me, I heard Rachel gasp. Both she and Mantella had arrived. Mantella pushed past her as he peered down on the dying vampire.

'Why's he taking so long to die?' I asked.

He looked down on him curiously, no differently to how he might scrutinise a malfunctioning machine. 'Well, we could hack his head off. That'll probably finish him off.'

'Fucking do it then!'

He jumped into action, reaching under his jacket behind his back to produce a large hatchet. He made a few swift hacks, plunging it unhesitatingly into Ziggy's neck. The defeated monster's greying flesh was turning somewhat malleable, like plasticine, so it was with ease that Mantella soon broke his head clean off.

'Yeah, there we go. He's definitely dead now,' he announced casually.

'Did we do it in time?' I asked him. 'Am I okay?'

He stood there and sort of shrugged his shoulders. 'How do you feel?'

'How am I feeling? I think it's going to take a long fucking time to reflect on this night and work out what the hell I'm feeling about all this!'

He stepped over Ziggy's body towards me, taking out his torch and shining it into my eyes.

'You look fine to me,' he said. 'Got a sudden craving for human blood? Try extending your canines.'

'How the fuck do I do that?'

'I don't know. I'm not a vampire. I don't know how the hell they do it.'

I wrinkled up my lip as I exposed my upper row of teeth, jutting them forward. He looked on at me and just shook his head. He slapped his hand on my shoulder.

'Looks like you're clear, Melody.'

I turned round to Rachel. She stared down quietly at Ziggy's corpse as it continued to dissolve into mush. I gave her a hug. As nonchalant as she was about her relationship with the guy, I figured she would feel something tearing away at her emotions with seeing her lover dead after discovering he was secretly a supernatural creature. It was a bit of a mind-twister, no matter how carefree you were.

She clung on to me tightly. 'We did it, Mel. I can't believe we did it.' She sniffed, and I pressed her tighter to me.

'Shit, Rach. They don't come any closer than that.'

Right at that moment, a figure hobbled into the doorway. It was Kerrish, anticipation in his features before he examined the scene in the hallway, at which point the tension in his body turned to one of sheer relief. We both shared a smile. It occurred to me I'd never seen a smile on his face before. It was like I was meeting the real Kerrish for the very first time.

As I joined him back on the pavement, he slid down against the front of the house to catch his breath, his injured leg stretched out before him.

'Thank you, Kerrish,' I said. All his death threats, all his pushing me around and locking me up against my will had now been forgotten. Ultimately, he was the one to have saved my life.

'Next time be more careful, Miss Freeman. Stay away from those vamps.'

'He's just disappointed,' Rachel said as she also joined us out there. 'Disappointed that he won't get to use his handcuffs on you anymore.'

Chapter 27

The curtains around us had started to twitch, so before too many nosey neighbours came out to get a closer gawp at the drama, or before any of them phoned the police, the four of us hobbled to the car and drove back to *The Hooded Claw*. I knew we'd succeeded, that we'd undone the infection and I would not be transforming into a vampire, but after all I'd been through, I wanted undeniable proof. I wanted to *see* it.

So we returned to the operations room and for the third time I gave them a blood sample so Mantella could again run his detection test. I needed to witness the same result we'd seen with Rachel: nothing. Dud blood. Regular, uninfected, human haemoglobin that didn't go whizz-bang crazy when Mantella splashed his magical potion on it.

We'd all gone way past our tired stage by now so our bodies didn't know what the hell was going on or what time it was. I didn't want to live by the clock anymore, as events had forced me to tonight. Although a new day was emerging and I was massively in debt with my sleep, I had the rest of my life to catch up on that.

Donna had fucked off home. In fact, she'd already left by the time we'd got back. Kerrish must have texted with the news that we'd terminated the vampire in time, but the miserable bag evidently wasn't interested in having a celebratory drink and rejoicing with us. She just wanted her beauty sleep.

With another cupful extracted from my poor veins, I sat with Rachel and Kerrish as we waited for Mantella to bring the mixture for my third and final test. Third time lucky! As ever, Rachel was in a playful mood.

'So, Kerrish, now that Mel's got clean blood, does that mean it would be safe for you to shag her?'

'Rachel!' I scolded her, worried what else this sleep-deprived girl would come out with. What kind of monster had we unleashed in her?

'I'm just asking. I mean, it was clear that earlier he saw you as nothing more than something to ram his wood into. I wondered if he sees you any differently now.'

The poor guy sighed as he closed his eyes and put his head in his hands.

'I'll ram something into your neck if you don't shut up, girl,' I replied.

'Okay, but seriously,' she went on with faux sincerity. 'We definitely can't catch nothing from this skank now, no? For example, it's all right to kiss her, yeah?'

Kerrish still wasn't rising to it.

'Didn't stop you kissing me in the cell,' I muttered to her.

He slid his hand down onto his chin as he stared at me. 'What did you say?'

'What?' I responded, suddenly feeling sick by the urgency in his voice.

'Did you say you kissed Rachel while you were infected?'

'Y... yeah.'

'What?' Rachel asked in a high-pitched tone.

'Oh Jesus,' Kerrish sighed.

Rachel and I stared at each other in disbelief. Had we really sowed the seeds of some sickening twist to this whole affair? Had I passed on my infection to my friend? I suddenly recalled Mantella talking about the virus, how it could be transmitted through bodily fluids. And then I'd gone ahead and kissed her!

Oh shit. How could I have been so stupid? Kerrish slid his chair backwards, and I readied myself as I anticipated him brandishing a stake as he'd abruptly done when he'd despatched with Veronica. All this time we'd rushed to save my life, and all along the virus was lying patiently in wait in Rachel's blood.

'Oh my God,' she whined. 'Am I a fucking vampire?'

I saw it all happening like it was in slow motion. The wooden stake in Kerrish's hand. It rising high above his head as it angled at Rachel. He swiped it down, lunging towards her heart...

And then he calmly placed it down on the table. 'Nah, I'm messing with you,' he said. 'You're not a vampire.'

'Holy... fucking... moly,' I uttered, my heart hammering away in overdrive. I really didn't think I could take any more of this. 'You bastard, Kerrish!'

Rachel started laughing. 'Dip me in duck shit. That was a good one. You are one twisted son of a gun, Kerrish.'

Mantella now approached the table, having been quietly observing the joke. 'Nice one, Kerrish. Yeah, you're fine, Rachel. If she had passed the virus on to you, it would have died when we undid her infection,' he nerdily informed us.

'Are you sure?' she asked, still laughing. 'Think I want to take this test again as well now.'

'You're okay,' Kerrish reassured her. 'I guess this will count for both of you then. It's not like there's actually a precedent for this situation.'

'The potion is all ready,' Mantella announced.

'Can I do this?' I asked. He handed me the flask, and I stood, taking a few deep breaths. Holding it before me, I focussed on the mark on my hand, the strange symbol that had led me here in the first place. Would it already be fading away from my skin?

I twisted my wrist and watched the potion drip into my blood. This time there was no flash, bang or puff of smoke. Instead, the four of us just stared dumbly at this innocuous mixture.

'Well, I don't know about everyone else,' Rachel yawned, leaning back in her chair as she checked her watch. 'But I think it's about time I called it a day.'

Chapter 28

We said goodbye to Kerrish and Mantella, leaving them to finish up in their operations room. Mantella had got coffees for him and his buddy, but I really didn't want any caffeine right now. I just needed my bed. I never understood why people would get a coffee when they woke up in the middle of the night or after doing an all-nighter. How do you wind down again right after you've put caffeine into your system?

They probably had to write up their reports or the results of tonight's findings from our many experiments, or maybe they had more vampire hunting operations to plan for Saturday night. I also sensed that Mantella was eager to get the word out amongst the Vihn Angel community, let all their counterparts across the world know that the myth was true: the infected could become uninfected again.

As we walked through the deserted lounge area, I had that sensation of longing beginning to form in my brain. Would I see Kerrish ever again? Why was I even wondering that?

At least I knew where to find him again. It wasn't like we were going our separate ways and he would be lost in a sea of city strangers. There was nothing to stop me calling in on him at *The Claw*. All that back and forth with our mobile phones tonight and none of us had swapped numbers. Not to my knowledge, that was. I shouldn't have put it past Rachel getting Mantella's number when we'd become separated in *Satan's Cellar*. I bet the two were already Facebook friends and following each other on Twitter.

I hoped Kerrish would come my way again, that he would make a move, that I would walk through the campus one day and find him there waiting for me. On that level, though, I couldn't read him at all. After everything he'd been through with me tonight and being enlightened on the various twisted shit I got up to, I doubted he was now viewing me as potential girlfriend material. Neither would I, to be fair.

As though picking up on my thoughts on Kerrish,

Rachel said, 'He fancies you.'

'Who?'

She rolled her eyes at me. 'You know who I mean. Come on, you really think he would have done all that if he didn't want to lose you to the vampires? And then rush out again when we only had nineteen minutes left? Wanted to be your knight in shining armour, didn't he?'

'You reckon? Well, maybe he's not my type,' I said, angling my face away.

'Yeah, whatever. You ain't kidding me, sunshine.'

We reached the front door. Rachel unlocked it and opened up. Someone stood there, waiting, as though they knew we were about to appear.

It was the kooky guy who worked at *The Fog*. The same guy I'd later seen in the café and who'd warned me I needed to search out the Vihn Angels because he sensed my life was in danger. Xander. The mind reader. It felt like a whole week ago that I'd been talking to him. But what could he want now?

'Melody, hi,' he said in his soft voice.

'Hi, Xander. Were you waiting for me? How did you know I was here?'

'Oh, I just...' his eyes lowered, and he mumbled something I couldn't hear.

'Nine o'clock on a Saturday morning and you just knew I'd be at *The Hooded Claw*? Somewhere that's not even open right now.' He had told me to go looking for the Vihn Angels, I supposed, and this was their headquarters. But I didn't think Xander realised that fact else he would have informed me of that off the bat, surely.

His eyes remained on his hands, and as I looked down, I noticed that he was holding something. A pen.

'I just wanted to give you this,' he said. 'You left it in *Joe's Parlour*.'

'My Harry Potter pen. Oh my God, you brought it back for me!'

'Yeah. Here you go.'

'Well, everything *definitely* is all right with the world again,' Rachel chipped in, the sarcasm dripping from her words.

'It's my favourite pen,' I replied overenthusiastically, like a giddy schoolgirl. I turned back to him. 'Thank you, Xander. That was very kind of you.'

'No problem,' he said. 'Anyway, I should be...' With that he left. I didn't get to tell him anything else, nothing about my night, nothing about how the warning he gave me had led me on a crazy journey to save my life from an undead existence. I guess he already knew all that.

'He's friggin' weird,' Rachel muttered as we both leaned out the doorway, gazing after him as he drifted away, the unsung hero of this whole adventure.

'Yep. Come on, Rach, let's get back home.'

We stepped out and closed the big wooden door, walking across the square in the crisp February air as we searched for a taxi. I was happy to hoof it all the way back to our dorm, but Rachel typically found walking an unnatural activity. I supposed that we did look like two chicks doing the Saturday morning walk of shame. Not that I cared. Having snatched my life back from the jaws of vampirism, I felt rather radiant. The ability to amble through the city in the dawn sun felt like a privilege for me after all I'd gone through.

'I am so looking forward to my bed,' I said.

'Think I'll just collapse straight into mine without taking a shower. I don't care about all the nasty stuff I've been covered in tonight.'

'You know, Rach,' I started, my mind getting into a philosophical mood, 'a night like this puts things in perspective. You don't realise what you have, you know? This whole life thing, it really is a special gift.'

'Never know what you've got until it's gone. Think I shared something on Facebook that said that once,' she replied. I had no idea if she was being cynical or if she was genuinely resonating with what I was saying.

'I really don't want to be in this situation again. From now on it's going to be different.'

'I'm hearing you, girl.'

'I realise I'm not quite twenty yet, but I feel like I've grown up ten years in one night. Time to settle down.'

'Totally.' She stopped walking as her eyebrows

furrowed together. She then turned back to me and said, 'I was so scared that I'd lost you, Mel. When we were locked up in that cell I came to a realisation. It was like I was having a holy epiphany moment or something. Hit me like a heavenly ray.' She fell silent. She seemed genuinely moved, and that was not something you typically saw in Rachel.

'What was it?' I prompted her.

'I just completely saw that...' Her phone interrupted her, undoubtedly tearing her train of thought so far off the rails that it would never get back on track ever again. Yep, that thought was as gone now as the train that had veered into the ravine at the end of *Back to the Future 3*. She answered the phone.

'Oh, hey there! How are you?... Yeah, he told you we'd seen him last night?... Yeah! How cray was that?... Oh, he's really nice, your dad.' She put the phone on her shoulder momentarily and whispered to me, 'It's Sam Sherborne.' Putting it back to her ear, she resumed her conversation with David's daughter. 'Yeah... Yeah... Definitely!... Yeah, we'll tell you all about it... Yeah!... Uh, let me think a moment... Yeah, I'm not doing anything. Let's do it! Okay, great, we'll see you later.'

'What did she want?' I asked as she hung up.

'Okay, that is tonight sorted. We need to get home and grab some sleep and then we are meeting up with Sam and we are hitting up *The Mercury Lounge*. Two for one on shots all night, baby!'

My jaw dropped open. 'Rachel?'

'It'll be great to catch up with her. It's going to be an awesome night. She said she's bringing her new boyfriend. I think she wants to show him off.'

'You seriously want to go out again... *tonight*?'

'Yyyeah?'

'But... after all we've just been through?'

'Oh, come on, Mel. Don't tell me you're going to get all boring and sensible now? Is that what you were trying to tell me?'

I sighed. What the hell. You only live once. Or twice in my case.

'Fuck it,' I replied. 'Let's do it.'

Get a Free Joseph Kiel eBook

Visit my website www.josephkiel.com and sign up to my mailing list to receive a free Joseph Kiel eBook.

Into the Fires is a standalone prequel to my *Dark Harbour* book series, a supernatural thriller about a man on the run from the mob in a mysterious seaside town.

Signing up to my readers' club won't result in endless spammy emails, so don't worry. Never miss a new release. You can unsubscribe at any time.

Connect With Joseph Kiel

Twitter (@Joseph_Kiel)

Facebook (/josephkielauthor)

www.josephkiel.com